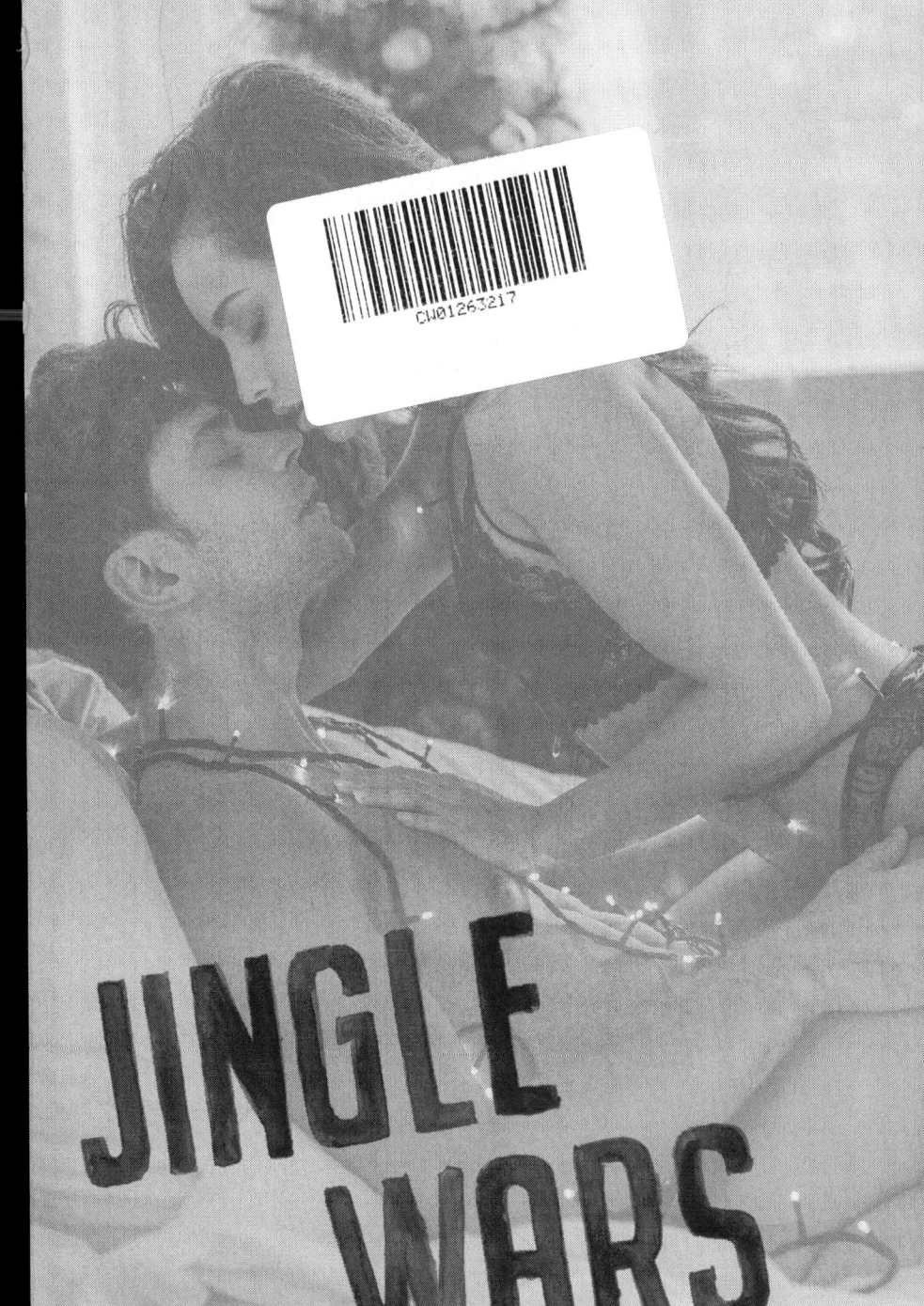

JINGLE WARS

R. HOLMES & VERONICA EDEN

Copyright © 2020 by R. Holmes and Veronica Eden

All rights reserved.

No part of this book may be reproduced in any form or by any electronic or mechanical means, including information storage and retrieval systems, without written permission from the authors, except for the use of brief quotations in a book review.

This is a work of fiction. Names, characters, places, businesses, companies, organizations, locales, events and incidents either are the product of the authors' imagination or used fictitiously. Any resemblances to actual persons, living or dead, is unintentional and co-incidental. The authors do not have any control over and do not assume any responsibility for authors' or third-party websites or their content.

Cover Design: Najla Qamber, Qamber Designs

CONTENTS

About the Book	vii
Playlist	ix
1. Finn	1
2. Freya	7
3. Finn	13
4. Freya	23
5. Freya	31
6. Finn	39
7. Freya	49
8. Finn	63
9. Freya	73
10. Freya	81
11. Finn	95
12. Finn	105
13. Freya	113
14. Finn	125
15. Freya	135
16. Finn	149
17. Freya	157
18. Finn	169
19. Freya	181
20. Finn	193
21. Finn	199
22. Freya	207
23. Finn	217
24. Freya	229
25. Finn	237
26. Freya	243
27. Finn	253
28. Freya	261

Epilogue	271
Epilogue	275
Acknowledgments	283
About R. Holmes	287
Also by R. Holmes	289
About Veronica Eden	291
Also by Veronica Eden	293

ABOUT THE BOOK

From bestselling authors R. Holmes & Veronica Eden comes an all-new steamy new adult enemies-to-lovers holiday romcom standalone.

Two inns, one town, and there's not enough room for the both of them.

Add in a reindeer-ish donkey, a Christmas competition, and a rivalry to end all rivalries and you're bound to end up in disaster, right?

Finn Mayberry has enough on his plate trying to keep his Grandparents inn afloat. The last thing he needed was some California state of mind starlet bulldozing into his town and throwing up a five-star resort right next to his family's inn.

But, now she's here and he can't get her out of his town or his head.

ABOUT THE BOOK

Freya Anderson took one look at the snowcapped mountains of Hollyridge and fell in love. She's finally here and ready to take on the task of proving to her father that she can handle running Alpine.

She never expected to make enemies with the sinfully delicious lumberjack of a man who runs the inn next door. He's moody, impossible and completely off limits.

There can only be one winner, but you know what they say. All is fair in love and... Jingle Wars?

Playlist

Dominick the Donkey (The Italian Christmas Donkey)—Lou Monte
Holly Jolly Christmas—Michael Bublé
Let It Snow—Liam Payne
Like It's Christmas—Jonas Brothers
Bring Me Love—John Legend
Run Run Rudolph—Kelly Clarkson
Last Christmas—James TW
Champion—Bishop Briggs
Confident—Demi Lovato
Sleigh Ride—Carpenters
Have Yourself A Merry Little Christmas—Haley Reinhart
My Only Wish (This Year)—Britney Spears
Best of You—Andy Grammer & Elle King
My Favorite Things—Kelly Clarkson
Be Your Love—Bishop Briggs
Baby, It's Cold Outside—Brett Eldredge & Meghan Trainor
Stuck with U—Ariana Grande & Justin Bieber
Never Tear Us Apart—Bishop Briggs
All I Want for Christmas Is You—Mariah Carey
White Christmas—George Ezra
Make It To Christmas—Alessia Cara

PLAYLIST

Blue Christmas—Michael Bublé
You Make It Feel Like Christmas—Gwen Stefani & Blake Shelton
Winter Things—Ariana Grande
I'll Be Home for Christmas—Rascal Flatts

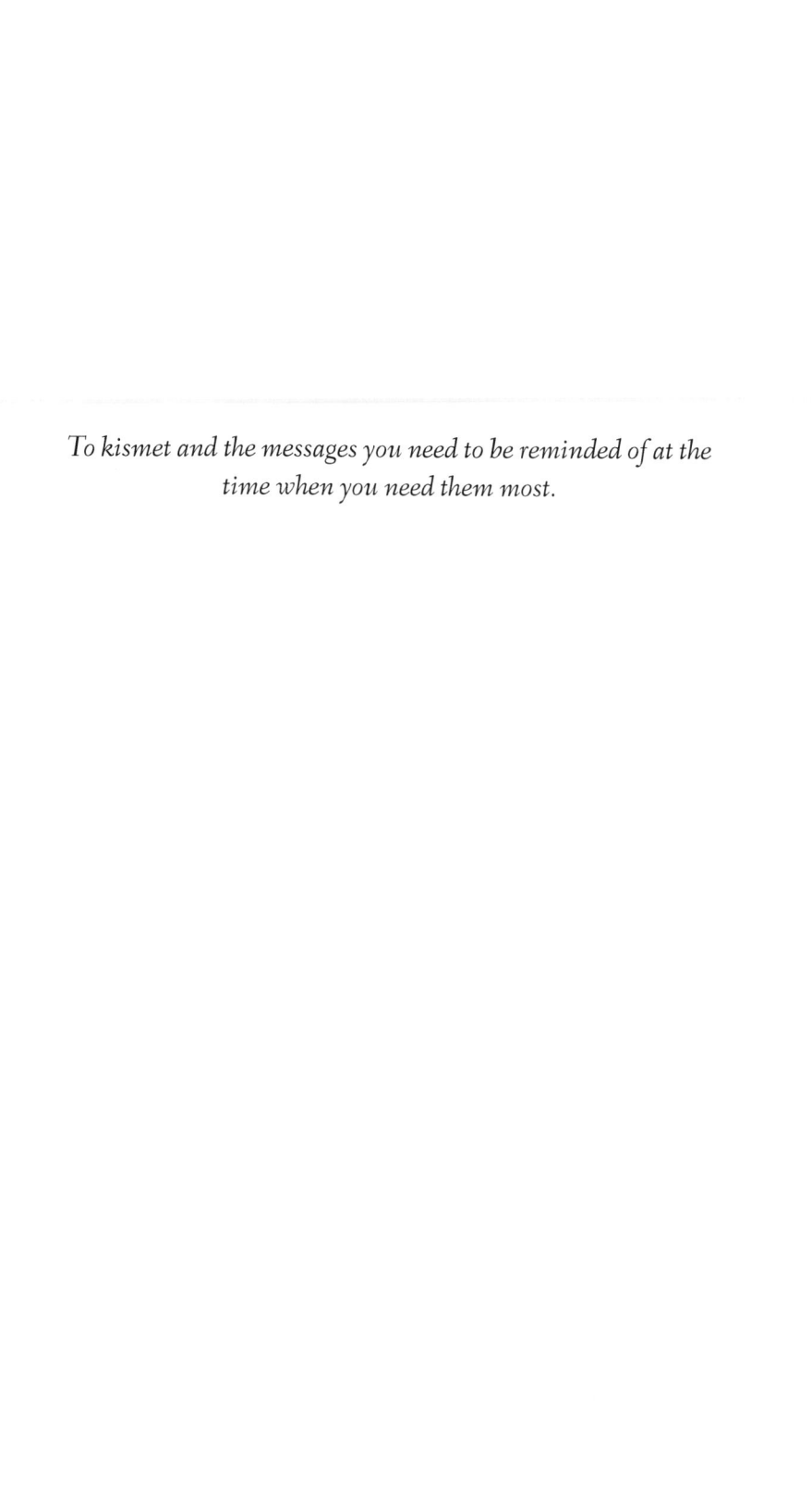

To kismet and the messages you need to be reminded of at the time when you need them most.

Chapter One
Finn

"Grams, seriously, there's nothing up here." Once again, my eyes search the dim, musty smelling attic for the specific decoration that she's asking for. There's practically everything else you can imagine, but no donkey riding a snowmobile. I've been up here for at least thirty minutes and each time I tell her it's not here she just hollers at me to look harder, because I'm missing it.

Right... Because donkeys riding a damn snowmobile are easy to miss.

"Oh Finn, shucks, just move some stuff around. I know your Gramps put it up there somewhere," she calls up to me.

I hear her muttering under her breath. As much as I love this woman, my patience is wearing about as thin as this reindeer sweater that she insisted we wear while we begin decorating for the Christmas season. One thing I've learned is that you don't tell Grams no. Well, unless you want to be eating sandwiches for a week. Wicked woman, bribing us with food.

"Are you sure Gramps put it up here? Remember last time when you swore that Gramps was the one to misplace the extension cord? Except you forgot you lent it to the bingo hall for their light display?"

I close my eyes, grab the bridge of my nose, and let out a disgruntled sigh.

"Don't sass me, Finn Michael!" she exclaims. I can hear the feigned exasperation in her voice from up here.

Christ.

Even though I know it's not here, I move a few more miscellaneous boxes around and look through them quickly. In the dim light, I can't make out much and I'm using my hands to feel my way through the attic. Of course, I catch my big toe on a wooden beam and the pain radiates up my leg.

"Shit! Ah, damn it!" I curse, grabbing my throbbing foot.

"Finn Michael Mayberry!" Grams calls up the ladder, chastising me.

Jesus, get me down from this damn attic.

My final sweep of the attic reveals no donkeys and definitely not one riding a snowmobile, so I head back down the rickety ladder extended from the attic. The old wood creaks and groans under my weight and I make a mental note to add it to the never-ending list of things around here to fix.

Every time the wind blows, something else breaks or is on the verge of breaking, and there's not enough time nor money to go around.

"Finn, you in here?" My Gramps calls out from the living room. He's been working in the front all morning fixing and arranging everything exactly to Grams' liking until she came in here and put me on the mission of finding the damn donkey.

"In here, Harold!" she yells from her chair in the corner, where she's knitting yet another Christmas sweater of some sort.

"Finn, my boy, thank you for all of your help. You know how much your Grams and I appreciate you," Gramps says as he walks through the hallway door. Snow covers his shoulders and sits in the hair of his white beard. His red, wind-whipped cheeks make him look like a jolly version of everyone's favorite fat man. He's sporting one of Grams' newest creations, a sweater of a Christmas tree with actual fuzzy pom poms knitted into it. He's been grumbling all morning because they keep getting caught on everything. As much as he complains, he'd wear it regardless because he'd do anything for Grams. He walks over and claps me on the back, giving me a warm smile.

It's November first and that means the start of the Christmas season here at Mayberry Inn. Grams and Gramps have owned this inn since they were younger than I am now. I've lived in Hollyridge my entire life, and the Mayberry is where I grew up. I ran down these hallways with toys, and played with the guests' children on the front lawn having snowball wars until we were frozen solid from the cold.

Every memory from my childhood has a piece of this place, so I guess it's only right that it's my turn to take some of the reins, literally and figuratively. My grandparents are getting older and with Gramps' heart problems in addition to the scare that we recently had with said heart problems, they're forced to take a step back and not work so hard.

And that's where I come in. Now the place I once called home growing up is where I find myself once more. When they called, I packed up my small one-bedroom apartment and moved back in. Now, this will be my first year as the person running the inn. I'm determined to make Grams and Gramps proud and to make sure that this place is around for a lot longer. I've been using any free time that I have to do repairs. Paint, fix holes, work on the plumbing. I'm the first to rise and the last to lay my head down at night, but it'll pay off.

"It's nothing Gramps. We'll have this place fixed up in no time. I just wish you would've asked for my help earlier."

"Well, I tried to do it all myself, but you know this old ticker isn't allowing me to do much of anything anymore. With your Grams here on my back, I need to follow the doctors order and let my body rest," he says, his face falling ever so slightly. My heart squeezes at Gramps crestfallen face. I hate seeing him feel like this.

When you've put your heart and soul in something for the last fifty years, only to be told that your body won't allow you to anymore... It's a tough thing to wrap your head around. That's why I want to be here to help them as much as I can. It's up to me to restore the inn to its original glory.

"Don't worry Gramps." I give him a reassuring smile.

Grams looks up over the rim of her thin, gold metal framed glasses and says, "You know, Finn, me and the ladies at Pokeno last week were just talking about you."

And here we go...

"Mary Ellen has a granddaughter that is coming to visit for the holidays. I think it would be so lovely if you took her out and showed her the town."

"Christ. Grams, I do not need you setting me up with your friends' grandchildren. I am perfectly capable of finding a woman."

She grins ever so slightly. "I know that Finn, but you're creepin' in on thirty. You know that they consider women geriatric when they have children over thirty?" She huffs. "All the women in the town fawn all over you, why don't you just pick one already?"

Why am I single at twenty-seven? Because there's not a woman in this town that interests me enough to keep her around longer than the night. I wouldn't call myself a player or anything of the sort because my grandparents taught me to respect a woman. But I'm up front. They know exactly what they're in for from the start. I'm not looking for anything serious. The Mayberry is what has my full attention and I don't have time for any distractions.

"C'mon Grams. You know you're the only woman in my life." I grin.

Grams loves me, I know it, but the meddling drives me insane

She rolls her eyes and huffs, "Would you please do it, Finn? For me?"

This guilt trip is taking a turn for the worse, quickly. The look on her face is one that makes me feel bad and I haven't even done anything wrong. Dammit Grams.

"Fine. But it's not a date," I mutter.

Her face lights up and she hastily puts her knitting on the table beside her, then stands.

"Oh, I have to go call Mary Ellen and tell her! She will be so excited." She squeals then leaves me and Gramps standing there, off to gossip with her friends.

Gramps looks at me and laughs, clapping me on the shoulder once more. "Welcome to the past fifty years of my life, son. You do a lot of things you don't want to do for the women that you love."

Tell me about it.

It's late by the time we get all of the decorations unboxed and Saint Nick, the inn's resident mascot and reindeer/donkey has been tended to. With the house silent and still, I sit down in front of the crackling fire, thankful for the quiet moments that are rare in a house filled with people at all times. It's been an adjustment from having my own peaceful solitude to the hustle and bustle of guests. Even though bookings through what is usually the Mayberry's prime tourist season have been...light. Which worries me more than anything. Usually the inn is completely booked, no vacancies. That was my first sign that something wasn't right.

One thing that my grandparents have always believed in is family. The Mayberry may not be the biggest, or the fanciest inn in Hollyridge. It may have a few loose floorboards, and need a new coat of paint, but it's always been a place where guests can come to feel welcomed. Since the Mayberry's foundation is built on tradition, people enjoy coming here to spend quality time with their families. Each year we get a wave of the same familiar faces as families make visiting their own personal tradition.

But for the past few years...business has slowed down. Greatly.

Kids get older, they get iPads, Instagram and TikTok, or whatever the hell they call it, and then spending face to face quality time with their families isn't very high on their list of priorities and yeah, I get it. Today's generation is much different than the one I was raised in. But that's what we're trying so hard to do here, preserve a place that is filled with love, tradition, and the real Christmas spirit. One that doesn't include TikTok.

Although it's hard to stay positive and cheery when the bills I see Gramps carry in every day weigh heavily on us all. We have three months and then the bank is going to foreclose on the property and everything that Grams and Gramps worked so hard to build. So, it's up to me to save the inn and make a legacy that our family can be proud of. No pressure, right?

Chapter Two
Freya

The real estate listings for this quaint little mountain town are like freaking unicorns. There and gone in a blink. Something that might've been a vodka cranberry soda-induced mirage.

This is the third time I've lost out on a place in the two weeks since I arrived in Hollyridge, Montana. I got here just in time for the holiday season.

With a dejected sigh, I toss my phone to the faux fur chair matching the one I'm curled up in. For the time being, I dash my dreams of an Insta-worthy rustic cabin to call my own, and turn to the floor-to-ceiling window overlooking the snowy mountainside view. A Michael Bublé song plays in the background on the flatscreen during a scene from 12 Dates of Christmas, the cheerful holiday soundtrack filtering through the speaker system while I wallow. Even a fun holiday romcom movie can't lift my spirits like they usually do, my go-to favorite pick-me-up lacking the usual mood-lifting magic it brings me.

My new friend Riley swears I'll be able to see wild elk from my window, but they're as elusive as the Zillow listings around here. The only thing I've spotted from my window is a donkey, and that's not what I came all this way for.

Elk aren't real reindeer, but with their pronged horns, it's close enough for me to pretend I'm witnessing some Christmas magic from my favorite movies with my own eyes in *real* snow.

The corner of my mouth lifts. I pull my highlighted brown hair half up in a messy knot and cross my legs, admiring my new knit socks from the outfitter shop downstairs.

I didn't expect Montana to be so cold. Those street fashion Pinterest girls lied to me in their chic sweater dresses and thigh high boots when I was packing to come out here from California. I finally broke down and grabbed them to help my winter-challenged ass warm up. The cream cable-knit knee socks go perfect with my fuzzy pink coat.

I arrange my legs so they're kicked over the side of the low lounge chair and snap a shot that captures the view and part of my room—*Scandinavian Winter*, an all-white dreamscape with modern touches. Each one at the property has a name instead of a number, creating a home away from home experience tailored to our guests' needs.

"Perfect," I murmur, editing it and adding it to the hotel's Instagram feed with the caption *getting cozy in one of our rooms with a view, plan your stay today for a dreamy winter escape* #thealpinehollyridge #winterwonderland.

It's better this way. My hashtag cabin style home decor dreams can wait. First, I've got goals to smash.

Staying at the Alpine, Dad's latest crown jewel in his hotel empire, I can get a better feel for running the place.

It's the reason I came here. This is my big chance to not be seen as my father's daughter working for him. The one I've fought tooth and nail to earn, to prove to Dad I'm perfectly capable of managing a property. It only took me until I was twenty-five and blue in the face for him to finally listen.

Thank god, because that desperate shade of blue so doesn't go with my SoCal tan complexion.

I half-heartedly watch the movie for a few minutes before I give up and turn it off. I'm in serious mourning over that perfect cabin.

Maybe what I need after the letdown from the real estate listings is some fun. The resort offers a full spectrum of amenities to cater to our guests. They can create their perfect vacation whether they like the spa with our natural hot spring or are the adventurous type with winter sports.

Two weeks into my new residence in Hollyridge and I haven't braved the outdoors yet. Looking at pictures of snowy mountains on my phone and actually standing at the foot of one blanketed in snow are two very different experiences. I open the hotel's app on my phone and browse the amenities, swiping past snowboarding with lifted brows.

"Surfing, yes. Snowboarding? I don't think so. Losing balance on a surfboard isn't as scary as face planting into the snowy mountainside at top speed." Dragging my teeth over my lip absently, I tilt my head. "Why don't we have sled dogs? That would be fun. I could totally chill with dogs in the snow."

Mental note, debut the Alpine's own sled dog team next year. It'll have a kids center, where Balto will play on a projector. *Hell yes.* It's making me nostalgic just thinking about Balto making it back to town with our own pack of dogs at the resort.

With thoughts of the future attraction at the resort filling my head, I keep flicking through the options for something to do.

There are almost too many choices, giving me a sense of decision paralysis when faced with the unfamiliar. Winter in California is nothing like it is here in Montana.

I debate texting Riley for some "moral support". Translation: I love Christmas, but I have no idea *how* to do all these winter activities on offer at the Alpine Mountain Resort.

For all that I've traveled the world for Dad and the company, I've always been so focused on working twice as hard as any of the other executives. There's never been time for distractions, recreational or otherwise, not when I have to do everything in my power to make sure no one thinks I haven't earned my spot at the table fair and square. Dad responds to nothing short of better than my best.

It wasn't any different growing up, either. Dad lives and breathes his empire of hotels around the country. He built his renowned reputation with money and power as his building blocks, sacrificing the time to make family memories in favor of his own personal form of world domination. I don't think we've spent a Christmas together as a family since I was ten, after my parents divorced and split our family down the middle—me living with Dad because I was the oldest and my younger brothers going with Mom when she left.

Spending so many Christmases alone, I fostered a serious love of feel-good holiday movies—from nostalgic classics to cheesy romances to the hilarious comedies, I love them all and they are my strongest memories of growing up.

The only reason I was finally given the opportunity to take over this property is because Dad's health has been declining since the resort was built. Two of the older, more experienced senior executives fought to take the Alpine, but in the end Dad gave it to me with a gruff command.

Cue my internal happy dance. On the outside I was a cool little California cucumber amidst the stubborn grumbling of my colleagues. *Screw them; I freaking earned this.*

I'm the only one in Montana. Me. Not those douchebags who have always looked down on me.

If I'm going to run this resort my way to show Dad I'm ready for more, I want to familiarize myself with everything. The guests will have trouble telling me apart from the locals in Hollyridge within another month.

My mouth curls into a satisfied smile. *Damn right, girl.* I mentally give myself a confident fist pump.

No safety nets this time. It's everything I've been working for. Time to crush it.

Feeling better about my missed unicorn cabin, I send a text to Riley after all. I need a girls night and she's my only friend in town.

Freya: You're looking at the resident of the Scandinavian Winter room for the foreseeable future because Zillow hates me [confetti emoji]. Hot toddy and hot spring soak date?
Riley: You had me at hot toddy. Hell yes, I need to get all steamy and wet [smirk emoji]

A laugh bursts from me at her response, and I get up to change into a strappy gold designer bikini that sets off my tan. The resort robe is plush and luxurious with a dark green embroidered mountain from our logo. I let out a hum of pleasure as I wrap it tight around myself.

Armed with my phone, always prepared to start an Instagram Live to showcase the hotel, I lock the door to my home for now and head to meet up with my new friend.

Riley is on my staff at the resort, doubling as a part-time ski instructor as well as the teacher for our art classes. The first day I met her, when I accidentally walked right in during the middle of a pottery class, we clicked immediately.

Thank god, because I am so in need of some friends around here.

In the elevator, a cute guy gives me a casual flick of his eyes.

I offer him a smirk that always leaves men wanting more, but it's all he'll get from me. One, I don't hook up with guests. Learned that lesson the hard way at our property in Hawaii. Two, I don't have time for relationships. I haven't in a while, not since college two years ago, and even that wasn't really serious. I've been too focused on making Dad see me to worry about a boyfriend.

It's just me and the trusty vibe to keep me warm at night, rather than solid muscles and hot lips making me shiver. Good thing my imagination runs wild with fantasies of what I'd do with a rugged, sexy guy in my cute rustic cabin, snowed in on a chilly winter night. At the thought, a rush of hot and cold tingles spread over my skin, and a pulse of heat tugs in my belly. *Oof, yes please Mr. Mountain Man.*

Flipping my hair over my shoulder, I exit the elevator with my mood lifting by the second.

As I walk through the luxurious lobby full of leather, wood, and stone accents to set the atmospheric mood of Hollyridge's mountain locale, a thrill rushes through me.

I get to be in charge of all of this.

I can't wait to get started. My mind is already brimming with ideas.

Chapter Three
Finn

Hollyridge is a sleepy, tourist town tucked away, deep in the Montana mountains. Our small town is surrounded by huge, snow-capped mountains, crystal blue lakes that have frozen for winter, tall pine trees coated with a fresh coat of fluffy snow. It's straight out of a painting.

The best thing about Hollyridge is the quiet, peaceful serene that feels like nowhere else. Unlike most other tourist towns, its small-town charm is still untouched by the rest of the world. You can walk down the street and see people without their phones glued to their faces. They're taking in the sights, window shopping, and spending time with friends.

Today, town square is packed and excitement buzzes through the air. Even old Dr. Thomas at the local family-owned medical practice was all smiles when Mrs. Moore was here this morning, flirtin', pretending she hasn't been married to Ed for the last forty years. Nothing new, those two. Doc

Thomas is as grumpy as they come but it seems like the approaching Christmas season has everyone in high spirits, including him.

"Finn Mayberry!"

I hear a loud, high-pitched voice behind me. It takes everything inside me not to let out the groan that's threatening to bust out at the sound of her voice. I'd know that voice anywhere. Ella Arnold. A few meaningless nights together and she's hanging on like the modern day black plague. I avoid her in all ways possible, which is extremely hard to do in a town this size. And the fact that she owns the one and *only* Christmas store in town, and Grams likes to send me for things at least once a week? I unfortunately see a lot more of Ella than I care to. She's about one late night roll by my house from a full blown stalker.

"Ella, how are you?" I give her a polite smile and pray to God she doesn't think I'm flirting or something crazy. Knowing her... she mistakes politeness for more. Trust me, the only thing I want from Ella is for her to forget she even knows me.

She giggles and lazily twirls a loose piece of hair around her finger. The reason I don't want to be with Ella has absolutely nothing to do with her looks. She's beautiful, always has been. Her long, honey-colored hair falls in waves past her waist. Her simple light pink sweater paired with tight jeans shows off every curve she has, and let's be honest showcases an ass that made me come back for more, more than once. Hell, if she wasn't so damn crazy I might have entertained something serious, but when she started to show up at my apartment at random hours of the night, I knew I needed to cut her loose and fast. I think she has some notion in her head that we'll end up together like soulmates or something. Bat shit fucking crazy, this one.

"I'm good. Just getting things ready for a busy Christmas

season. You know, with the store and stuff." She smiles warmly and then we stand there awkwardly for a few beats before I break the thick silence.

"Well, it was great talking to you. I've gotta get home to Grams, she sent me into town for some supplies." I lift the grocery bags I'm holding.

She nods. "Oh okay. Right. Did you see the Jingle Wars announcement this year?"

I haven't, but it's not like I've been paying much attention anyway. I never do. I hate that stupid competition and wish they'd find a new town to host it in. Jingle Wars started as a small competition years ago, just a silly local tradition. Now that it has gained national attention in recent years, it's growing bigger like it's the next Shark Tank, inviting local businesses to compete for bigger prizes. Although, it does bring a ton of traffic to the town, so I try not to complain much. Without the crowd that it brings in, I think this tiny town would disappear right off the map.

"Nah, I haven't had much of a chance. Grams is keeping me real busy at the inn." I make sure to emphasize "real busy" so hopefully she takes the hint and stops calling ten times a day. Fat chance there though.

She leans in closer and whispers in a hushed voice, "Apparently there's some big time sponsor this year and the grand prize is one hundred thousand dollars. Can you believe it?"

A hundred k? Seriously?

"Ella, I've got to run, but it was nice talking to you." I don't let her get in another word before I'm headed in the opposite direction. I make my way through the crowd to town square until I see the huge bulletin board that sits in the middle. There's a poster advertising for Jingle Wars. For the first time I'm interested.

A hundred thousand dollars is a lot of money. The poster

reads a grand prize for the winner of three "Christmas" themed competitions that will be announced within the next few days.

I wonder who the silent donor is?

I'm taking a copy of the flyer that's pinned to the board and turning to head back to the inn when I collide with something warm, fuzzy, and soft.

"Oh—*crap!*"

Everything happens in slow motion, a flurry of limbs and chaos. I reach out for the woman who's collided with me, and catch her before she can hit the ground.

"Oh my God, I'm so sorry!" she cries as I set her back on her feet and help steady her. She adjusts the thin cardigan that she's wearing, and only then do I get my bearings enough to realize how beautiful she is.

Beautiful, and not a resident of Hollyridge. I would know her if she was. I'd never forget her face if I'd seen it before.

She's around five foot tall, give or take an inch or two. Much shorter than my six two. So much that I have to look down at her. Bright blue eyes framed by thick, dark lashes peer back at me. Her cheeks and nose are red from the cold, and snowflakes cling to her lashes. Pink, lush lips that I immediately want to kiss draw my attention. They compliment her dark, highlighted wavy hair that falls down her back. I'm taken aback by her beauty. Her attire on the other hand? It immediately catches my attention. Definitely not intended for a Montana winter. Her fuzzy, pale pink cardigan is paired with simple black leggings that hug her curves, not that I got much of a glance in the scuffle. She's wearing a pair of furry UGG boots that are soaked through from the snow. How she's not shivering, I have no idea. I'm cold just looking at her.

"It's no problem, that ice can be slippery without the right shoes." I grin and glance down at her UGGs.

She laughs, then her boot catches another piece of ice, almost causing her to fall once more. I reach out and steady her before she ends up on her ass. Obviously beautiful, but sensible not so much...

Don't be an ass Finn, maybe she's just a tourist and doesn't know any better.

"These damn shoes! Thank you, seriously." Her cheeks turn another shade darker and she's obviously flustered, but damn if it doesn't make her that much more attractive.

"It's no problem. It looks like you're probably not from around here," I tell her, gesturing to her attire.

"Is it that obvious?" She wrinkles her nose and looks down at her feet.

I laugh, offering a nonchalant shrug. "Maybe a little. You have to be freezing. Hollyridge winters are no joke."

"I am," she admits, fiddling with the buttons on her cardigan. "I wasn't planning on coming into town, but I was going stir crazy. Wanted to see for myself everything Hollyridge has to offer." She holds up her phone and offers a beaming smile. Bouncing on the balls of her feet excitedly, she shows me her phone. "I swear I can't stop taking pictures of everything. My Insta feed is so cute right now."

"Ah, yeah, it's a great place. To visit or to live. Friendly people, good food, lot's to see. I'm Finn by the way." I extend my hand to her and she places her small, albeit freezing fingers in mine. A shiver runs down my spine.

"Sorry for the ice fingers. I'm Freya. It's nice to meet you."

I spend the next few minutes pointing out some of the popular spots in town square that my family and I like to go to. There's so much more to Hollyridge than what I can show her from the town square.

This girl is beautiful. The way her eyes light up at the

simpleness that Hollyridge has to offer immediately makes me want to get to know her further. See what else gets such an easy reaction from her.

"You know what? You should let me show you around sometime. Introduce you to the non-tourist version of Hollyridge," I tell her before I can second guess what I'm doing. I just asked her on a date. Sort of.

"That's so sweet. They aren't kidding about how welcoming everyone is here, huh? You know, my schedule is actually super tight this week, but that would be nice. Maybe we can meet over there, at The Coffee Spirit? Friday around four?" She gives me another bright smile, still fiddling with the buttons on her cardigan.

Just from the few minutes around her I can tell she's confident, and sure of herself. The sexiest thing about a woman is the confidence she exudes.

"Yeah, that sounds great." I grin.

There. Done. An *actual* date with someone who I wasn't set up with through my Grams on bingo night. She'll be proud.

I bite back a laugh at the thought.

"Well, I have to get back home with this stuff but it was nice to meet you, Freya. I'll see you next week." I toss her a flirty grin and she responds with a cheeky smile of her own. I turn back and start my way home, but sneak one more look at Freya over my shoulder and see her snap a photo of the Jingle Wars poster. This stupid competition was looking more and more appealing by the second.

* * *

"Dude, you're telling me you met a hot new piece of ass in this little bitty town and you didn't think to ask her if she had a sister?" My annoying best friend scoffs, then slams his beer down on the bar for dramatic effect.

"West, I talked to her for like ten minutes. We planned to meet up for coffee and for me to show her around. Not a lot happened in those ten minutes." I didn't want to say much more and jinx it because even though he's annoying, he's right.

New people constantly pass through, but very few stay longer than a few days, maybe a week at most.

"While I was in town today, I ran into Ella Arnold, unfucking fortunately, but she told me that the Jingle Wars grand prize this year is a hundred thousand dollars."

"No shit huh?" West takes another pull of his beer, but his attention is on the bartender, Aria, who's talking to another patron at the end of the bar.

"Yeah, I thought about maybe joining this year."

He throws his head back and laughs until he has tears in his eyes. Asshole.

"Why the fuck is that so funny?" I mutter.

He wipes his eyes. "Dude, you literally hate the competition. You bitch about it every year until I'm ready to beat my head on this bar."

"I just think it's such a ridiculous thing to have people compete in fucking Christmas games for money. Like show animals or some shit."

"You boys need another refill?" Aria asks from the other side of the bar.

West shakes his head no, but doesn't speak. The air has turned icy and I can feel the tense vibes between the both of them. Once she's gone I turn to him.

"What was that? Are you boning her?"

He hesitates for a moment, then downs the rest of his beer in one large sip.

"Complicated shit man. Women."

Ain't that the truth.

West has had his share of women problems, starting with Riley Tucker when she was chasing him around the playground. Twenty years later and he's the one doing all the chasing.

"Welcome to my life. At least your eighty year old grandmother isn't setting you up at the bingo hall bro." I grin.

"Yep, you're right. Doesn't she need our help with some lights or some shit tonight?" he asks.

"Damn, I forgot. Yeah, let's get out of here before she throws all the cookies away. You know she's always bribing me with food."

"She knows the way to my heart."

After I finish off my drink, we leave the bar and head home.

When we pull up in the driveway of the inn, Grams is waiting on the front porch, knitting. She's bundled in a sweater with her heated blanket and I shake my head. This woman will worry me crazy. It's cold as shit outside and she's out here like she's on the beach somewhere. The sun has already dipped below the clouds and night is setting in, causing the temperatures to drop.

"Hey Grams," West greets her, dropping a peck on her cheek.

"Why, West Andrew Collins, it's been far too long since you've shown your face around here. Lots of things for you to fix." She smiles.

"I'm here now to make up for lost time." He shoots her a wink and she rolls her eyes in response.

"How about I go and make you boys some hot cocoa for all the hard work that you're going to be doing?" She smiles warmly, like she didn't just half ass bribe us with delicious treats. As usual, my stomach is a damn traitor and as always I'm a sucker for anything that Grams bakes.

She sets down her knitting and rises from the rocker.

"Alright boys, ready to get started? I've got *lots* for you to do."

West and I share a look. Anything for the women we love, right?

Chapter Four
Freya

In a matter of days, the town square at the heart of Hollyridge looks completely different. It was festive before with its cheerful seasonal flags on lamp posts and wreaths on doors, but now it's like the holiday season has exploded from every crevice, flooding the small square with a sea of red, green, gold, and silver. The Jingle Wars competition begins today, the one the posters plastered throughout town have been advertising, inviting businesses to strut their holiday spirit for a national audience.

And I signed up.

I saw the advertisement three days ago when I almost busted my ass on the slippery sidewalk in my soaked UGG boots, too focused on taking the perfect shot for the resort's Instagram story, and I couldn't get Jingle Wars out of my head.

Finn stuck in my thoughts after meeting him, too. I don't need distractions that are tall, look like they can throw me over their shoulder, and have that sexy beard with hints of red shot through the brown, but...he's totally my lumberjack fantasy wrapped up in a muscular, climb-me-like-a-tree package. The kind that has me biting my lip anytime he pops into my head. Total panty-melter with a charming smile and he literally swept me off my feet.

I mean, I was falling—ungracefully as hell, seriously, who knew UGGs have zero traction—but there was definite feet-sweeping going on. I'd be lying if I tried to play it like I'm not looking forward to our coffee date.

After he shows me around town, hopefully he's down to show me other things, like the backseat of his truck and his bedroom.

Hell, I'll take the hallway. Finn has WSE—wall-sex energy. It's written all over him.

I sink my teeth into my lower lip and momentarily lose myself thinking about how his scruff would scrape against the sensitive skin of my inner thighs and my neck. He might have that handsome gentleman's smile that melts me, but, god, I bet he knows how to kiss dirty.

My thirsty ass brain is in overdrive at the first chance of some non-vibe action. *Down girl.* But who wouldn't be attracted to Finn? He's incredibly handsome.

My goals come first, though. They have to. *Don't let yourself stray from why you're here,* I remind myself, shaking my head as I wander the bustling square with Riley.

The hundred grand prize isn't that important to me, but the recognition and publicity? Huge. Representing the Alpine in this Christmas-on-crack competition—Riley's word's, not mine—is the edge I need for my efforts with the resort. If I win the competition, the marketing I can do with the social proof to back it up will bring fantastic buzz to the Anderson Resorts brand.

An icy breeze moves through the grassy area behind the gazebo where a backstage area has been set up. It cuts through my thin, off the shoulder gray Chanel sweater, skating down my spine. I hold the warm cardboard cup of coffee with both hands and brace against the instinct to shiver. I'm freezing in my outfit, but the red leather pants and Santa Baby-level heels are worth it. Impressions are everything in business and marketing, so I want to look good for the competition's first airing where the contestants are introduced.

A stage is set up in front of the huge gazebo, both structures decked out in garlands of fresh cut pine and red velvet ribbons. Holiday songs blast from a speaker system before the broadcast with the host begins. The crowd of people filling the live audience gathered in front of the stage create a low murmur floating in and out as we walk around in the production area.

"You know," I say to Riley, "when you said this town loved this competition, I didn't think you meant it would be like this."

Riley shrugs as a woman in a volunteer shirt with honey blonde curls shot through with gray waves to her. I've seen the volunteer woman running the bakery when I've ventured into town in the last couple of days. She makes sinfully good bear claws and I might be addicted. The show volunteer-slash-bakery owner isn't the only person Riley recognizes. This whole competition really has taken over the quaint little town of Hollyridge.

"Yeah, it's always been loved like this by locals. But then the tourists get a bigger kick out of it every year, so it keeps growing. Look at it now." Riley nods at the camera crew setting up. "All professional and shit with filming teams. It used to be on the public service station when I was in high school and put on by local volunteers. Now it's a big to-do." She tilts her head. "But I would've thought something like this wouldn't surprise you, Hollywood."

She keeps calling me that to tease me. Ever since I walked into her pottery class at the Alpine on my first day, when I was looking for one of my lobby managers, phone pressed to my ear as I talked while sending an email on my tablet. Exec life waits for no one. It took me a full two minutes to realize I'd interrupted the class. Riley had told me where to find the business center, assuming I was a lost suit, only to find out I was her new boss when I took my sunglasses off.

My nose wrinkles. "Ew. I didn't live in the Hills. Before here, I lived in Malibu."

"*Ew*," Riley mimics, exaggerating my California accent, which sounds hilarious in her soft Montana drawl.

I poke her side with an amused sound. "Not everyone in California is just walking around movie sets all the time. I'm too busy in the office at Anderson Resorts, so this is new for me."

"You're all about diving in, huh?"

"I'm a take life by the horns kinda gal," I say, imitating a twangy accent. "I'm bringing home the blue ribbon for the Alpine family, baby."

Riley smiles, the corners of her pretty green eyes crinkling. "I hope this isn't like the first time you rode the ski lift yesterday."

I release a dramatic, scandalized gasp, pressing a palm to my exposed collarbones. "Traitor! How could you? You promised to *never* speak of that debacle ever again. That thing is like a death trap. There has to be a safer way up a mountain." My coffee sloshes in the cup as I gesture wildly. "Honestly, you guys are crazy for ever getting on it."

During the Ski Lift Incident, she had keeled over in hysterics. Even as one of the part-time ski instructors, she couldn't get me on that thing again. Who ever thought it was a good idea to dangle people from a swinging basket on a cable high above the mountainside?

She releases a hearty cackle and shakes her head. "Who put you in charge of a winter resort? You're the opposite of all things winter."

My amusement at our banter disappears as the weight of my doubt slams into me unexpectedly. I clear my throat and flick my nail against the plastic lid of my cup.

Goals are only wishes we dream up if they're unconquerable.

I swallow past the lump forming in my throat. This is silly to get all twisted up over. Sometimes it hits me out of nowhere when I least expect it, because I focus so hard on work.

I'm not a little girl pining for my parents at Christmas every time I watch a holiday movie wishing my family could be perfect like that. I'm the woman who works her ass off to achieve what she sets out to do.

"My father."

"Well, jeez, don't go sulking like someone pissed in your Starbucks cup." She nudges my shoulder. "Buck up, buttercup."

I shake my shoulders out and offer her a smile. "You're right. I'm sorry for being a downer. I think I'm nervous."

"You? *Psh*. Girl, you exude confidence."

This time my smile is more genuine as my worries melt back into the shadows of my mind where they belong. I give them a mental middle finger. "Thanks. This'll be good. I can do this."

"Anytime."

Another chilly breeze blows through the square, making me shudder. The tip of my nose is cold. I hope it doesn't start to run when I'm on stage for the broadcast.

"You'll be an icicle before you're even called up," Riley points out with a smirk, bundled in her double-lined parka.

She flashed me the fleece interior in my room at the Alpine before we left to come downtown for the filming. I want nothing more than to tear her coat open and sink into the warmth, sharing the coat with my friend, but that would be giving in and the weather won't beat me.

Riley's head tilts, gaze skating over me from head to toe. "A cute icicle though. All the guys will want to lick you for a taste."

With a smirk, I pop my hip out and pose. "That's the idea. I'm up there as a visual representation of how great the Alpine is. Marketing is all about subtle psychological messages, and I, my friend, have mastered the art."

"Sex sells," Riley adds. "It's already working. You've definitely caught my friend's eye."

I follow her line of sight and my cheeks flush. Finn, my walking rugged mountain man wet dream, admires my red leather pants from several feet away while he brushes off one of the production company's makeup artists buzzing around him. The corner of my mouth curls up. See? Entering this competition was the best idea.

Suck it, doubts.

When he drags his eyes up to meet mine, I give him a cheeky wink.

Caught you, I mouth with a hint of flirtiness across the distance separating us.

His gaze slides over me once more, unapologetic about checking me out in a way that has my insides heating up pleasantly, then shrugs and offers me a rueful smile.

Oof. Double oof! The charm rolls off him in waves so strong, I feel my heart skipping a beat from all the way over here where Riley and I stand.

Her breathy puff of laughter breaks me from the seductive Finn-induced spell. When I glance at her, she drinks deeply from her coffee with her brows raised.

"What?" I ask.

"Nothing. Just witnessing another victim of Finn's drool all over her designer sweater. It's a time-honored pastime in Hollyridge for our hometown heartthrob. Townie or tourist, no one is safe from his dimples and warm whiskey-eyes," Riley says with all the sageness of a town elder. "I've seen the best of us go down in all the years I've known him."

A protest catches in my throat as I hastily swipe around my lips painted with matte longwear lipstick, checking my fingers. No smudges. We're golden. "I am not drooling. I am —*admiring*."

Riley laughs again. "Yeah, okay."

"Besides, who wouldn't?" I make a subtle gesture in Finn's direction, where the makeup artist has wrangled him for a touch up anyway. A snort escapes me at the sight of him grimacing while her powder brush swipes over his nose. It doesn't make him any less hot. "That dude is stacked and I'm one hundred percent here for it."

His ass in those dark jeans? Here for it. That sexy deep voice? Here. For. It.

Riley's shoulders shake with her snickering. "See? Another victim of his hunky status. Nah, none for me, thanks. I've been friends with him too long and know too many of his gross guy habits."

Before I can say more, a man with thick-rimmed glasses, a headset, and a clipboard materializes at my side.

"We're ready for the contestants to line up now," he says. "We're live in ten with the host."

"Okay, thank you."

He moves on to tap the shoulders of several other contestants, including Finn. People start moving over to the stage and forming a line as they're herded by the production team.

Riley takes my unfinished coffee and I lift my brows. "Showtime."

Chapter Five
Freya

"Knock 'em dead, killer," Riley says.

"I think you're supposed to say break a leg for good luck," I say.

She pulls a face. "Why on earth would I want you to get hurt? I'm already worried as it is, you can't even manage a ski lift ride."

My mouth pops open and I hold up a finger. "Never! Again!" I hiss, eyes darting around to make sure no one heard her. "Quit harshing my vibe, dude! Now I'll get all nervous again."

Setting our coffees on a picnic table, Riley takes me by the shoulders and gives me a little shake. "Get a hold of yourself. This ain't the boss ass bitch who showed up in my pottery class. Go on now." She spins me and smacks my ass as I stumble in the four inch heels. "Show the world who you are."

She's right. Dad probably isn't watching, even though I

texted him the details and a livestream link. But that doesn't mean I'm not going to show him anyway.

I sidle up next to Finn as the headset guy reappears to put us in order of how we're being called to the stage. The host stands nearby in a bright red suit with coat tails and a top hat. He's a portly man with a white whiskery beard.

"Fancy meeting you here," I say to Finn. I hold up my fists and pretend to box. "I guess this makes you my rival now. May the best Christmas lover win."

He grunts, scratching the back of his head. His demeanor is off from how easy-going he seemed when we met, his body language stiff. "Yeah. This was kind of last minute. Not my usual thing."

"What?" I fake a shocked gasp and plant my hands on my hips. Leaning close, I look side to side and whisper, "Are you saying you're *not* a Christmas lover? The wolf in lamb's wool sneaking in?"

Finn's lips twitch and he swipes his fingers around his mouth, tracing his scruff. He relaxes, losing the tense set of his shoulders. I bite my lip and flutter my lashes up at him. A warm ember glows in the pit of my stomach just being around him.

Or maybe that's because he smells fucking fantastic—cedar and spice, adding to the whole outdoorsy lumberjack hottie vibe. *Yes, please.*

I press closer, whipping out my phone. "Let's take a behind the scenes selfie. I bet the hashtag for the competition is poppin'. We'll give the viewers a little reality TV drama. Maybe they'll start shipping us. Do you think they'd put your name first or mine in our portmanteau?"

"Uh, what?" Finn blinks at me in the wake of my rapid rambling, his hand automatically finding my waist.

Mm, big hands. I shake my head and beam at him. *Jesus. Cool it, brain, you thirsty bitch.*

"Come on, let's do it!" I elbow his side as I tease him. "You can't be much older than me to not know what a selfie is. Definitely not old enough to call Daddy—"

"*What?*" Finn chokes and squeezes my waist, practically massaging it. Damn, that feels nice. With a rough, almost growled cough, he clears his throat. His eyes go wide and his thick brows rise into his wind-tousled brown hair line as he stares at me with intensity burning in his gaze. "You—"

Laughter bursts from me and I lean into his side. "Sorry, oh my god. The look on your face. Too easy! But for real, let's take a selfie."

As soon as I've snapped a photo of us snuggled together, a trilling trumpet takes over the holiday soundtrack, drawing everyone's attention.

"It's starting," Finn says. A determined look settles on his face, a crease forming between his eyebrows and the corners of his mouth tipping down.

The host jogs onto the stage, waving for the crowd that cheers for him. He's more spry than I would've guessed. Maybe the beard is dyed. Or these country boys are just made of sturdier stock than the people I know his age.

"Ladies and gentleman, holiday enthusiasts far and wide, welcome back for another year of Jingle Wars! Your favorite Christmas competition that tests hopefuls every year to be crowned the champion of the best holiday of the year," the host announces with flair. "We're live in Hollyridge, Montana and the contestants are lined up backstage waiting to meet you. I'm Cornelius Frost, your host! This year we're bigger than ever with competitions you voted on to challenge our contestants."

While he talks, I post my photo with Finn to social media, tagging the competition. The cold still bites through my clothes, so I huddle close to him to absorb some of his body heat.

"You know, I'm surprised you're here, too," Finn says. "First you're tripping over snow, and now you're competing in this?"

I shrug. "I like trying new things. It seemed like the perfect way to prove something to my dad." My lips pull to the side as I hesitate, searching for a way to phrase it. I don't know Finn very well, and I can't unload my family baggage on him all willy nilly. "I have to be loud to get his attention."

"So a game show?" Finn frowns, studying me. After a beat, he nods to the stage, where the first person in line is climbing the steps for their introduction. "This thing gets pretty intense and wild. Last year there was a camping challenge in the woods." His deep brown gaze slides over me, lingering on my exposed neckline from the off-shoulder designer sweater. "Are you sure you're up for something out of your element if you're not used to a Montana winter?"

My mouth pops open to give him an immediate denial, then closes so I can think first. I purse my lips. It's true. I've discovered how averse I am to real winter nonstop since arriving in Hollyridge from California, but I'm not letting anything stop me, not my doubts, or the company's vulture executives biting at my heels—or Finn, no matter how good his intentions.

The tall snow-capped peaks catch my eye from above the shop roofs in the square. There's something about looking at these majestic mountains surrounding town that gives me the drive I need to keep going. I can do it.

"The chivalry is appreciated, but unnecessary. I can handle myself just fine, thanks."

Finn tilts his head to the side and holds his hands up. "Alright, darlin'. Meant no harm."

"And now for our next contestant!" Cornelius' voice booms over the loudspeaker. "Let's welcome Finn!"

"You're up," the guy with the headset prompts.

Before he heads for the stage, Finn seems to give himself a pep talk, flexing his hands. The stiffness from before returns as he takes the steps two at a time.

"That's the spirit! Give the audience a wave!" Cornelius makes a sweeping gesture with his arm.

From my vantage point off-stage, I catch Finn's grimace. He lifts his hand as if he's a robot. He hasn't struck me as the shy type, but he's definitely not cool with the cameras pushing in on him as Cornelius introduces him.

"You're here to represent a local favorite, Mayberry Inn," Cornelius says, coming to Finn's side to clap him on the shoulder.

The business he's representing makes me blink. Mayberry. That's the picturesque bed and breakfast next door to the Alpine, isn't it? The hashtag cabin goals one. Finn never told me his last name when we met. I knew the inn was Alpine's neighbor, but I didn't realize that meant *Finn* was my neighbor, too.

"Your family's history runs through Hollyridge. Both locals and visitors from out of town are fans of Grams Mayberry's famous cookies and the resident reindeer," Cornelius continues. "Jingle Wars is glad to see you join our ranks for your chance at winning the game, Finn."

"Uh, yeah." Finn shifts his weight. "Thanks."

"Any messages for our audience?"

When he shakes his head, I practically bounce in place. The tall heels make it difficult, throwing my balance off slightly. *Dude, that was your marketing opening!* If he's here for his family's business same as I am, why isn't he taking every chance to put himself out there? It's Marketing 101.

"Time to bring out our next winter warrior hopeful, then!" Cornelius checks the prompter screen set up next to one of the cameras. "Let's give a warm Hollyridge welcome to rival the

California sunshine, where our next contestant hails from. Let's introduce Freya!"

I give my blow out a fluff to perk up my styled bombshell curls and stride onto the stage to strut my stuff. My smile is so wide my cheeks cramp as I give the crowd a holler and wave.

"Thank you, Cornelius! Howdy, y'all!" Could've been better in my delivery, even though I practiced that. *It's ok, girl, just keep it together.* Reality TV is all about fake it til you make it. I follow Cornelius' silent invitation to take my place next to Finn in the lineup, allowing his comforting woodsy cologne to calm me down. "I'm so excited to be here! There's nothing I love more than the holiday season!"

"Cute as a button, too, isn't she folks?" Cornelius grins into his microphone. "You're here to represent a newer business in town, the Alpine Mountain Resort."

Finn was stiff before, but I feel the undeniable shift in the air when he goes absolutely rigid beside me.

A rough breath leaves him and he mutters something unintelligible under his breath. I throw him a quick glance and am taken aback by the iciness in his gaze. The warmth of his brown eyes is gone, swallowed by a frozen lake of cold regard.

"That's right, Mr. Frost." Ignoring Finn, I switch on marketing mode, my voice taking on a perkier quality than my usual tone. "We're a luxury lifestyle resort to meet all the needs of vacationers with a number of amenities. Whether you come to Hollyridge to unwind, take advantage of its historic shopping district, or are adventurous thrill-seekers looking to take on the beautiful Montana mountain range, allow the Alpine to be your home away from home."

Finn scoffs softly. My eyes flick to him. What is his deal?

"Fantastic. Welcome to Jingle Wars," Cornelius says. "Let's meet our next contestants before we go over the rules!"

I tune the rest of the host's words out as the next few

people are brought up. Attempts to catch Finn's eye are fruitless. He's even turned slightly away from me to give me his shoulder. *What the hell crawled up his ass!*

This can't be nerves from the spotlight. Something about him changed as soon as I was introduced. The corners of my mouth tug down, but I force them back up into a smile for the cameras, compartmentalizing Finn's attitude until the opening ceremony broadcast is finished.

Cornelius Frost runs through the rules after the introductions. "We'll have three rounds of challenges between now and our finale, when we crown our Jingle Wars winner just in time for Christmas. The competition is tough, contestants, so bring your holiday A game for the chance at our grand prize this year: one hundred thousand dollars."

The crowd seated on benches in front of the stage applaud. My focus is all over the place. Finn's low grumbling keeps distracting me. He's growing tenser by the second and I'm starting to worry that I've awoken a bear.

"Who's ready to hear about our first challenge?" Cornelius addresses the audience. Their cheers crescendo. "That's the spirit! Misty, my dear, if you please?"

A young woman dressed up as an elf pulls a gold cord on a plush velvet drape covering a table at the side of the stage. The curtain draws back to reveal a gilded frame of a perfectly trimmed Christmas tree.

"For our first challenge, which will be in a week and a half, our contestants will venture into the wilderness. The true mark of any holiday enthusiast is their ability to pick out the perfect tree." He turns to pace in front of the lineup with dramatic flourish. "The catch is you'll only have three hours to find your choice, cut it down, and bring it to the judging area to decorate. Trees must be complete before the iconic Jingle Bell in the square tolls, or you'll be disqualified."

Woods? Cutting down trees? I chew the inside of my lip. Ok, maybe I didn't think this whole competition thing through before diving in. I take in the framed photo of the decorated tree and realize this might be out of my depth.

I've never had a real Christmas tree. What if I suck at picking one out? Hell, what if I can't cut it down? I fight the urge to twist my fingers anxiously, a nervous habit I kicked long ago.

Every Christmas movie I've ever fallen in love with has prepared me for this moment. My favorite comfort showed me what I was missing out on whenever I was lonely. The momentary anxiety bleeds away, replaced by a burst of anticipation.

So what if I haven't done it for real? I've seen pretty much every holiday movie ever made. I was *born* to pick out the perfect tree.

Bolstered by the surge of confidence, I throw Finn an excited look, only to be reminded of the sudden stick up his butt. His surly expression tries to strangle my enthusiasm. I narrow my eyes. Is this him challenging me? I'm here to win this.

"Be sure to tune in for round one for a holly jolly good time! I'm Cornelius Frost and this is Jingle Wars!"

Our host does a twirl and then someone off-stage yells *cut*. In a flurry of motion, the contestants head for the steps to leave the stage.

Finn brushes by me without a word, eating up the length of the stage in quick strides of his long legs. I have to double-time it to catch up with my much shorter legs and these heels. He's not getting away from me that easily without an explanation.

As he stalks down the steps, I chase after him with conviction burning in my chest.

Chapter Six
Finn

"You," I seethe, whipping around to face my surprising foe. The second I step off the stage, she's at my heels.

I feel betrayed and I don't even know why, but it fucking burns. The fire whipping around my wounded pride.

"Oh, hey, Finn." She props a hand on her hip. "I see we aren't going to have a friendly, neighborly rivalry. I didn't realize you lived next to my resort."

Freya looks up at me through her dark, deceitful eyes paired with a sickly sweet smile painted in red. She has the audacity to look me in the eye and not feel even remotely bad for what she's done. What she's *doing*.

Doesn't matter that she's so fuckable, a perfect present in a pretty bright red bow waiting to be unwrapped. Now that I know who she is, *what* she is, our would be date is out of the question.

Freya is a traitor.

A traitor of the worst kind. One who goes against everything that Hollyridge is.

And after the revelation on the stage, I realize that she's my new neighbor. She's the reason that Grams and Gramps might lose the inn.

It's been bad enough with that damn resort opening next door, bad enough when my friend Riley had to start working there to pay her bills, but this…this is the icing on the fucking cake.

"How about we skip the sweet neighbor shit. I see right through it. You knew I owned the inn next door," I accuse. My voice must be louder than intended because the people walking around us pause to look on to our soon to be argument.

Her dark eyebrows furrow with confusion. "Actually I didn't know that, not until they introduced you. But I wasn't aware that I shouldn't be friendly to my neighbor."

"Oh that's rich. Your "neighbor" that you have no problem stealing business from and trying to drive our business into the ground, right?" I scoff.

Her eyes darken at my accusation and she steps closer to me before she speaks. I try my best not to watch her tits rise against her gray sweater as she crosses her arms across her chest. "You are seriously being an asshole, Finn Mayberry. Way to be warm and welcoming to your new neighbor." She throws her hands up in exasperation. "I haven't done anything wrong!"

"Did you pick your land just because we were next to it? Easy competition?" My teeth grit together in frustration.

"How self centered of you. We chose our land because it's prime real estate. I can't help it if somehow you've gotten it in your head that I am out to get you or your inn."

Freya steps closer, and so do I. Our toes meet. An inch more and her amazing, completely off limits tits would be pressed against my chest.

The thought of that does nothing but make me more angry, and horny. Two lethal combinations.

"Right. You chose the piece of land directly next to ours and set up shop. Did it ever occur to you that as a small business, we would be directly affected? Of course not. You come here in your Mercedes, throw up a five star resort with little consideration to the people who have worked their entire lives for what they have. Daddy's money isn't so common 'round here, Princess."

My face is centimeters from her, even while looking down on her and I can feel the rise and fall of her heaving chest with each pant. I'm so pissed I want to put her over my knee and spank her here, right now, just to teach her an important life lesson to keep your friends close, and your enemies closer.

Because that's exactly what we are now. Enemies.

"You are such an asshole. I'm trying to run my family business, same as you are. Don't make assumptions. You don't know me, Finn, and now you never will." She narrows those striking blue eyes and huffs.

"Well great. Consider our date cancelled. It's never happening," I spit back at her. "I'm not fraternizing with my enemy. " I feel my blood pressure rising with each second I have to spend in her presence. My hands tighten into fists at my side on their own accord.

"Fine. I don't care." She doesn't step back, remaining toe to toe with me, a mutinous look on her face like she's ready to throw down. I'd like to see her pint-sized, five-nothing ass try.

"Fine," I say back, fueling her annoyance.

Good. Be annoyed. *Hate me for all I care.*

Because she just started a war.

Before she can leave, I get one last jab in. "You are so out of your element here, Princess. With your fancy clothes, and high heels, and holier than thou attitude. You won't make it through the first round of this competition. You started a war that you won't be able to finish."

"We'll see about that. May the best one win."

She turns on her heel and stomps off, leaving me standing there, no less angry than I was ten minutes ago.

A whole lot angrier, in fact, and even more determined to win this stupid competition.

* * *

Hours later, I'm still somewhat annoyed. Every time I hammer another nail into the wood, I feel my frustration dissipate slightly. Then I look over and see her towering resort looming over me and I'm mad all over again.

Grams walks over to the ladder I'm on, peering up at me with an amused look on her face.

"Hammering awful loud out here, Finn. Everything alright?" She asks.

Hammer. Hammer. Hammer.

"Yep, everything's great, Grams."

Another string of Christmas lights, another nail. Maybe if I make the inn ten times better than her resort, we can win back some of our business. Or maybe if she wasn't so damn beautiful, I could think straight for five minutes, and that just makes me hate her even more.

"Finn, did you hear me? You're gonna hammer a finger clean off. Come on down from that ladder before we end up in the emergency room and you know tonight is Pokeno night."

I sigh, then set the hammer and nails down on the shelf of the ladder before climbing back down. I guess now is the best time as any to tell her about Jingle Wars. It's up to me to save the Mayberry.

"I've been thinking today Grams..." I trail off as I follow her inside to the warmth of the inn. It's cold as shit out here, but lights don't hang themselves.

Grams busies herself in the kitchen alongside Bell, our chef, making what looks like chocolate chip cookies. My favorite. She always tries to have treats available to the guests. Part of her "homey" touch. Even if we only have a few guests right now...it doesn't stop her from making way more cookies than needed.

"I'm sure you've heard by now... I entered the Jingle Wars competition..."

She stops stirring and looks at me, unblinking, then throws her head back and busts out laughing. She laughs and laughs until Bell joins her and they both have tears streaming down their faces.

"Glad you find this amusing Grams," I mutter.

"Oh Finn, honey," she coos as she walks over and pulls me into a hug. "Of course, I heard. But why in the world would you join the competition? I know you are not a fan."

"The grand prize is a hundred thousand dollars this year. We could fix the inn, we could pay the remainder of the mortgage off and everything would be alright." My voice breaks when an unexpected bout of emotion hits me full force. If anything in the world could make me soft, it's my Grams.

Her eyes water, and fill with tears. Real ones this time, not from laughing. She pulls back to look at me. I know she's not one to show how stressed or worried she really is, but I see it. It's there in her eyes every time a stack of mail is brought in. Or when something breaks. I'm doing this for my Grams. So I can take the worry from her shoulders.

She brings a hand to my face, "Darling Finn. You are doing more than enough around here to help Gramps and I. You don't need to enter that competition, we will figure it out dear, we always do."

That's the point. They shouldn't *have* to figure things out. It's not their fault someone decided to build a resort right next to the inn and cause bookings to plummet. They shouldn't have to worry, or struggle when they've spent their entire lives putting everything into this inn.

"Don't worry about a thing Grams, I'm going to take care of it. Now, I'm gonna go take care of Saint and the stalls and talk with Gramps. I'll be back later for some of those cookies, 'kay?" I give her a wink and walk out the kitchen into the dining room. I try my best to downplay the emotion because I can't stand to see the tears in her eyes.

She'll have me crying in the kitchen like a damn pussy.

I find Gramps in the stalls, petting Saint—the real star of the show here at the Mayberry. Really, a donkey is what brings people back here. Not the quiet, quaint inn. Not Grams' chocolate chip cookies and hot cocoa, or even the fact that Gramps is basically Santa in the flesh. A damn donkey.

I won't lie though, that damn donkey is the best friend I've ever had. He's as old as me but still as perky as the day we got him. Which, we never really intended to do. Get a donkey that is. Gramps was driving back on County road one snowy night and Saint stumbled out across the road. His mother died and he was left alone, freezing and starving. Gramps brought him back to the inn and nursed him back to life. Bottle fed him and all. Now, he's a permanent part of the Mayberry as much as me, Grams, and Gramps.

"How's it goin Gramps?" I ask as I join him in Saint's stall. I pick a few carrots up from his treat bucket and feed them to him. He loves carrots, but don't let him fool you, he loves Jolly Ranchers the most. It's our secret and I don't tell anyone because I'm about ninety percent sure that donkeys shouldn't have them, but hey we all have our vices.

"Finn, my boy! Good, good. Just brushing Saint Nick here."

He brings the brush across his coat in leisurely strokes. Saint's ears twitch and he lets out a hee-haw.

"It's funny, this donkey has heard a many of things over the years. He listens and never has much to say, but it's everything that I need to hear. Never thought he'd be a part of the family the way that he is." He pats Saint Nick in a loving gesture.

"Talked to Grams just now." I pause and pet Saint gently. "I entered Jingle Wars."

Gramps looks up from his job of brushing and laughs. "Bet she had a lot to say about that."

I grin. "You know Grams, she speaks her mind."

"What made you decide to do that?"

We'll lose the Mayberry if I don't.

I don't want to worry Gramps, but looking over the numbers last night, things are a lot worse than he originally let on. So I give him the watered down version that won't make his heart give out.

"The grand prize is a hundred thousand. That would solve every problem we have and then some. Hell, it's just a few "Christmas" games, and that money is too much to pass up."

Gramps nods, but doesn't offer any words of wisdom for me. This is a sensitive subject for him because he feels like I'm having to pick up slack, but his heart just can't take it. I'd rather do everything at this inn than lose my Gramps.

"What the hell is that awful smell?" I hear a high-pitched whine from the fence that runs between our property and the resort.

Gramps and I both look up to see none other than the traitor herself standing at the fence, trying to peer over the top at us. It's almost as tall as her but I see her eyes, dark and demure, peeping over the top.

"Fuck me," I mutter and Gramps laughs.

We walk over to the fence and Gramps greets Freya.

"Howdy, can I help you ma'am?"

"I'm sorry, but the stench. I was out here arranging some chairs for our bonfire, and I couldn't help but smell." Her nose wrinkles in distaste.

"Sorry about that, back here are the stalls where Saint Nick is." He gestures toward the donkey.

"A donkey?" Freya asks, eyes wide.

"Yes ma'am. He likes resident reindeer, though." Gramps winks at her.

"You dress him up?" Light fills her blue eyes. "That's so cute!"

"You hear that, Saint? She thinks you're cute." Gramps chuckles and turns back to Freya. "You'll have to see him when he's all dressed up."

Stop being so nice to the enemy Gramps!

"Freya," I say curtly.

Her eyes turn to mine and a scowl replaces the smirk on her face. "Finn."

"Well, I see you two have met." Gramps grins.

Freya shoots daggers my way with her eyes, which I return with daggers of my own.

"I'll leave you to it, I've got to get some of those cookies your Grams was working on. Nice to meet you, Freya."

She smiles at him, a genuine one that was wide and bright enough to almost knock me on my ass.

"Nice to meet you too, Mr. Mayberry!" She waves as he walks away. Once he's gone, she squints at me. "Wish I could say the same for you, Finn."

"Go back to your fancy resort and leave the real work to me, traitor. Shouldn't you be practicing getting your hands dirty? I know you're not used to having to do things yourself."

"Ugh!" She groans. "You are impossible. I'll see you at the

competition. And you know, you really shouldn't underestimate females, that's sexist you ass!"

She marches away and my eyes watch her ass with each stomp she makes. Fuck me, she's got a great ass, but her mouth...

This is going to be one long ass winter.

Chapter Seven
Freya

The Jingle Wars tree picking challenge is in less than a week and a half, but I don't have time to wait around for it. There's so much I want to do with the resort to drive up bookings now.

"Keep the ideas coming," I say to the group gathered for our meeting, tapping the bluetooth pen on the iPad Pro in my lap where I'm jotting down notes for our marketing and content creation plan for the month. "I love where we're going with this."

It's a new routine I'm instating, getting the Alpine staff involved for fresh ideas and authentic stories for our brand message. We're all seated around a crackling fire pit on the terrace down the hill from the main resort building. The one close to the fence line where I met Mr. Mayberry and his donkey last night

And Finn.

My grip tightens on the pen for a moment. *Breathe, sis.* I blow out slowly, focusing on the sharp snapping and popping of the glowing logs. Between the warmth emanating from the fire and the maroon plaid wool poncho wrapped around me, I'm comfortably cozy in the Montana chill.

"We could do a drone following the instructors down the runs," one of the senior snowboarding teachers suggests. "Show off the runs and the classes."

I snap my fingers and point at him with enthusiasm. "Perfect! Do five clips, we'll drop one a week to drive up the hype for people who want to be just as badass on the slopes. And someone make sure we have a drone on hand. Do y'all know how to film as you go or do we need a film crew?"

"Bet your fancy staff love being bossed around like that, Princess."

That deep, raspy voice wipes the energetic smile from my face. *Finn.* How long has he been eavesdropping on us?

With my eyes slitted, I crane my neck around, finding him leaning casually against the fence post while he absently strokes the soft looking fur between his donkey's ears.

The adorable donkey is dressed up with a red blanket trimmed in white and green felt reindeer antlers attached to his head.

Fuck. Saint Nick looks so damn cute! My fingers twitch for my phone to take a picture. I can't, though. Finn would know he won in his stupid pissing contest against me if I stooped to fawning over his donkey.

He feeds the donkey an apple slice he cut from the shiny red fruit he's holding with a pocket knife, then carves off another piece for himself, eating it right off the blade with his eyes locked on me.

Oh, Santa freaking baby, how is even that small gesture sexy? I don't know, but it is.

His dark hair is even messier today, unruly ends curling around his ears as he drags a hand through it. The whole look he's got going on from his tan canvas coat to his beaten up leather boots does unfair things to my insides.

"I'm not bossy," I snap once I break myself free of the stupid Finn-induced drool fest.

Bad brain. No more lumberjack lusting.

Throwing Riley a subtle glance, I play off swiping the sides of my mouth like I'm not checking to make sure I haven't embarrassed myself. She waggles her eyebrows, catching me red-handed. Shit.

I admit, I'm a thirsty bitch and I'm not blind—Finn is hot as hell. But I'll be damned if I'm not also a pathetic one. This man is not the charmer he pretended to be when he caught me in his strong arms. Underneath the handsome rugged exterior is a stubborn grouch with enough brittle pinecones shoved so far up his ass you can smell the sickly sweet sap seeping out of his pores.

"Sure you're not, traitor," Finn says. "That what they call business savvy back in California board rooms? Because around these parts, it's called bossy."

"Well, what you are is called *rude*." I hop off the arm of the adirondack chair I was perched on, striding over to the fence line separating my resort's property from his family inn. "All you've done is make assumptions about me, and I'm getting sick of it."

The corner of Finn's mouth pulls up to one side in a sardonic curve as he folds both arms over the top of the fence, leaning his weight on the wood. My brows pinch together in annoyance. He's using his height to undermine me because I'm not tall enough to get in his face to challenge him, but I won't back down. Curling my fingers over the top of the fence on either side of his folded arms, I push as high as I can on tiptoe to see over the fence. Finn's gaze bounces between my eyes, then dips down to my lips for a beat. There's a flash of surprise there and gone in a second before he settles his thick brows back into a sour expression.

"You need to get over yourself," I say.

"Do I now?" His voice is a low rumble from this close.

It occurs to me how this might look to my staff. Instead of meeting this jerk eye to eye, it could also appear intimate, like we're about to kiss. Crap. If I lean back, he wins.

The bright glint in his eye and the twitch of his lips has me guessing he's drawing the same conclusions. I tighten my grip on the wood to stave off the frustration simmering beneath my skin.

"I won't repeat myself," I say firmly. "I told you before, my Dad's company picked this land because it was the right choice for the hotel we were planning to open."

"Bullshit. I looked up your company. They deal in hotspot cities and the last four resorts opened were in Hawaii, Palm Beach, Los Angeles, and the Hamptons. That's not counting the international ones. We might have bustling tourism in Hollyridge, but it's nothing compared to the locations you people usually target." I blink and open my mouth, my brain kicking into gear as if I'm facing off with one of Dad's executives. Finn beats me to the chase. "What's that look for? Didn't think I would research the competition stealing my business from me?"

"I—no. It's just..." There's no way I'll compliment him for doing exactly what I would do first if I were in his shoes. I lick my lips and huff. "I just thought you were a caveman cowboy, that's all."

Finn snorts. "Is that all?" He shakes his head and pushes off the fence, addressing the donkey nudging at his coat with little grunts in search of more treats. I squeeze the fence to keep from reaching out to pet him. "You hear that, Saint?"

Up close, the donkey dressed as a reindeer is even cuter.

Once again my fingers itch to take out my phone. A high-pitched, excited sound builds in my chest, but I shove it down. This is torture. Any animal in a costume gets me hyped, and Finn's donkey is no exception. I love reindeer and I haven't seen any of the elk Riley promised. The donkey's barn nearby could pass as cabin-like. This is almost too much for me to handle.

"Alright, Princess. As much as I enjoy these little chats, Saint Nick and I have to get down to town square for the annual Christmas Kickoff led by the mayor. It's a real local favorite. The kids always look forward to his transformation from donkey to reindeer." He inclines his head with a polite gesture that comes off patronizing. Dick. "Y'all have a good day now."

First he insults me, then he torments me with the temptation of his cute donkey playing dress up. The frustration rises to a boiling point.

As Finn leads Saint Nick away up the winding trail, I fume. *Princess.* I hate that nickname he gave me. He hasn't stopped with it since he found out who I am, deciding he hates everything about me without even knowing me.

I'm not a princess. The goddess I'm named for might be associated with love and beauty, but she's also a goddess of war and this is my siege.

"You're going down, Finn Mayberry," I murmur. "This is war."

Swinging back to the group seated around the fire pit, who all act like they weren't hanging on that whole exchange between us, I wave my hands. "Let's come back at this in a couple of days to hammer out the rest of this month's marketing plan. Thank you for your time, everyone."

I wish I could go up to my room and hunker down with a holiday movie marathon. They always have made me feel better. But my marathon, complete with a mug of hot cocoa, will have to wait because I have a lot of work to do around here.

Riley falls into step beside me as I head back up the hill to the main building. "So what was that all about?"

I wave her off. "He's got a stick up his ass about this whole Jingle Wars competition. And he's mad my father branched out with a new hotel here." I push my fingers into my hair. "I mean, he even called me his enemy! Like how ridiculous is he? Who talks like that?"

Riley laughs, the husky sound a welcome comfort, even if she doesn't have the sympathy I'm looking for. I suppose I shouldn't expect her to pick sides between friends. She pats my shoulder. I sigh, hooking my arm with hers.

"That's Finn," she explains. "He's always been like that. Same with our best friend, West. I grew up with them both." Her shoulder hitches. "Once Finn gets something in his head, it's always been hard to steer him otherwise. He can be as stubborn as their donkey, Saint."

"Well he should learn to be flexible and open to change. It lets the good energy in," I grumble. "Good energy leads to new opportunities."

Maybe that annoys me so much because of how hard I've worked over the years. I couldn't just be skilled and well-versed in the industry I work in, I had to be better than the other men.

"Don't let him get to you. He'll figure himself out once he realizes you're not going anywhere. He's not really a mean guy."

"He can do whatever. I don't care if he likes me or not. But I'm definitely here to stay."

"That's it, girl." Riley checks her hip against mine, lifting my mood. "Let's go to the spa and get smoothies."

"Sounds perfect."

* * *

The whine of the drill makes me wince, but I give the work crew a thumbs up. The new sign installation at the entrance to the Alpine looks awesome. It's huge and at night it will be brightly lit with a neon mountain from our modern-style logo.

I stand off to the side of their work area, shuffling my weight from foot to foot in my knee-high suede boots, regretting dashing outside in a designer sweater dress with a short hem and a shaggy white faux fur coat thrown over it. So much for starting to get used to the Montana weather. At least these short chunky-heeled boots have better protection than my cozy UGGs, but those are the only flat shoes I own.

A loud engine rumbles behind me, followed by a screech as a big truck skids across the salted asphalt, sending a spray of muddy sleet into the air that lands inches from my damp suede boots. Finn throws the door open and stomps around the front, engine still running.

"You've gotta be fucking kidding me," he grits out, then stabs a finger toward the sign being installed. "What the hell do you think you're doing?"

"Standing," I sass, crossing my arms. It's mostly to show him he can't intimidate me, but also because I'm freezing. I rushed out here so fast I didn't think about the fresh snowfall from this morning. He certainly looks warmer than I feel in two layers of thick checkered flannel beneath his open utility jacket. "Is that a problem?"

"Don't give me that lip," he demands. "You're putting up this big ass sign. How are you gonna tell me you aren't actively trying to steal our business with this shit?"

"You have a sign!"

"So did you!"

"Well, I wanted a better one."

"There! Right fucking there." Finn stalks up to me so we're practically pressed together.

The scent of his spicy cologne hits me full force, almost making me dizzy enough to grab a hold of him to keep from swooning. *Shit, why does he have to smell so good?* I don't have the height advantage of my high heels today and he towers over me.

His words come out as a growl. "See? A better one. Bigger. You know exactly what you're doing here, Traitor. Don't think I don't see it."

I huff, blowing highlighted flyaways from my face. "I only do what benefits my resort."

"Don't I fuckin' know it," he says severely as he glares down at me, anger rolling off him in waves. His gaze flicks down, studying me for a beat, lingering on my curves and the hemline of my dress. If possible, his face contorts into an even angrier expression. "Don't you know how to dress, damn it?"

A scoff bursts from me as I put on a show of examining my designer outfit. I know I'm cold, but when Finn challenges me I just want to go off. He calls on every stubborn bone in my body.

"What's wrong, big guy? Don't know fashion when you see it? It's called *style*."

At my snarky tone, he grips me by my upper arms, leaning close enough to kiss me as he hisses, "Put some real goddamn clothes on before you freeze that perky little ass off in the snow, traitor."

For a second his deep whiskey-colored eyes dart to the workers watching us curiously, then his attention is back on me.

Is that jealousy burning in his gaze? Impossible. He hates me as much as I hate him.

"No." I squirm, but his grasp is strong. "Fuck you for thinking you can tell me what to do, you controlling dick."

"*Yes*," he rumbles. "Your thighs and knees are all pink exposed to the cold like that."

"Worried about my well-being now?" I tilt my head to the side, shoving down the little burst of pleasure he elicits in me. "Is this because you know I'm totally going to win that first challenge picking the best tree out there? Good. You should be nervous."

A rough laugh falls from Finn's lips and he releases me as if I'm boiling hot. He swipes his fingers over his reddish-brown scruff, covering his mouth with his hand. With a grumble he whirls away, only to double back with his thick brows flat over his eyes.

"You know what, that high and mighty act ain't gonna fly. This is getting real. You should just drop out now to save your pride." He waves to the tree line across the street, where the woods border both our properties. "This isn't cutesy glamping or light hiking for your Facebook likes, Princess. No way in hell are you cut out to trek through the woods and chop down a tree." He gestures to my shoes. "Not in those."

"You'll just have to wait and see."

Finn jerks his head back at the conviction in my tone.

He thinks he can tell me what I can and can't do? Hell no! I didn't grow up fighting to prove myself every second to Dad to be told I can't do something now.

"Fine. Don't say I didn't warn you."

With the satisfaction of the final word, he glances once more at the workers installing the new sign, then goes back to his truck. He throws it into gear and another spray of sleet kicks up from the tires as he whips the truck onto the road and pulls into the nearby driveway for Mayberry Inn next door.

I sigh and turn back to the workmen. "It looks great. Thank you guys. I'll be up at my office in the main lobby if you need me."

* * *

The next morning as I'm heading out in my Mercedes to go to town, Finn is installing a new sign. His arm swings with confidence, bringing the hammer down with force. The sign is bigger than the previous one they had, and handcrafted with the Mayberry Inn logo burned into the freshly stained wood.

A sharp tug on my heartstrings has me frozen, foot on the brake as I watch him work. He swipes a forearm over his head to wipe away a shine of sweat curling his tousled hair.

My sign for the Alpine might be shiny and professionally commissioned, but...it's not handcrafted. I didn't put my own energy into making it, as I suspect Finn did.

I grip the steering wheel and smother the unwanted feelings. My jaw works side to side. "That's how you want to play it, big guy? Okay. Fine."

We don't need to wait for the first Jingle Wars challenge. Finn wanted a war? I'll give him one.

By the end of the day, I have a giant lit tree up next to my sign in all its festive glory. But then he follows with one of his own—a freshly cut one I watch him unload from the bed of his truck with a friend.

The following days continue like that. We one-up each other in petty little ways. Neither of us is willing to back down. May the best hotel win.

On Friday, there's a holiday bazaar in the town square. Hollyridge is as charming as ever, and I've been happily snapping away and adding to the Alpine's Instagram story in short bursts all afternoon on my breaks from the sponsored booth I bought in a prime spot across from the bakery. As customers spill out, they have a direct line of sight to Riley and I dressed in hilarious ugly Christmas sweaters.

It works like a charm to draw in the tourists wanting a picture of us for their social media memories.

"These were such a good idea," I tell her, grabbing another selfie of us for the Alpine's Facebook page. "Thanks for doing this with me."

Riley's sweater is green with actual stuffed reindeer sticking out from random spots. She wanted to put two red-nosed Rudolph plushies protruding from her tits, but I vetoed in favor of keeping it family friendly until later, when we have a staff party. My sweater is Grinch-themed after my favorite movie in a hideous color with a fuzzy fur collar going on, complete with a matching Max the dog purse. It lights up and sings the tune to the Grinch's theme song when I press a hidden button in the hem.

"I wouldn't leave my girl alone. You're still getting to know everyone in town. Besides, there was no way I was missing you strutting your stuff in that hideous sweater. It's hilarious," Riley says. "You're so cute, but the sweater is so, *so* ugly."

"That's the idea!" If I were an emoji, right now I'd be that purple smirking devil in my self-satisfaction. "Make it so they can't look away."

Riley's attention drifts around the decorated stalls and booths. "Oh, look. See that? That's Ella. I bet she's here for the parade with Finn. She's always all over him."

"Well, she can have him. Hi!" I greet a young couple passing by. It takes effort to push Finn from my mind and inject the necessary amount of warmth and excitement into my voice. Once I have their attention, they come over to grab a cookie from our plate. We have brownies to pull out next, keeping people stopping by with different treats every hour for the chance to win a golden ticket inside for a free night at the resort. "Try one. Are you having fun?"

As if Riley summoned him with gossip, I catch sight of Finn

over the young couple's shoulders, missing their answer. A sigh leaves me before I can stop it. Our eyes meet and it's like the whole crowded square disappears for a few tense seconds.

Finn has a burgundy Mayberry Inn hoodie on with dark jeans and his rugged beat up boots. It's unfair how attractive he is. Riley wasn't kidding about his heartthrob status in Hollyridge, either. He's pulling plenty of attention as he leads Saint Nick through the crowd. Kids and tourists flock to him to pet the donkey dressed as a reindeer, who loves the fawning fans.

When they're close to our booth, he stops. Saint Nick leans in, nostrils working when he catches a whiff of the cookies.

"Not for you, buddy," Finn murmurs, redirecting Saint Nick away from the sugary treats. He surveys us and the table. "Of course you'd be here."

"Yup." I pop the *p*, then offer him the plate. "Want a chance to win a golden ticket?"

"What's the prize?"

"A free night at our luxury mountain resort. Stay in style."

He scoffs, head jerking slightly. "Yeah, no."

As he turns away, I stop him. The temptation was hard enough to resist before, but now it's impossible. "Can I pet Saint?"

I swallow at the astonished look he gives me when he turns back. Apprehension zips up my spine. Is he going to refuse my request? I lick my lips and step out from the booth.

"You want to pet Saint?" he repeats.

"Yes." My hopeful gaze bounces from him to the donkey. "Please."

Finn is stunned silent. He shrugs and nods. As soon as I have permission, a muffled excited squeal shakes my whole body. I take another step closer, holding out my palm to the donkey.

"Hi, Saint." I beam as his velvet-soft nose pushes into my hand. "Oh my god," I whisper in a strangled voice. "So soft." As the donkey bumps against my palm, licking it, I laugh in delight. "He likes me!"

Being accepted by a donkey might be the usual to someone like Finn, but it makes tears prick my eyes. I probably look crazy, eyes glistening because I'm stroking a donkey dressed as a reindeer, but it makes warm joy pour into my heart. I think I get why the Grinch was amazed when he felt his heart grow three sizes. This feels just like that.

Finn watches with a strange expression. Without the anger, it does funny things to my chest, igniting butterflies. At last he mutters, "Saint, you're a traitor."

It doesn't hold any heat. He allows me to keep petting his donkey for a few more minutes.

"Well, I've got to..." Finn nods his head to a red sleigh with the Mayberry logo on the side painted in gold. "Saint Nick is the resident reindeer, after all. He needs to pull the sleigh."

"Right. Okay." I give the donkey one more scratch behind the ears and murmur to him for being a good boy. "Thanks."

Once I return to my booth, my attention strays to Finn and his donkey-drawn sleigh more than once. Everytime I look at him, my stomach flips.

Chapter Eight
Finn

"Welcome to day one of Jingle Wars everyone! I am so glad everyone could make it out, and we are so excited to get the festivities going! Gather around Christmas fanatics, because this is a competition that you *don't* want to miss!" Cornelius Frost, the host, says into the microphone, addressing the crowd.

Once again I find myself on the stage decorated with more tinsel and garland than the entire town needs, shoved front and center between frosty and my icy enemy. Once again feeling like a show animal for the second time in less than two weeks. Even though fresh snow blankets the ground, I'm sweating like Heat Miser's got me by the damn balls. My second time on this stage, and it's not any easier this time. If anything, I'm more fucking nervous knowing what's at stake. The reason I did this stupid competition in the first place.

The Mayberry.

I hate being up here in the spotlight, but as a contestant we're required to be here on stage while they're kicking the show off. This year is a hell of a lot more over the top and everything has to be shown "camera ready" like a tried and true game show.

If that wasn't bad enough, of course Freya is standing directly across from me in another pair of UGG boots and a plush fur coat, looking every bit out of place as she has each time that I've seen her thus far. Princess isn't used to snow and freezing ground, but one good time on her ass and she'll change her tune from chic to sensible.

Women.

Her frigid gaze catches mine and she glares at me, shooting icicles directly my way. If looks could kill, I'd be dead on the spot. What's worse is she's even hotter when she's scowling. *Shit.*

Why does my traitorous enemy have to look so good in those damn furry boots?

"As you know, the first competition will not only test brawn, but your creativeness. Your own personalized touch on a tree that says everything about you and your Christmas spirit. You will be required to cut your own tree down, get it to the stage, and decorate it as the best darn Christmas tree this town has ever seen! Good luck to all of our competitors and may the jolliest one win!" Cornelius starts the giant clock that sits hauntingly in the middle of the stage.

Two hours and fifty nine minutes shows with the seconds ticking by slowly. I'm not wasting one of those seconds and giving Freya the chance to get a one up on me.

Can't wait to see how her tiny ass plans on dragging a whole ass tree out of the forest.

I, unlike, my sworn enemy, came dressed and prepared for today's competition. Sensible and smart.

Long johns, jeans, heavy duty work boots, a thick thermal jacket with work gloves and a hat that provides warmth. Ugly as sin, but it works better than some name brand designer shit that looks good and doesn't warm my ass.

Freya prances down from the stage in her matching furry pom pom beanie and gloves, and heads back behind the stage, only stopping to grab the bag provided by the hosts to actually cut the tree down. They didn't want anyone saying that someone cheated or had unfair advantage, so they provided the tools. Which, I don't mind much because a bow saw is a bow saw. But, one thing I have that Miss Princess doesn't?

Grams.

She and I spent half the night buried in boxes and boxes of Christmas shit, picking out the perfect ornaments, the best tinsel, and a tree topper that will steal the show all on it's own. Grams is the Christmas angel of Hollyridge and no one, even Freya, can compete with that. She's my secret weapon.

I make my way into the forest with my bag of tools and start searching for the perfect tree. I know they'll judge it on fullness, height, and how fresh the leaves are on top of how we put our flair on the tree. Just like anyone would when they cut down a tree for their house, and I'm betting Freya won't know that since all she knows are sunny beaches and margaritas.

Matter of fact, I'm counting on it.

There are a few contestants walking around, checking trees out. I see Mr. Nelson from the hardware store, dressed in his signature overalls and bright red ear muffs. Never seen him without them. Ella's here too, dragging a guy behind her that I haven't seen before but hell, I'm not getting close enough to ask questions. She almost broke her neck trying to wave at me earlier today, but I pretended I didn't see her.

Crisis number one of the day averted.

The fresh, fluffy snow that blankets the forest floor crunches beneath my boots as I move deeper into the woods. There are plenty of trees that I pass that look "okay", but none of them are what is going to win me this competition and I'm not stopping until I find the one.

I walk further and further into the trees until the voices fade out behind me. The temperature begins to drop, the farther I walk into the forest where the trees thicken and begin to block out some of the sun. My breath forms a cloud in front of me as I walk and there, right in front of me, I see the tree that will win it all. It's over six feet tall, thick and full, with healthy green needles.

I hear a high-pitched squeak behind me, and then I'm pushed forcefully out of the way as Freya darts past me, making a beeline for the tree that I just picked out.

"Oh hell no!" I cry and take off after her, and just before she makes it to the tree, my arms circle her waist and I pull her back against me. I wasn't expecting her to come so freely and we both topple to a tangled pile on the snowy forest floor. Her tight little body is perched perfectly on top of mine and I feel my dick come to life between us.

Fuck, I hope she doesn't notice. Who gets hard from their smart mouth traitor of an enemy? Me, that's who.

Her cheeks are flushed red and I wonder if it's me or the cool air that's made them that way. I want to make her other cheeks pink as I spank her ass.

Shit, Finn, cut it out. She was just trying to steal your tree. Stop getting distracted.

That's probably her game plan, to distract me with her ass and lure me in like the true siren she is.

"Finn, let me up!" she complains, trying and failing to escape my hold. My arms are still wrapped around her tightly.

"So that's how it's going to be then? You're going to cheat your way to the top?" I can see the delicate pulse of her throat pound as her breath quickens. Only then do I realize how close she is to my face. Her pink, pouty lips are just a breath away from mine.

If I was going to kiss her, if I wanted to kiss her, I could do so with barely moving. I could capture her lips in a kiss that would sear us both with the heat. But I don't kiss liars, cheaters, or people who want to steal my livelihood, so that won't be happening. My grip on her waist loosens and she wiggles against me trying to sit up. My dick is so hard against my jeans, she had to have felt it digging into her and the incessant wiggling she'd doing does nothing but make me strain harder against my waistband.

"I didn't cheat!" she exclaims, finally untangling herself from me when our trance is broken.

Her hair is mussed from our hands on scuffle, and her ridiculous pompom beanie is nowhere to be found. She looks ready to explode from anger or frustration, and that serves her right, since I'm feeling the same, just in a *very* different way.

"Looks that way to me." I brush the snow and leaves off of my jeans as I stand. My ass is completely soaking wet, along with my back after laying in the freezing ass snow.

"You're such a child. You can't claim a tree from a hundred yards away, Finn. I saw it before you did anyway, which automatically makes it mine." She smirks. "Now, if you'll excuse me I've got a tree to chop down. See ya!"

This girl will be the death of me. I'm two seconds from having a damn coronary.

"No." I jog over and stand in front of her, in front of MY tree, blocking her from touching it. I fold my arms across my chest and tell her, "You are not cutting my tree down."

A look crosses across her face that I can only describe as utter determination and then it's gone, like it never happened. She shrugs nonchalantly. "Fine, it's an ugly tree anyway."

Turning on her heel she starts back towards town. I sigh

heavily. I never wanted to join this damn competition to begin with, and now that this infuriating woman is involved, I want to be here even less. If it wasn't for my family, I would've told her to kiss my ass. *Even though it's really her ass I'd rather be kissing, but she'll never know that.*

Before I can even blink, she turns around and sprints at me full speed, tackling me like a fucking linebacker and almost knocks me clear off my feet. I'm so shocked that she just sumo wrestled me that I lose my footing and am on my back once more, with her sitting on top of me. But this time, it feels intense. Like all of the fresh forest air around us has been sucked out. The warm apex between her thighs is pressed tightly against me and I stifle a groan.

She leans in closer, whispering, "Listen here, Finn Mayberry. You can have this damn tree. But let's be clear, it's because I'm letting you have it. Not because it was yours first. Because I'm a strong, independent woman and I don't need to lie or steal my way to win this competition. I'm going to win it fair and square, and when you lose you're going to tell me you're sorry for being such an asshole and trying to sabotage me."

"Sabotage you? You are insane. I didn't sabotage anything!" I exclaim, sitting up on my elbows abruptly, causing friction against my dick and this time I do groan out loud. I bring my hand to her neck and slide it against her smooth, warm skin until it's wrapped around her nape, then pull her to me until she's a centimeter from my lips.

"Don't think for one second that I'm letting you win, Traitor. No matter how much of a fit you throw. That won't work here, not with me, not in Hollyridge."

She swallows, and her little pink tongue darts out to wet her lips. Her pupils dilate, and I know she's feeling every bit of what I'm feeling, plus some. I read her body and everything it tells me.

"This is my town. We're playing this by my rules and you might not realize it yet, but you will." I ever so slightly brush my lips against her, a mere whisper against her lips and a shudder racks her body.

I remove her from my lap abruptly and stand, offering her my back while I adjust myself so it isn't completely obvious that while I may hate her, my dick sure doesn't.

When I turn back, she's on her feet, heading back in the direction she came.

Finn: 1

Freya: 0

* * *

With so much time wasted, I get straight to work cutting the tree down, and netting it. One way to make my trek back to town square easier. I wasn't going to drag the tree and let it get destroyed in my walk back, I was going to hoist the entire damn thing on my shoulder and carry it back. Even for me at six two, that was no easy feat. By the time I make it out of the forest and to the grassy area that's designated for the remainder of the competition I'm sweating and sore. My shoulder has a permanent crick from carrying that heavy damn tree for so long.

There are only a handful of people that have made it back and put their tree in its stand, and even less who have started to decorate so I feel a small sense of pride that I was able to make it back on good time, even after the she-devil tried so hard to make me lose.

I waste no more time watching the competition and begin setting the tree up, just like Grams told me. When I bend down to tighten the bolts at the base of the tree stand I see Freya make her way out of the edge of the forest. Her hair is standing in all directions, there are small sticks and leaves sticking out of it and maybe even a damn critter by the size of the rat's nest that's poking out the side. She's dragging a tree that's twice her size behind her and I'll be damned, I'm sorta impressed. I can't believe she got that thing all the way out of the forest by herself. She makes sure to stick her tongue out at me like a damn child, but heads to her station and gets right to work.

I look back at my boxes and focus on finishing before the time runs out. Each and every ornament is packed with care and labeled with what is inside, so I won't waste time trying to figure out it's contents. Grams even included berries she got for me to hang and I lose myself in my task. Before I know it, the iconic Jingle Bell is sounding. It's over. No more time. And somehow, thankfully, I've just put the topper on and my tree is officially done, just as the bell has sounded.

"Alright folks, time is up!" Cornelius says from the center of the stage, then walks down to where us contestants are still standing by our now decorated trees. I look around at the competition, and seeing everyone's hard work makes me just a bit nervous that I won't make the cut. Freya's standing in front of her tree wearing a bright smile. Damn it, it doesn't look half bad for an out of townie.

"The judges will deliberate for thirty minutes and choose our top three contestants! Feel free to look around at the local vendor booths and stop at The Coffee Spirit for a cup of hot coffee or cocoa!"

All of our audience disperses, visiting the tables and milling around while we wait. Apparently while we wait, Freya is going to ignore me and act like I don't exist, and that's perfectly fine with me. Not like I have anything to say to her anyways, not after what I said during our scuffle in the woods. I like seeing her off kilter, her hair disheveled, her makeup smudged. I can tell she spends so much time trying to perfect everything and what she needs is a hard dose of reality.

One I'd happily deliver.

The time passes quickly, and I busy myself scrolling on my phone on Facebook, the one and *only* social media app that I have. Even then, I barely post. Social media as a whole makes me cringe. I only use it to keep up with old classmates and friends who got out of this town and traveled the world, got married, had kids.

"Places everyone, we're going live in the count of 20," the assistant with her bright pink clipboard tells us all, shooing us into our places. "Okay three...two...one."

"We are live here on the set of Jingle Wars! Our judges have spent the last thirty minutes deliberating on who is making the top three cut! We have so much talent here today, I know their choice couldn't have been easy! I have the three contestants who will continue on to round two right here in this envelope. Are we ready to find out?" Cornelius asks the crowd, then points his microphone in their direction. The crowd yells and claps excitedly in response.

The speakers pound with a drum roll and the crowd starts to clap, each one getting increasingly louder as he pulls the card from the sealed envelope.

"The first contestant proceeding to round two in third place is... Freya Anderson! Congratulations! Please take your spot on the stage."

Freya squeals excitedly and skips over to the stage.

Damn it.

I'll never forgive myself if she wins this competition, not when she was the one who distracted me from the finish line. I can't afford distractions when the entire fate of the Mayberry rests on my shoulders.

"The next contestant to advance into round two is... Marcus Godrey! Congratulations!"

Shit.

This is my last chance. If they don't call my name, the hope of saving the inn is gone.

A knot forms in my stomach, and I feel like I'm going to hurl right where I stand. I'm more nervous than I've ever been in my life with the enormity of what is truly at stake.

"Taking first place in our very first competition and advancing to round two is... Hollyridge's finest, FINN MAYBERRY! Congratulations, Finn! Get your handsome tail up here!"

My cheeks heat as I make my way up to the stage, joining Freya and the other contestant. She doesn't look as triumphant as she did whenever I wasn't here on the stage next to her. I don't even give a shit right now, all I care about is that I fucking made it through this stupid competition and I have a fighting chance to do what I promised Grams and Gramps I would... Save. The. Mayberry, no matter what it takes.

Chapter Nine
Freya

Finn wins. After all my effort and hard work, he takes first place in the challenge.

My brief burst of confidence at making the cut for top three wavers with him standing beside me. I have to admit, even though I put my all into decorating my first real tree, his is... His tree is perfect. It has so much heart and soul. It *is* the Christmas spirit in tree form.

But Finn winning this round can't take away from something even more important to me. Today's experience was a magic I can't describe, trekking into the quiet forest to search amongst the trees for one that spoke to me. Excitement still bubbles in my chest when I picture the moment I touched the soft green pine needles of my tree, smelled the fresh scent. Some sticky sap still coats the heel of my palm, proof of my hard work. The movies I love don't do the sense of accomplishment justice.

Now that I have an actual taste of the real experience I missed out on, I'll cherish this memory for the rest of my life.

The bright glow is enough to keep me distracted from my soaking wet UGG boots and how damn cold I've been since rolling around with my rival in the snow.

I was worried I wouldn't make it after Finn gave me shit, but I still did it. I found the biggest tree I could, got it back to the judging area with some creative maneuvering, and advanced no thanks to him.

True, I couldn't have the one I first spotted—the one he claimed, that big…stupid…sexy jerk who smells like spice and has soft warm lips. I shake my head. *Reel in the thirsting.*

Did he mean to sort of kiss me as a distraction? The brush of his lips on mine and faint scrape of his scruff against my skin as he told me we're playing by his rules is branded in my mind. As Cornelius flirts with the crowd, I press my chilled fingers to my lips.

He didn't mean it. There's no way. He probably wanted to fight dirty. The corners of my mouth turn down. Anything to sabotage me.

"So there we have it, your semi-finalists of Jingle Wars!" Cornelius pauses for the crowd to clap. "We're one step closer to crowning our king or queen. What festive feats will they face next? Well, I'm glad you asked!"

I push the near-kiss with Finn to the back of my mind and listen closely as Mr. Frost presents the next round of the competition.

"Hollyridge is a town of longstanding history, known for its holiday tourism. For the next challenge, our contestants will be sent on a scavenger hunt," Cornelius announces, waving to the same table with a velvet curtain. "But this won't be just any scavenger hunt. It's the Hollyridge Merrymaker Trail, a local favorite! Misty?"

The girl in the elf costume pulls back the curtain to reveal an illustrated map of the town with landmarks.

Cornelius Frost points to each as he talks. "This scavenger hunt will have our contestants visiting local businesses in Hollyridge. But we have a special bonus surprise we'll be revealing on the day of the challenge!" He winks at us. "Once they complete the trail and find all the points on the map, our judges will determine who is passing to the final round."

A scavenger hunt? Yes! A thrilling sense of anticipation rises. I have this one in the bag, no doubt. I'm totally back in the game to win this.

"Tune in next time for round two, our semi-finalist challenge!" With that, the broadcast ends and Cornelius gives the three of us a nod to leave the stage.

Once I'm moving again, it's hard to ignore the sogginess in each frigid, squishy step. Are my toes numb? They might be. I can't tell anymore. I grimace, hopping off the last step.

"Ew," I mumble, lifting one wet foot.

I'm pretty sure this time my UGGs are ruined beyond repair. They're muddy and gross, the color of the suede indistinguishable.

"What's wrong, Princess?" Finn's voice carries a heavy dose of sarcastic bite. "The woods not what you expected?"

I turn to find him behind me, smirking. The smug bastard is proud of his win.

"Nothing. I'm perfectly fine." Folding my arms, I tip my face up. A crinkled, dead leaf falls from somewhere on my once-fluffy faux fur coat, but I hold Finn's stare with a challenge in my eyes. "I made the top three, didn't I? So I'm great."

"Peachy fuckin' keen, I'd bet," Finn says, the corner of his mouth lifting higher. "You cold?"

"No," I answer stubbornly.

"No?"

Ugh, that knowing, arrogant lilt in his voice! It makes my mind jump back to straddling him in on the snowy ground, wrapped in his arms against his hard body. His warm, muscular arms. *I have had it up to here with you, brain. You're in time out.* I take a step closer to him with narrowed eyes.

"No." I glance around after my voice rises with more sharpness than I intended.

Finn brings this side out of me. The one that makes me want to fight tooth and nail to be seen and heard.

He snorts. "Sure. That's real believable when your fuzzy slippers are soaked through from the snow."

Without asking, he reaches forward and picks a twig out of my tangled hair. A shiver runs down my spine, but I'm not sure if it's from the chill in the air or from the way he's looking at me. I lift my chin a fraction higher. Twigs are rustic chic right? That's me.

Amusement lights up Finn's eyes for a few moments before fading back to dismissal. His brows furrow. "Why the hell are you even doing this? It doesn't seem like you need the money."

There's something about that making him angrier, driving away any shred of humor, as if he's remembered why we hate each other. Well, screw him. I can't control that I have money, but it's not like I haven't worked my ass off for everything I've earned.

I'd argue he's luckier—he's the one with a loving family, after all. Money doesn't give cozy hugs when you need to be reminded someone cares for you.

Finn might be in this competition for the prize, but I'm the one who needs this edge to impress Dad.

Rolling my eyes, I move to shove past him. "It doesn't matter. Why do you care?"

Before I get far, Finn has an arm hooked around me, stopping me in my tracks. I struggle with a grunt, but he easily herds me back two steps so my back is pressed against the cool wooden frame of the gazebo, his big hands planted on either side of my head. A pine garland wrapped with silver tinsel blocks us from view.

My chest rises and falls with each breath as we stare each other down, and my heart skips a beat.

"What are you doing? Let me out of here. I want to go take a long hot bath and get out of these dirty clothes."

Finn's deep brown eyes flare with heat. He holds my gaze, then drops it in favor of dragging his attention down to my body to my skintight leggings. I almost feel his eyes like a sensual caress as his gaze moves back up to meet mine again. He lifts a hand and plucks more sticks and leaves from my hair.

The bustling town square disappears around us, the world narrowing down to Finn, me, and a tether cinching tighter between us.

"I told you," he rumbles, the rough sound of his voice piercing me. My clit throbs in response. He sighs. "You should stop now. Save yourself the trouble of having your pride bruised. I don't want to see your pouting face when you lose to me."

Peering up at him through my lashes, I pull my mouth to the side in a crooked grin. "Oh, caveman. The only one of us who'll be bruised is you."

We're close enough I can see his pupils dilate, feel the shift in his breathing when his head inclines another inch to erase what little distance is left between us. To prove my point, I reach up to cup his neck, thumbs grazing his jaw. It's warm beneath my icicle fingers. His focus drops to my mouth and my grin stretches.

Without warning, I dig my nails in, just enough to be uncomfortable, not break the skin. "I'm a fighter, Finn Mayberry. I have no problem fighting you to the end."

"We'll see about that, Traitor," Finn rasps, a hint of arousal clear in his tone.

I lick my lips and he releases a near-silent groan. I'm only aware of it because I feel the rumbling vibration beneath my hands. The invisible cinch pulls tighter, his chest brushing against mine. He drops the stick he fished from my messy hair and traces my jaw with his thumb, angling my face up. My lashes flutter and my chest caves.

He's going to—

"Don't you two look cozy."

The friendly voice laced with laughter has us flying apart. I smack the back of my head against the gazebo.

"Ow." I wince, holding the back of my skull.

Finn reaches for me on instinct, then drops his arm like a stone in water. A bewildered, guilty look settles on his face. "Grams, I—No—It wasn't—"

He takes two big steps away from me, putting ample space between us, then rubs his forehead. My eyes bounce between him and the woman who interrupted before he kissed me. He said Grams, so that would make her Mrs. Mayberry. She's a beautiful older woman with laugh lines and her eyes crinkle at the corners with her smile.

Everything about her immediately makes me want to hug her.

"Well, um." I hook my thumb in a vague direction that is *anywhere but here*. "I'm just gonna. Yeah. I need to go."

"Make sure you drink something warm after you get yourself cleaned up. Don't let your bath water get too hot, or you'll burn fresh out of the cold. You have to go slowly to warm back up," Mrs. Mayberry says, taking in my state, lingering on my soggy UGG boots. "And after that, double up on your socks, wrap up in a blanket, and plant your bottom in front of the fireplace, you hear now?"

"I—" An unexpected lump forms in my throat. No one's ever looked out for me like that before. This is unfamiliar and a wave of dormant emotions slam into me. "Yes, ma'am. Thank you."

Before the tears stinging my eyes and clogging my throat are noticeable, I hurry off. As I leave, her comment to Finn reaches my ears.

"It's nice to see you both getting along."

"That's not what I'd call it..." Finn mutters.

Chapter Ten
Freya

After filming the first round challenge on Sunday, it takes a few days to get my head back in the game with Finn getting deeper under my skin. He's a distraction. One I can't grant any power over me if I want to surpass Dad's expectations with the Alpine.

But if he'd kissed me? I think I would've let him. Hell, I would've kissed *back*.

There's no denying it. My body was all too eager to arch for him. His cedar and spice scent is so intoxicating, I probably would have climbed my lumberjack neighbor like a tree right there in the town square.

Damn Finn Mayberry. Damn his scruff, and that cocky grin when he thinks he's right. Damn everything about that infuriating man.

On Thursday, I brace my hands on the white granite counter in the bathroom of my room at the Alpine. With the competition, I've given up my search for the perfect cabin to call my own. The *Scandinavian Winter* room is still my home. For now.

Twitter notifications flood my locked phone screen with mentions and trending hashtags about Finn and I. It was a joke when I suggested the Jingle Wars audience might ship us, but I didn't expect it to actually happen. Since the tree challenge, my notifications have been blowing up. Who knows what vibe we gave off at the broadcast. I was too busy bouncing between living and breathing the winter spirit and shooting daggers at Finn. On live TV.

Going by some of these tweets, people have the distinct idea we're either boning every second we get, or we're five minutes from it.

"Yeah right," I say with a breathy laugh.

Don't be lyin', girl.

My brain needs to cool its tits. "Don't @ me, Brain Freya, it's not happening. Quit calling me out." I point at my reflection in the large mirror, manicured brows raised in a *don't try me* expression. "No matter how many sexy as fuck almost-kisses we share, I won't cross that line with him."

The put together version of myself in the mirror doesn't answer, but I still sense the judgy gaze. I'm a mess. Ever since I got to Hollyridge, it's like I've lost the edge I've spent the last two years cultivating since graduating college in California.

"Okay, enough moping."

And enough talking to myself.

I have to finish getting ready for today's special Facebook Live event at the Alpine. We're unveiling a new amenity for our guests: a virtual sleigh ride through the mountains surrounding Hollyridge filmed by a professional drone crew.

It's an idea I got after seeing Finn and Saint Nick at the bazaar for the donkey-drawn sleigh ride.

I wasn't going to debut it so soon. On my meticulous

marketing plan the big reveal of our new attraction was supposed to tie in with Christmas Eve. But after I just scraped through in the first round of the Jingle Wars competition, I felt this was what we needed to get back on people's radar again.

A nasty voice in my head creeps in, whispering doubts that claw at my cracked confidence. *Why are you here? No matter how hard you work, it's not good enough. Dad doesn't care. Give up.*

"No," I hiss, squeezing the hard counter. Pushing down the inner critic, I grab a berry red matte lipstick from the makeup spread on the sink. I perfect it and pucker at my reflection. "Be bold and show 'em all."

I fluff my highlighted dark hair, styled in bouncy soft curls, and check the false lashes making my bright blue eyes pop. Perfectly camera-ready with a little extra makeup than I wear day to day.

Snagging my phone from the countertop, I head into the bedroom and put on knee-high black suede boots to go with my cable knit designer sweater dress. I've learned my lesson, adding a pair of deep red tights with white snowflakes and a cozy forest green wool wrap for when we step outside with the live reveal of the sleigh situated on the patio behind the lobby, next to the outdoor bar.

Movement outside the window catches my eye and I freeze. There, in the tree line. An elk steps out.

My breath catches. "Wow. They are real."

It's a majestic sight, one I can't look away from for several seconds. The elk lifts its head, almost as if it's meeting my eye, then moves on. It disappears as fast as it appeared.

Is the spirit of winter sending me a sign? It sure feels like it.

Grinning wide as a giddy excitement blooms in my chest, I head downstairs with my mood soaring high.

The lobby is buzzing with energy from the guests enjoying

the hot cider and gingerbread cookies set out for snacks every day at three. A sign next to the front desk advertises the Facebook Live event for the new experience at the resort.

Riley stands by the stacked stone fireplace to the side of the room with a handsome man with a dimpled smile and blonde, unruly hair. I recognize him as the same friend that helped Finn with the tree he put up in response to mine next to his inn's sign. He leans a shoulder against the stonework and whatever he says makes her laugh hard. She leans close to respond. They must know each other well, because they seem comfortable together, standing near enough their bodies brush when they shift. When the guy looks away at an attractive woman, though, Riley's gaze hardens and her shoulders move with the force of her huffed exhale.

As I head for the sign, Finn walks in, casting a look around the Alpine lobby decked out in rustic touches and seasonal decor. My stomach clenches in surprise.

Sweet Santa's elves, does he always have to look so good?

Once his searching gaze finds Riley and the other man in the corner by the fireplace, he joins them. He pauses for a second, gesturing to Riley's green fleece pullover with the Alpine resort logo in white on the chest. She swats his hand away and rolls her eyes while the guy with them chuckles.

I don't even know why he's here. He can't be stopping by for a simple, neighborly cup of sugar. But it's time to start, so I'll have to grill him about it after the grand unveiling.

Keeping my camera-ready smile plastered in place by sheer force of will, I start my introduction to the small crowd of resort guests gathered. "Hi everyone! Who's excited for today's big reveal?" A little boy in front with a missing tooth cheers loudly. I laugh. "Well, all right, then! That's what I like to hear. We're going live to share this with our guests far and wide so they know what a gem Hollyridge is to visit for their next vacation.

Will you help me out? I need a special volunteer to try it out with."

The little boy beams and pumps his fist in the air. "Yes!"

A ripple of amusement moves through the gathered audience. I set my phone up on a short handheld tripod and tap the live button on my phone screen. Once it's all ready to go, my smile grows wider.

"Hi, Alpine friends and family!" I wave to the phone screen as viewers join the stream.

From the corner of my eye I spot Finn crossing his arms. He doesn't sit in one of the leather armchairs by the roaring fire, standing stiffly, staring me down like a big moody shadow while I host the livestream.

No pressure.

"For those of you watching from somewhere else in the world, we miss you! Come to your favorite home away from home at one of our Anderson Resorts locations."

Did he really just scoff? *Oh my god, focus!*

"I'm Freya Anderson and we're coming at you live from the Alpine Mountain Resort in breathtakingly beautiful Hollyridge, Montana. I'm for real, folks, if you've never seen the snowy northwestern mountain country, you need to get here for the winter season!" Leaning close like I'm divulging a secret, I add, "But don't be like me, fooled by Pinterest street fashion bloggers. If you're from somewhere warm, pack accordingly. But we've got you covered if you forget your second and maybe third layer of socks at the Alpine Outfitters right in our lobby."

The people around me titter at my anecdote. This time it's undeniable that Finn rolls his eyes. I turn my back on him and change the angle to show off the guests.

"We've got some of our Alpine friends and family in residence joining me for today's special event. I have a helper who will give me a hand testing out our newest attraction to entertain you during your visit. There's never a shortage of events and activities at the Alpine." Starting for the tinted glass doors at the back of the lobby that lead to the rest of the resort grounds, I address both the in person guests and my phone. "Who's ready for the surprise? Let's go see it!"

Out back on the patio, space heaters put off a comfortable blanket of warmth to protect the outdoor bar area from the weather. A green curtain hides the sleigh. I give a brief tour of one of the Alpine's three fully stocked bars with award-winning mixologists for the livestream, then stop next to the green curtain.

Finn, Riley, and their friend followed us out, but Finn remains by the door with a wary expression, his thick brows pinched together.

"Ok, it's time for the grand reveal!" I tug a hidden tie and the curtain flutters to the ground, unveiling a large shiny red sleigh, one fit for Santa Claus himself. A clear screen creates a bubble around the top and a small projector is ready to go at the press of a button. "This is the Alpine's virtual sleigh ride! Hop in with the whole family for a beautiful scenic tour of the Montana countryside surrounding Hollyridge."

The guests clap and murmur. My little helper steps forward, examining the gleaming glossy veneer. He meets my eye.

"Is this...Santa's sleigh?" His voice is hushed in awe.

I give him a bright smile. "That's right. He's letting us borrow it until Christmas."

"Wow," he says.

"Ready to help me take it for a spin?"

"Yes!" He jumps up and down, his hair flopping across his forehead.

Turning back to my phone, I ask, "How about our online

viewers, are you excited to see what this can do?" I pause and feel a relief pour through me when the comments scroll. It all seems positive. "Great! Let's hop in and see if we can hear the sleigh bells jingling."

I slide onto the plush seat cushion first, followed by the little boy as his mother helps him climb up.

"Okay, push that big button," I say.

My helper vibrates with excitement for the importance of his job. He smacks his hand down on the button, making me laugh. I adjust the phone so the livestream can see what's happening as the screen lights up.

The sleigh has state of the art graphics technology to allow for a see-through screen from the outside, but a crisp picture inside. It steals my breath when the drone makes its first swoop from the mountaintop, following the flight of a hawk and soaring over a herd of elk. The view is stunning.

"*Whoa*," the little boy gasps beside me when we tail a snowboarder down one of the Alpine's ski runs.

Pride glows like an ember in my chest as we are taken on a virtual experience unlike any other, ending our ride in the quaint town square. When the video ends, we hop out of the sleigh.

"What did you think?" I ask the boy.

"So cool! When we went like *whoosh* and flew so high over the trees, I liked that part best."

"Thanks for helping me, dude. High five." He hits his hand against mine and I turn back to my phone. "Book your stay today at the Alpine Mountain Resort in Hollyridge to enjoy our newest attraction. Thanks for joining us live!"

After I sign off and put my phone away, I catch sight of Finn. Riley and the other guy have disappeared, but Finn lurks at the edge of the patio.

He looks *pissed*. More furious than I've ever seen him. The intense scowl has me falling back a step.

A tug on my sweater dress draws my attention. My little helper points to the sleigh.

"Can we go again?"

I give him a soft smile. "Yeah, bud. You can go as many times as you want."

With an eager sound, he takes off to grab his mom's hand.

When I look up to find Finn, he's gone. An uneasy knot twists in my stomach, but I ignore it. This is what it takes to achieve my goals. That's what is important to focus on right now, not my gruff neighbor and his opinion on anything I do.

* * *

Like total party animals, Riley and I are hanging out in my room at the Alpine Friday night.

"Want to have a holiday movie marathon?" I suggest from my sprawl on the bed. Riley is in one of the faux fur chairs, angled toward the bed with her feet crossed at the ankle on the mattress. "Romcoms or classics or cartoons?"

Riley snorts. "Girl, I don't know anyone that loves the holiday season as much as you do. Not even Grams Mayberry is as dedicated as you, and she's like our queen of Christmas around here. No. We are not spending our Friday night off watching movies holed up in your room. Especially not Christmas movies."

A gasp drops from my lips as I scramble to sit up. "What! But they're the best! They have *all* the feels, Riley."

"They're so cheesy." She shrugs. "Unless it's like Die Hard, I'm not a fan."

I drop back to the bed, moaning in horror, then prop on my

elbows. "Dude. These are the only holiday memories I have. I love them. I even watch them when it's not winter."

"Wait, seriously?" Riley stares at me. After considering me, she hums. "I guess The Grinch Who Stole Christmas isn't so bad. The Grinch is a mood."

"You're a Scrooge," I say. "Holiday movies are the perfect movie. No matter how lonely or sad or depressed you are, they're like a big hug. When your family is divorced and too focused on themselves year-round, they're all you have."

With a stricken expression, Riley climbs onto the bed and pulls me into a hug. "Okay, damn. Come here, we'll hug it out. But I still don't want to watch holiday movies."

"Fine, as long as you refrain from harshing my holiday-loving vibe in the future."

"Deal."

I shift around to face her, leaning my head on my hand. "So who was that guy in the lobby yesterday?"

"That was West," Riley says. "He and Finn were there to pick me up. We all grew up together and have been friends since we were kids."

"Friends? That's not what the pining look on your face says," I tease. "Are you crushing on him? He's cute! Those dimples."

She snorts as I fan myself dramatically. "No, we've, uh." She shakes her head as a complicated expression contorts her pretty features. "No. We're just friends."

Before I can prod her for more, my phone rings. Dad pops up on the caller ID. "Hang on. I've gotta get this." I scoot to the edge of the bed and answer. "Hi Dad."

"Freya." His voice is gruff and crackles with mucus. That means it's not a good day with his health. A spike of worry wedges into my gut. I open my mouth to ask if he's okay, but he recovers and snaps over the line. "You've been out at the Montana property for over a month. I'm calling for a report."

I hold back a sigh. Dad is always all business, no time for fluff. Or family affection. No *hi, honey, how are you* or *I miss you* conversations.

"I've been sending my reports weekly since I took over management."

Tension settles in my shoulders and I get up to pace. It's one of the anxious habits I can't kick whenever I'm on the phone with Dad. It helps focus me, keeping my nerves from spiraling.

"I want to hear it from you. I saw the online event yesterday and I wasn't impressed."

"I—Dad, it's—"

"The brand isn't about fluff, Freya. You either do it according to the guidelines or you don't do it at all. I can't have different properties offering surprises like this."

The pressure of my emotions sear my throat. Damn it. I will not cry because of him. I thought I burned that out of myself years ago.

Maybe it's because this is the first time I don't have a safety net, the first I've been allowed full control to do things my way, with my ideas for what makes a fun and modern experience for resort guests.

"Dad, it was a hit. Bookings jumped five percent overnight."

"I don't care. That's not sustainable. It's the shiny effect. You showed off something new, and people want it. Will you keep offering new things when you have none?"

"But my marketing plan—"

"Damn it, Freya. It's always like this with you. Always so frivolous and scattered in your ideas when you should only be focused on overseeing things." He breaks off into a hacking cough. After he catches his breath, he continues. "And what's this fucking reality TV competition you're in? I sent you to Montana to manage the resort, not as a vacation."

"Yes sir," I murmur tightly.

"Maybe this was too much for you to handle. If you're not up to the task, I'll send someone else. Someone I trust."

The call ends before I can respond. He doesn't even say goodbye, just hangs up. Everything is on his time and his dime.

I blow out a heavy breath and press my forehead to the cool window, peering out through blurry vision. I thought I was doing everything right. This is a wake up call that I need to win the competition more than ever to make Dad understand what he can't see.

"You okay?"

I jump at Riley's question, forgetting I wasn't alone. My voice comes out hoarse when I answer. "Yeah. Peachy."

Peachy fuckin' keen, Finn's voice echoes in my head. I swallow past the lump and swipe my tears away.

"All right doom and gloom. That's it, we're going out."

"I don't know, I think I might go to bed early. I have a lot of work to do."

"Nope." Riley goes to my closet and pulls out the red leather pants I wore for the first Jingle Wars filming. "We're going to cheer you up. Time to let loose. Your depression buster medicine might be feel-good movies, but mine is dancing it out." Spinning to face me while she holds one of my lowcut sweaters against her chest, she grins. "Are you going to hole up or come with me?"

Reluctantly, I smile, taking the sweater. "Going with you."

"Atta girl." Riley smacks my backside and nudges me to the bathroom. "Go get sexy as hell. We're going all out tonight."

* * *

As soon as I set sight on Moose's, the bar Riley pulled up to, I love it. The sign is lit with galvanized pendant lamps and inside it's like an old world western saloon. It's lively with music, people dancing on the worn floor, and a glorious mechanical bull in one corner.

"Oh my god," I gush. "This is amazing."

"This is where everyone in town goes to have fun," Riley says, waving to people she knows.

"Riles! Get your cute lil' butt over here, girl," a weathered woman calls from behind the bar. Another girl closer to our age and covered in tattoos is working beside her, talking to the patrons on the stools at the bar. "Been too long."

"Sorry Miss May, I've been busy with work and keeping this one company." Riley nods to me with a smirk. "This is Freya. She's new to Hollyridge and owns the Alpine."

"That fancy place you teach art and skiing at?" May asks as she pours a beer from the tap in a mason jar. Once she's done, she leans an elbow on the bar and plops the fresh drink in front of Riley. "Welcome to town, Freya. How come you took so long to stop in to say hello?"

I blink in surprise. "Um. No reason. I'm sorry."

May grins. She's missing a tooth, but her smile is warm and welcoming. It's comforting and I find myself returning her smile.

"Just be sure you realize the error of your ways and come see me every Friday from now on."

"Of course," I say. "I hear it's the place to be."

"May isn't kidding." Riley sips her beer as May hands me a drink across the bartop. "She'll come hunt you down if you stay away too long."

May laughs and moves down the bar to see to a man with a scraggly salt and pepper beard.

"Thanks for taking me out." I clink my beer with Riley's. "This is great."

"Damn right."

Riley immediately gets pulled into two conversations back to back with other locals, introducing me to one of the oldest residents in Hollyridge and a girl she went to school with.

Everyone is friendly at Moose's. I've never felt so accepted in my life. It's almost enough to knock me back on my ass in overwhelming relief, but I'd rather take that mechanical bull in the corner by its horns. Actually, on closer inspection those horns are moose horns. The mechanical bull is a mechanical moose.

Riley was right about coming out. I need to dance it out and let loose rather than wallowing in misery by myself. It's something I need to work on—learning to accept that it's ok to lean on others for help rather than doing everything on my own.

I slam my empty mason jar on the bar not long after we arrived. "Let's dance!"

"Hell yes!"

Riley follows me, rolling her body in a side shuffle as we move to the dance floor. Before long, our hips are moving and our hands are up, clapping on the beat. Riley dances better than I can, but I keep up with her, rolling my hips in sensual sways.

A laugh drops from my lips as I spin and dip, sticking my ass out. When I come up, a familiar face in the door makes me pause.

Finn.

"Shots," I announce and Riley cheers. She takes my hand and leads me back to the bar. I press up on my tiptoes. "Miss May? Can we get two shots of tequila please."

Finn and his friend West are watching us. Finn looked annoyed when he walked in, but now at the other end of the bar, they sneak intense looks our way. Those guys must think they're being surreptitious, but the art of subtlety is lost on both of them. They might as well have binoculars for how often their gazes flick our way as Riley and I down our shots.

Well, he can look all he wants. I'm determined to have a good time tonight.

Chapter Eleven
Finn

As if this week could get any worse.

Well, that's what I said before I walked into Moose's for some beers with the guys and saw Freya and Riley on the dance floor laughing and singing with each other. My enthusiasm for guys night was promptly replaced with irritation at the sight of my painstakingly beautiful rival. Freya's eyes locked with my own the second I stepped foot through the door.

Every time her hips swayed with the beat, I grew more annoyed and more horny by the second. It seems like every place I go, somehow Freya ends up there as well. That's the problem with small towns.

So, you can understand why I'm in a sour mood the second my ass hits the barstool, and it's all downhill from there.

"Fuck, Riley's here." West groans when he finally drags his eyes from Aria and spots Riley perched on her stool next to Freya.

The history between those two is so long and complicated

that it would take me an entire case of beer to explain and even then we would only be scratching the surface. I like Riley, she's cool. Her spunky "take no shit" attitude is everything that West can't handle. The dynamic between them is hilarious, but for the most part I stay far away from that shit. I listen when my dude needs an ear, but other than that I'm out.

"Maybe she won't notice you." I grin and signal the bartender over, only to realize she's the same girl from the other night when we were here. Except, Riley already has.

"Damn it. This is not going to end well," West hisses once Aria approaches.

She's the total and complete opposite of West's type. Short, dark hair, tattoos up and down both arms, a piercing in her nose and lips. West has a more reserved...type. Don't get me wrong, she's hot as shit and I can see why he's giving her fuck me eyes from next to me at the bar, but with Riley just across the room? He's insane.

"Dude, you better figure your shit out. Also, Riley just spotted you and she looks like she may actually kill you."

His eyes go wide and then Riley is hopping off her barstool, drink in hand, accompanied by the siren herself, headed our way.

Jesus H.

"Remind me to kick your ass for this later, yeah?" I whisper loudly to him as they walk up.

"Mmm, fancy meeting you here West..." Riley heckles him.

Both of them enter into the most intense stare off I've seen in my life, and I can't imagine how uncomfortable Freya is feeling, especially since she doesn't know either of them well enough to understand their history.

"Riley, uh, can we talk?" West asks, rising from his stool, stepping closer to Riley and she takes a step back.

Freya elbows her in the side, and she rolls her eyes, like

she's annoyed that her friend is pushing her to give him what he's asking for.

"Fine. Five minutes. Freya, I'll be right back, okay?"

Freya nods and shifts around in her red leather pants uncomfortably.

Glad it isn't just awkward for me.

"This is weird," Freya says quietly.

I look over at her and notice how quiet she's being, which I've learned is weird for her. I feel bad for being a dick, almost.

Maybe a little.

"Sit. Those two will be a while." I nod my head to where they're bickering in the corner and Riley is pushing him while they argue.

"I didn't realize things were so... intense with them. She gave me the whole 'just friends' spiel." She laughs lightly.

"Who knows, I can't keep up with them two. I stay out of it as much as possible."

Aria comes over to check on us, and I order two shots of tequila with lime and a beer.

"You gonna drink both of those by yourself?" she asks.

"Nope, we're gonna take them together. I don't feel like drinking alone, do you?"

When Aria brings the shot glasses over to us accompanied with lime, I push one towards Freya and she raises an eyebrow.

"We're not gonna fight about it?"

"Might. Right now, I just want to drink some tequila," I tell her. I pick up my shot and hold it up, waiting for her to join me in a toast.

She eyes me warily, as if waiting for the other shoe to drop, but hesitantly picks up her shot glass and clinks it against mine, then tosses it back in one long sip.

Damn.

I'm so surprised that I haven't even taken my own shot yet.

She sucks on her lime and my dick immediately hardens beneath my jeans. She squeezes her eyes shut then slams her glass down on the table.

"Wow. I'm convinced that there's really nothing that tequila can't fix."

With my eyes about to bulge out of my head, I toss my shot back and welcome the fiery path that burns down my throat.

"Look, they're gone." Freya motions over to where Riley and West were just arguing and now there's no one there. My eyes scan the crowd and I don't see either of them in the building.

I groan. "Looks like it's just us then."

I know exactly where those two assholes are and now I'm stuck without a ride at a bar with my sworn enemy. Great.

Signaling Aria, I order another round of shots. If I'm going to be stuck here, I might as well get drunk in the process.

After another round of shots, or is it two rounds?

"Fourth round, Finn Mayberry." Freya giggles next to me.

I've lost track of how many shots of tequila we're on, all I know is that Freya is looking even more appealing sitting next to me. Her cheeks are flushed from the alcohol and her plump, lush lips are begging to be kissed. Every time she leans over the bar her tits rise against her cut out sweater and I have to bite back the groan that's ready to escape.

"I bet you another round of shots that you can't ride that moose past eight seconds." I grin and point to the large brown mechanical moose that sits in the middle of the bar. Its roped off area looks much like a boxing ring, but with soft cushioned flooring to break the fall of unsuspecting victims. As drunk as I've been at Moose's, never have I gotten on that damn thing, but wouldn't it be a fucking sight to see Freya on it with her tits bouncing?

"Oh?" She smiles confidently and hops off her barstool but wobbles slightly.

"You're gonna do it, really?" I ask when she places her small hand on my arm to steady herself, then pulls her hair back out of her face.

"I don't back down from a challenge, Finn Mayberry. That moose doesn't have shit on Freya Anderson." She grins.

Fuck, I want that feisty mouth wrapped around my dick.

"I mean... If you think you can do it, be my guest."

She grabs my hand, tugging me from the barstool. Laughing, I grab the beer and follow her over to the moose where Landon is setting up for the next rider.

"Finn Mayberry, you gonna ride ole Moosey tonight?" Landon laughs, but his eyes aren't on me, they're on Freya and my hackles immediately raise. Even though I shouldn't care that he's checking her out, part of me wants to punch him like a fucking caveman.

"Nope, my girl Freya is." I grin and toss an arm around her shoulders nonchalantly. I basically just pissed on the ground in front of her, staking my claim, and I have no damn clue why.

The tequila, it's got to be. I can't stand the beautiful liar.

Traitor.

The last person I should want *anything* to do with.

"Alrighty ma'am, well hop on up and I'll get it started."

Freya bites her lip and looks over at the moose hesitantly, unsure of what she's really gotten herself into. As usual.

"Ah ah, no backing out, a bet's a bet. Get your sweet ass up there." I push her towards the massive mechanical animal gently.

Her shoulders square and she reaches down and unzips her fuck me boots, kicking them off. She's ready to take on the moose.

"Landon, give you twenty bucks if you make sure she falls off in less than eight seconds." I grin, pulling my wallet out quickly while she's struggling to swing her leg over and mount the bull.

I wish it was me she was mounting instead.

Fuck Finn, get it together before you get a stiffy in front of the entire bar.

He takes the money from me quickly and stuffs it into the pocket of his jeans just as Freya manages to hop on. She grins a wide grin, ready to challenge me and holds on with both hands as he gives her a thumbs up, signaling he's about to begin. The moose lurches to a start slowly at first, but quickly begins to raise and lower and jolt her from side to side. Man, do those tits bounce. She's holding on for dear life when I nod at him and he cranks it up a notch until she's bucked off, sailing through the air landing in a heap at the cushion of the floor.

I'm laughing so hard tears roll down my face and I'm struggling to keep it together. Even fucking more because she's still laying on the floor on her back, breathless.

When I walk up and stand over her, extending my hand, she scowls at me and pushes herself to her feet, ignoring my help.

"You knew that stupid moose would buck me off! That's why you bet me." She huffs and stomps her way back over to her shoes, putting them on quickly.

"Maybe, maybe not." I shrug.

"Ugh, you are infuriating. You love to watch me make a fool of myself, don't you."

I lean into her, right where her dainty, diamond earrings are showing and whisper gruffly, "Maybe I just wanted to see how well you could ride, Princess."

I watch as a shiver runs down her body and I know it turned her on just as much as it did me. She smells like fucking cookies and something I can't put my finger on. All I know is I want more of it, I want her sweet scent all over me as she rides my dick. I run my nose against her soft jaw line, and brush my lips against the lobe of her ear.

"I need fresh air." She pulls away abruptly, leaving me standing alone in the middle of the bar, barreling out the back exit.

I follow behind her, not bothering to ask if she even wanted me there. I don't give a shit anymore. A man can only take so much and my resolve isn't nearly what it was this morning with the amount of tequila I have coursing through my veins.

The cold air assaults me the second I walk outside, nearly stealing my breath. I've lived in Hollyridge my entire life and I'm still not used to the cold. It's the bone-chilling kind that takes hours to shake once it's seeped into your body.

Freya's standing against the cold brick, her eyes squeezed tightly shut. The moisture of her breathless pants makes a soft cloud in front of her. I walk over and stop just in front of her until her eyes open up and meet mine.

Then, it's like all rationality has been sucked from the air. We collide together in a messy, raw fumble of chaos but it's every fucking thing I've waited on since she pranced her way into town. I can hate her tomorrow.

Her lips find mine in the dark of night and I'm a fucking goner for the girl in the faux fur and UGG boots. She snakes her arms around my neck, entwining with my hair and yanking me closer to her as her tongue darts out, begging me to open. I'm equally shocked that Freya wants to take the reins. Hell most girls are timid when it comes to showing a man what she wants but not Freya. She knows she's owning me.

I lift her off her feet and walk her backwards until her back hits the wall and pull my lips from hers, kissing a path down her throat until I get to her neck where I suck, bite, lick. The frenzied motions get me nowhere closer to where I want to be with her leather jacket and sweater in the way.

"Finn. What are we doing?" She pants as I nip at the sensitive spot of her collar bone.

"Shh. No talking," I whisper gruffly, taking her mouth once more. Her tongue dances with my own in a searing, breathless kiss.

"Finn? Freya?" I freeze whenever I hear West's voice from behind us.

Fuck.

I lower Freya gently to her feet and close her jacket some, since apparently in our scuffle I ripped it open for easier access.

"Wow." Riley snickers.

I drop my head against the wall beside Freya and groan.

Just what I need.

"Riley, I'll meet you inside, 'kay?" Freya says softly, picking up on my frustration.

"*Okay.*" Riley snorts again and then I hear the door slam behind them.

"Well, that was even more awkward than watching them pretend to fake hate each other," she says, laughing lightly.

"Uh, yeah." I straighten and do my best to fix my disheveled hair and jacket, so it isn't completely obvious what was happening outside the bar.

"Wanna talk about what just happened?" she asks me lightly, her eyes hesitant.

"Nope, let's pretend it never happened," I tell her, even though it's the last thing I want to pretend. West and Riley's interruption was like a splash of freezing water and exactly what I needed.

I was weak tonight. I gave in to temptation and I let Freya win. If I don't stop letting her under my skin and into my head, I'll lose this competition and then the Mayberry will be no more, all because I couldn't keep my dick in my pants. There's too much riding on this competition, not just notoriety and what the town will think. This is everything to my grandparents.

"Wow, I thought you'd at least wait until tomorrow to be a dick, Finn." She scoffs and storms off.

"Freya... Wait," I call out, trying to stop her but it's too late, she's already opening the door and stomping inside.

Great, now I've made an even bigger mess than the one I'm already in.

Chapter Twelve
Finn

"Grams, I'm back!" The warm heat of the inn hits me as soon as I step foot inside from the blizzard that rages on outside. I'm assaulted by the smell of fresh baked cookies and am even fucking more glad that I got back to the inn when I did. I quickly remove my damp, snow soaked jacket and gloves, then unlace my boots and leave them by the door. I've been down the road helping Mr. Walker all morning get their furnace back up and running and I'm chilled to the bone. The wind is killer.

Now that I'm home and on the way to being warm, all I can think about is one of Grams' secret recipe cookies. Working in the cold, freezing my balls off has worked up a serious appetite. I'm a growing boy, I need all the carbs. Specifically in the form of Grams' desserts.

I round the corner into the kitchen, ready to eat the entire plate. "Grams, did you make coo—"

I stop mid sentence when I see Freya standing next to Grams, both of them covered in flour, kneading a large round ball of dough. She looks up and gives me a shy smile, then Grams smiles widely, enjoying this way too fucking much.

This damn woman, playing matchmaker every chance she gets.

I haven't seen Freya since the other night at the bar, when I almost fucked her against the damn building then ruined it all in one second by opening my mouth. I should've handled it better. Even if it's what needed to happen, *had* to happen, I should've taken her feelings into consideration and not been an ass.

"Hi Finn! We're making your favorite cookies, the ones with the little strawberry filling, look," Grams says giddily, all too happy to have Freya by her side helping. She lifts the dough in her hands to show me. Typical Grams, trying to distract me with food while she gets away with murder.

"Uh... Sounds great Grams, can't wait. Freya, surprised to see you here...with my Grams...baking cookies in my kitchen..." I trail off, waiting for one of them to say something, or at least tell me what the hell is going on. It's...strange seeing Freya in my house and the idiot part of me who always thinks with his dick is more than happy to see her fitting in nicely.

Freya looks at me warily, still kneading her dough. "Your Grams saw me outside with the delivery guy and asked if I wanted to help her make some Christmas treats... I, well, I didn't have anything else to do, so I decided to come," she says quietly, and I feel like even more of an asshole for treating her the way I did. She doesn't seem to be mad, but more hurt and that's worse than being mad.

"Yes Finn, I did invite Freya over to make some treats and if you don't behave you won't be getting not a one of them." Grams gives me a stern look over her wire rimmed glasses.

"Just curious. Smells delicious." I watch as Freya and Grams talk quietly. She mimics everything that Grams tells her to, handling the dough with care. Like it's completely new to her.

"You ever made cookies before Freya?" I ask.

She bites her lip and her eyes flicker with sadness before recovering quickly. "Uh, no actually, this is my first time."

I caught the look that passed in her eyes before she answered, and suddenly, even though I know I shouldn't... I want to know what caused that sadness in her eyes.

"Well, good thing your next door neighbor supplies Christmas treats for the entire town, including all of the homeless for the holidays. Grams is always in the kitchen, isn't that right Grams?"

I give her my best grin and her eyes soften.

"Sure is. Least I could do for the town that's given us everything. Family and friends are everything to us Freya, there's nothing more important," she says, adding a cup of sugar to her mixing bowl.

"I love that. That's really special Grams," Freya whispers.

"Darn Santa's Sleigh!" Grams mutters. Her version of cursing.

"What's wrong?" I ask then turn away, trying to hide the cookie I snuck off of the plate.

"Put the cookie down, Finn. Those are for the shelter. I'm out of sugar and flour!"

And this is the part where she asks me to go back into town and fetch it for her, like a true errand boy. Bad thing is, she knows that I'll do it because I'd do anything for her.

Grumbling, I put the cookie back on the plate.

"Ooh Finn, how about you take Freya into town and get a few things for me? It would be the perfect time for her to pick up those Christmas decorations she was talking about earlier. Right Freya?"

Our eyes meet over the counter and she hesitates for a

moment then nods. "Yeah, that would be great, Grams. If you don't mind me tagging along, that is, Finn."

Not that Grams would give us much of a choice anyway. Freya was coming with me no matter what the second Grams brought it up. When she gets something in her head, there's no coming back from it.

"Sure, no problem. Let me just get my coat."

An awkward, heavy silence hangs in the air between us. Grams must pick up on the tension and she starts a never ending stream of conversation about her latest bingo hall drama. I use the distraction to head into the mudroom to gather my stuff. A few minutes later, Freya joins me in the mudroom with Grams following closely behind her.

Grams hands me the list she's written.

"Okay, here's the list of what I'll need, please make sure to get everything Finn, I would hate to have to send you back." She grins cheekily.

"Wouldn't dream of it, Grams. Be back soon." I drop a quick kiss to her cheek, and then open the door, gesturing to Freya.

"Ladies first."

Outside, the snow is falling at a steady pace, blanketing everything in sight. As beautiful as it is, it's fucking cold and I'm not looking forward to another trip to town. Especially while getting the silent treatment from Freya. I open her door and wait for her to get inside the cab of the truck, then shut it behind her and head around to my side. When I'm in and have the heater on full blast, she finally speaks.

"Listen, I wasn't trying to invade your personal space. Grams really did invite me over while I was out signing for a delivery."

Her face is a mask of seriousness and I can't read her expressions, but I know Grams and that's exactly something she would do.

"You don't have to explain yourself. I'm not upset." Tearing my gaze from her, I put the truck in reverse and pull onto the road heading into town.

"You know, Finn, I don't understand why you think I'm this horrid, terrible person that's destined to be your enemy," she says quietly.

Of course you don't.

My hands tighten on the wheel until my knuckles are white, but I say nothing, keeping my eyes on the road in front of me.

"When I was five years old, my parents got killed in a car accident," I say, finally breaking the silence. Her breath hitches with my revelation. "I was at the inn with Grams and Gramps. They were headed home from a movie. I was just a kid, too innocent to understand the world around me. I remember Grams breaking down at the front door when Sheriff Baker came to the door to tell them. He said the bridge was iced over, and they must have hit a patch of black ice and went over the embankment." My chest feels tighter revealing that, but also it feels good to tell her my truth.

I look over at her and see unshed tears filling her eyes. For the first time since meeting Freya, I see her for more than the neighbor next door that I'm supposed to hate. Everything is turning out to be more complicated, especially when I realize that I'm falling for a traitor. A beautiful, traitorous neighbor who despite all of that, is still off limits.

Now I realize just why I've spent so much time trying to hate her. She came to Hollyridge with the goal of making her resort the bigger, better resort. With all of the finest amenities money could buy. High tech sleigh rides, state of the art theatre system. Nothing that the Mayberry could compete with. My immediate distaste for her only grew when I saw not only was she my number one competition for the inn, but that she was trying to change Hollyridge as a whole. Attract more people, bring in more tourists. Take away the small-town, quiet place that my town has always been.

But I was wrong, that's not what Freya was doing. Seeing her vulnerable and her compassion, I know her heart has nothing but truth in it. She was never trying to hurt me or Hollyridge. She just didn't understand and now...I think she might.

"I went to the inn excited to spend the evening with Grams and Gramps, and then suddenly my parents were dead. From that moment on they took me in, they raised me. Every single thing about me, I owe to them. Everything Freya. Hell, I'm nothing without them. They made me a man. They raised me to be a man that I'm proud of." My voice is tight with emotion.

"That's why you're so close to them, because they're like your parents," she says softly. I hear emotion in her voice, which wasn't my intent, but I need her to understand why I'm participating in this stupid competition anyway.

I nod. "When I say I owe them everything, I mean it. Gramps is sick Freya. His heart... It's not doing good. He collapsed in the front yard recently and was hospitalized, and that's ultimately what made me move out of my apartment downtown and back into the inn. He just can't keep up with all of the maintenance, and Grams is on him to stay off his feet and relax, which just isn't in his vocabulary."

I laugh. "So I moved back in and have been doing anything and everything I can. Including letting Grams bribe me into dates with her friends' granddaughters in exchange for her cookies."

I swallow thickly. The memories of the past come barreling back as I tell Freya what's really been going on in my world. "The first week that I was here, I discovered a stack of bills that have gone unpaid for months. Gramps admitted that business hasn't been going well, and he's behind on the mortgage. Seeing the look on his face when he said that almost killed me. He's so full of pride."

Freya's eyes are wide and her lips are parted in shock. She truly had no idea things were like this bad at the inn.

"Him and Grams opened the inn almost fifty years ago, and have built a business from the ground up. Never had any help. And now it's like all his hard work is being ripped from him. He feels helpless. Hell, I feel helpless. Everything is falling apart. It seems like every time I fix one thing, something worse breaks." It feels strange to open up to her like this, but it also feels right.

"So that's why you joined the competition... For the prize money?" She looks at me compassionately. The unshed tears clinging to her lashes begin to fall. She's realizing that it isn't just "some" competition for me, and it's the only way to save my grandparents' Inn.

Nodding, I slow down as we drive across the very bridge that my parents were killed. Emotion hits me in a strong wave as we reach the other side.

"It's up to me to save the one thing my grandparents have worked their entire life for. That's why I have to win this competition. Why nothing can distract me from what I came here for." I hope she understands the meaning behind what I'm saying. That *she* is the distraction that I can't afford.

Freya's quiet the rest of our ride into town, staring out the window. I hate that I had to push her away, but the farther I get into this competition, the harder I have to work to make sure I'm the one who's on the stage collecting that prize money.

Nothing is going to stand in my way. Nothing will stop me from saving the inn. Even if it means pushing away Freya in the end.

Chapter Thirteen
Freya

At first when Grams Mayberry sent Finn and I on errands two days ago, I was cautious and unsure. I didn't know how to act around Finn after he'd been such a dick immediately after kissing me with wild abandon outside of Moose's last Friday. When he caught me in his kitchen with his grandmother, I thought he'd kick me out on my ass if it weren't for the promise of his favorite cookies.

But as we drove through the steady snowfall, he told me about his parents and his grandparents.

I could barely focus on the shopping we did for Grams, lost in my thoughts while Finn took us from store to store. When I couldn't remember the decorations I was supposed to get, he talked to the shop owner and took care of it for me, shooting me worried glances for my quietness.

My heart ached for him, tears springing to my eyes. As soon as I swiped them away, new ones would hit me. How could the world be so cruel, ripping away a young boy's parents, leaving him to face such a painful tragedy?

My family is...dysfunctional at best, too obsessed with money and renown to truly care about each other. My estranged brothers and I are a transaction, a business investment my parents completed and moved on from with their divorce. None of us talk to each other. *Really* talk, not what passes for conversation between Dad and I.

For all that I grew up lonely, I had my parents in some way or another. But Finn...

I ball my fists at my side to fight off the fresh wave of sadness threatening to swallow me whole as I walk the path leading to the Mayberry Inn from the Alpine's front entry drive.

Today I'm on a mission to see my handsome neighbor about a cup of sugar. A metaphoric one, intended as a peace offering. When Finn told me his reason for entering the Jingle Wars competition is all to give back to his grandparents for raising him and save his family's struggling inn, I understood so much more about who he is. He's an admirable man beneath the gruff moodiness.

I don't want Finn and his grandparents to lose the livelihood they built by hand, or lose the place Finn grew up.

The idea came to me while I was soaking in the hot spring last night, blowing bubbles with my lips beneath the surface of the steamy water while no one was looking.

It's a perfect plan. I want us to set up a joint event for the town. It will be sponsored by both his family inn and the Alpine, my way of showing Finn I don't want to steal his business or work in competition against him. We can work together.

As I march up the front walkway leading to Mayberry Inn's wraparound porch, I find Gramps talking to one of the inn's guests, an older man with a newsboy cap and a book tucked under his arm. Gramps is laughing with him, bundled in a parka and leaning on a snow shovel.

"Morning, Gramps," I call as I approach.

He lights up at the sight of me, stirring a happy glow of warmth in my chest. "Freya! Good mornin'. Ain't you bright-eyed and bushy-tailed." He tosses a glance to the inn's guest and his smile stretches wider when he looks back at me. "Pretty as ever, too."

Grinning, I tuck a piece of hair behind my ear. "Thank you. Yes, I am bright-eyed this morning. I'm taking on the day, sir."

"That's the spirit," Gramps says with a nod of approval. "Good to have your head on right, I always say."

His approval means more to me than I can say. First baking cookies with Grams Mayberry, and now being recognized by Gramps for having a good work ethic? The glow in my chest grows into a dancing little sun.

The conversation with Finn in his truck runs through my head as I take in the snow shovel in Gramps' hand and the freshly shoveled walkway. I don't know if I can say anything, but a fissure of worry runs through me at the thought of Gramps exerting himself with his heart problems.

"Where's Finn? I came by looking for him." I offer Gramps a wry smile. "Is he slacking off, leaving you to do all the work around here? Doesn't seem like him."

I know Finn works hard, but I don't want to hurt Gramps' pride if I fuss over him.

Gramps busts out in a hearty chuckle and the older man with him smiles. Gramps nods to the guest. "He's stuck inside, getting his ear talked off while this one's wife flirts with him. Same as every year since they started coming to stay at the inn. This is Warren Shepherd. He and Bertie love the mountain air."

"That we do," Mr. Shepherd says. He looks at Gramps and

his smile wanes. "Shame about this year being quieter around here."

I chew the inside of my lip, hit by a pang of guilt. This is exactly why I want to present my plan to Finn today. We don't have to work against each other. That's never what I wanted when I came here.

Gramps waves him off. "So it goes. You should enjoy the time to read your books on the porch without so many kids running around."

Mr. Shepherd's shoulders shake with amusement. "It'll be a blessing not to duck those snowball fights."

"I'm going to look for Finn. It was good to see you, Gramps. Nice meeting you, Mr. Shepherd, and I hope you enjoy your stay in Hollyridge." The corners of my mouth lift. "I'm new in town, but I can see why you fell in love with it here. It's great that you and your wife have a favorite place to visit."

Mr. Shepherd nods, holding up his book and ambling toward the rocking chairs on the wraparound porch.

"Don't be a stranger, now," Gramps says to me, waving as he heads for the side entrance around the back of the inn.

I continue toward the Mayberry. As soon as I reach the end of the walkway, the front door opens and Finn steps out, bundled in a coat. He takes me in, dressed in jeans and the bright red peacoat I finally bought in town, and blinks.

"Hey." I'm suddenly feeling a rush of awkwardness.

"You're over here twice in the same week?" Finn lifts his brows teasingly as he pulls the door shut behind him. The old wood planks creak as he saunters across the porch. His mouth curves into a lopsided, lazy smile. "You planning on moving in next?"

"Grams said I was welcome whenever," I say defensively, raising my chin, daring him to deny it.

The truth is, it felt so important and special when Grams

Mayberry invited me inside to bake cookies with her. She spent more time teaching me how to mix and handle the dough than I did helping. Each time I think of my first memory making cookies from scratch with her guiding me through the process, I'm struck by a nonstop surge of emotions welling in my throat. To her it might have been another afternoon spent baking cookies she's made hundreds of times, but to me it's immeasurable how much it meant.

I'm still afraid Finn will push me away more than he has, refuse to allow me to get to know his family. He said in the truck the other day I didn't have to explain myself, and he even opened up to me, but I'm wary he'll turn around and shut me out once more. He was quick to do it after the kiss, and has made it clear where his priorities lie.

We've reached some sort of gray middle area between the rivalry we were fostering and friendship. I think, anyway. Why would he tell me so much about his life and his financial struggles if he still thought of me as his enemy? Ever since that kiss, something changed between us.

If only he wanted that to happen between us again.

"By all means." He waves an arm, inviting me inside. "Go hang out with Grams."

"Actually, I'm here to see you."

He hitches a shoulder. "I'm on my way out."

His eyes narrow when he sees the shoveled path and he sighs something unintelligible under his breath. All I catch is *Gramps* and *stubborn old man*. When he steps off the weathered porch and brushes past me, I follow, holding onto my slouchy knit beanie so it doesn't slip off.

"It'll only take a minute."

"What do you want?" He walks fast on his longer legs, leaving me to shuffle double time to keep pace with him around the side of the inn.

"A potluck." We reach his truck and he angles his head to peer at me over his shoulder. "Let's put one together for Hollyridge. The holidays are a time people come together."

Finn swipes his fingers over his mouth, smoothing his scruff. It's thicker today, like he let it go a few more days between trimmings. "I have a lot to do today, Freya. I don't have much time to listen to this."

"Great, so I'll come with you," I shoot back, skirting around the front of the truck and opening the passenger door. "We'll multitask. I'll pitch the idea on the way."

His mouth hangs open at me inviting myself. I plop on the aged, cracked black leather bench seat, shifting a blanket aside to make room. Cedar and spice hits my nose. It smells like him inside, overwhelmingly so. As if his essence is soaked into these seats.

I was too on edge to appreciate it the other day, but now I'm taking notice.

"You can't just come with me." It comes out like he's talking through a laugh.

"Sure I can. I'm already in the truck. Hurry up and start it so we can blast the heat. It's freezing out here."

Finn remains quiet for another beat, raking his fingers through his tousled brown hair as his thoughts turn. After heaving an exasperated sigh, he yanks the door open on his side and climbs in. He ignores me pointedly as he turns the ignition and backs out of his parking spot. I like watching him in his truck, studying the familiar way he handles the gear shift and rests the heel of his palm over the wheel.

A moment later, he adjusts the dial to turn on the heat. I hum in content when I put my hands up in front of the vents. His attention slides to my profile.

"Where are we going?" I ask.

"Errands," Finn says.

"Again?"

"Not for Grams this time. There's always something to do."

As we pull out onto the main road from the inn's entrance, my gaze flits to the backseat. Before everything, when I was new to town, I fantasized about making out with Finn in his truck. It's cliché as hell, but it's still an appealing mental image. Maybe more so now that I know him better.

Especially now that I know the feel of his lips on mine.

After the kiss at the bar, with Finn's strong arms holding me up against the wall while his hands massaged my ass through the leather pants, and the heat of his ragged panting against my neck between biting kisses…yeah, I have all-new fantasies about my lumberjack neighbor.

The steamy thoughts fly from my head once I realize we're pulling into a farm after only a few minutes on the road. Two men are red in the face as they struggle with a huge tractor by the edge of a frozen pond. It seems stuck, or like it slid down the snowy incline.

Finn parks the truck a few feet away from them and gets out.

I shift sideways on the seat to watch him get rope and a big metal hook from the truck bed. "What sort of errands are you running?"

"Favors called in, mostly. We help each other out around here. Everyone has each other's backs." He cocks his head with a smirk, gaze flicking over me. "Going to stay in the truck, Princess?"

I suck my lower lip into my mouth. He still thinks I'm too good for hard work? "Nope." I hop down, glad I wore jeans today. "How long will this take?"

Finn releases a raspy chuckle. "About however long it takes, usually." He hesitates, studying me once more. "You can stay in the truck. It's okay."

"No thanks."

I walk off towards the two men by the tractor and he falls into step beside me with a smile playing in the corners of his mouth.

"You've just—got to—*argh!*" The older man on the left with gray hair peeking out from beneath his beanie kicks at the muddy wheel of the tractor that's stuck in the pond with broken ice surrounding it. "Blasted thing."

"All right now, Uncle Lyle. Don't get all tore up," Finn says with amusement lacing his tone. "We'll get it out."

"Oh, is he part of your family, too?" I stick out my hand, eager to meet more of Finn's relatives. "Hi, I'm Freya."

"Not really my uncle," Finn says as he circles around the tractor. "Just likes everyone to call him that."

"Ain't you a pretty little thing." Lyle takes my hand before I drop it and gives it a hearty shake. "Jared, ain't she pretty? That's my son."

"Come on." Finn's deep voice sounds from right behind me, his hand brushing over my hip through my wool coat. "Stop getting distracted. Let's get your tractor back to rights."

Without any life experience in pulling tractors from frozen ponds, I stand guard, watching as Finn and Jared point at different parts of the tractor while rigging the rope he brought to the back end.

"Freya." Finn's head pokes over one of the wheels. "Can you go to my truck and get the jug of rock salt? We need it for the traction."

"Right! On it." I hurry back to the truck and search the bed for it. The jug is heavy, but I manage with a little grunt, carrying it back. "Here."

"Thanks." Finn takes the rock salt and sprinkles it liberally on the snow by the wheels. "Ok, Jared, get on up and Lyle, you pull with my truck."

The three of them move quickly, driving the truck over and attaching the tractor with the rope and hook to the hitch.

As I'm watching Finn work with Lyle and his son, a funny sensation builds in my chest, encircling my heart. The man who I thought was stubborn and willing to play dirty isn't really who I thought he was at all.

He's so much more.

Finn is kind. Helpful. The sort of person who would give the shirt off his back to someone in need.

His grandparents did a great job raising him, especially in the wake of the tragedy that rocked their family. He's a good man.

I feel like I'm really allowed to see him now, as if he allowed me in past the fortress wall he erected around himself when he thought I was a threat.

The tractor moves from the pond, and Finn's concentration is on pushing. I only see it happen because I'm standing to the side out of the way, but something tells me to move. I jump in beside him just as his boot catches a slippery patch of the ground, gripping tight on his jacket so he won't lose his balance.

"Careful," I murmur. "You'll catch a cold for sure if you fall in the pond."

He blinks as he adjusts his footing and together we help push. He's probably doing more of the work, but I feel good standing beside him with my palms pressed to the cold metal as it inches up the incline while Jared drives and Lyle pulls with the truck. Together we get it away from the pond and back up the small hill.

"Thanks, Finn," Lyle says after we've finished. "Appreciate it. Tell Grams we said hello."

"No problem. You can call me whenever."

On our way back to the truck, I give his arm a playful tap. "That was some impressive brawn and problem solving."

He chuckles, the deep sound igniting a happy glow inside me. "That was nothing. You should've seen last year when I had to help deliver lambs at three in the morning."

My mouth pops open and I clutch his sleeve. "Really?"

Another laugh puffs out of him. He shakes his head, giving me a smile. A real smile, one that makes my heart stop and float off into la la land. *Big freaking oof.*

"You're so gullible sometimes. Bet you'd believe any good deed I told you about."

"Of course I would." I wait as he opens the passenger door for me. "That seems to be the type of person you are. Hard-working, helpful, and honest."

I don't know how I ever could've thought otherwise. He offers his hand to help me into the cab with a pleased look on his face.

Once we're back in the truck, I angle on the seat to face him with a grin. "Where to next?"

The corner of Finn's mouth lifts. "Other side of town. Grady Deerborne needs some extra hands to help with getting his furnace heating again."

He puts the truck in gear and we continue making stops, spending the day lending a helping hand and giving back to the residents of Hollyridge.

Working alongside him fills me with a sense of rightness.

My heartstrings tug insistently. This thing I feel for Finn is more than physical attraction. I keep getting flashes of future possibilities each time he smiles at me or puts his hand at the small of my back.

It's a future where I have everything I've wished for—a life to share with someone, a family, a home. One that isn't simply a place to hang my coat, but somewhere filled with love and memories I've made with the people closest to my heart.

My breath catches more than once at the force of longing

for these glimpses. They're the things I stopped hoping for a long time ago, when I was alone every holiday.

It's not until we're pulling back into the Alpine's entrance after dark several hours later that I realize I never fully explained my cosponsored potluck idea to Finn. He glances at me as the truck comes to a stop in front of the lobby entrance.

"Thanks for dropping me off so I didn't have to walk back."

"Sure," he murmurs.

With a soft reluctant groan, I pull the blanket off my lap. Finn watches me closely, an intensity burning in his warm whiskey-colored eyes. He reaches across the bench seat and brushes his fingers with mine as I fold the blanket. We sit in the stillness for a second.

Part of me wants to ask if he'll come inside, to my *Scandinavian Winter* room. Another part wishes he'll ask me to come with him back to his place.

I peek through my lashes and trace my thumb along his knuckles. My breathing syncs with the steady beat of my heart when he captures my fingers in his.

More than a kiss, I want to stay like this. In this moment, in his truck that smells like him, holding hands.

"Thanks for letting me tag along today." My quiet murmur breaks the spell keeping us captive. "I really like the people here." I release his hand and run my nail along the seams of the bench seat. "They make me feel like..."

"Like what?" Finn asks when I don't finish my sentence.

I blow out a breath and lick my lips. "Everyone here makes me feel like I have a place. Somewhere I should be. I've, um. Never had that." I rub at my nose, unable to remain still in my self-consciousness. "It's nice."

A worried crease forms between his brows as he stares at me. I offer him a smile and get out of the truck.

"Freya," he says, stopping me. I turn around, hand on the

door. He offers a crooked smile that has my stomach fluttering. "There's a town event coming up in a few days, the annual tree lighting. We always go, Grams and Gramps and me. Would you like to come with us?"

The bright, elated smile I give him almost hurts my cheeks. I lean back in the truck. "Really? That sounds amazing. This town is *perfect*," I gush. "These non-stop Christmas festivities are getting me so hyped." I pause for a second, touched that Finn would invite me along with his family to join in the fun. "Yes, I'd love to come!"

A chuckle rolls out of him at my enthusiasm for all things festive. "Well, alright then. Pick you up out front?"

"Sounds great."

He waits until I'm by the door, looking over my shoulder. Our gazes lock, making the world disappear for several seconds.

Then he drives off into the night. I head inside and move through the lobby of the Alpine, greeting guests and waving to my staff.

I meant what I told him. Hollyridge isn't simply a town on the map to me.

It's starting to feel like my home. The place I belong, where I've found somewhere to fit in and have the surrogate family I've never had with my own.

I wasn't supposed to stay here forever. The plan was to show Dad how capable I was so he'd start trusting my input for other properties we own.

But now? I'm not so sure I ever want to leave. I'm not sure I ever *could* leave.

This town has this way of charming visitors to stay, like as soon as you've stepped foot in it a piece of your heart feels like it belongs here—always has, always will. I've heard of people who travel feeling this way about different destinations they go, but this is the first time I'm experiencing that magic for myself.

Chapter Fourteen
Finn

"Finn, make sure you grab the thermos please," Grams instructs as she buttons Gramps' coat for him.

"Got it, Grams."

I'm packing the last few things into the truck before we head into town for Hollyridge's Annual Tree Lighting. It's the same night every year. A huge deal. Grams makes sure of it. She's on the festive committee in town, which she supplies most of the treats for, but she and the committee work tirelessly to make sure everything in town is as over the top decorated and "festive" as possible. Christmas threw up everywhere equals tourists which equals money for the town. Small-town charm sells, and Hollyridge is the coziest town this side of the mountains.

"Let's go, let's go... We're going to be late! Wait! Finn, can you grab the marshmallows from the pantry?" she asks over her shoulder as she shoos Gramps outside.

I sigh heavily. This woman.

Walking over to the pantry I open the door and search through more baking supplies than a damn bakery, searching for the marshmallows. Ah! Finally. They're nestled in the back behind a shit ton of sugar.

Wait. Didn't Grams send me and Freya for sugar the other day? She said she was out.

It dawns on me that my meddling Grams had sugar all along. She wanted to send me alone with Freya and she used sugar as the ruse. Sneaky, sneaky woman.

Grinning, I shut the pantry and walk outside joining my grandparents. I give her the bag of marshmallows.

"Grams, hold on, I have to run over and get Freya. Didn't want her to be home alone tonight," I say.

She gives me a look like *hm, I bet that's exactly why you're going to get her Finn Mayberry*, followed by a cheeky grin.

These women; gonna drive me crazy one of these days.

I trek through the thick snow across the resort's lawn to get Freya. She's waiting outside under the awning. Dressed in tight leather leggings and a red coat, she looks like any man's dream. *For fucking sure like mine.*

It's only been a few days since I saw her and God, she gets sexier every damn time I see her. In another over the top, non winter appropriate outfit she steals my breath.

Finn, get your shit under control. She's still the enemy.

"Hi Finn." She smiles.

Her dark curls frame her face, and I want to take her into my arms and kiss her until she's breathless. I can't help but be enamored by her. Her cheeks, red and flushed from the cold, match the red lipstick she's painted on her lush lips. The crimson color makes her eyes shine brighter. Tonight she's wearing makeup and even though I prefer her face bare, she looks breathtaking. Dark, thick lashes frame her eyes. Everything about this girl is perfection. But I'm beginning to see that

Freya's beauty isn't just skin deep. She's beautiful inside and out.

"Hi. Ready?" I ask.

She nods, and we walk together back towards the inn. Her shoulder brushes against my arm as we walk back together and she shoots me a playful grin.

"So, I gather tonight is an important night for Hollyridge? The resort is buzzing with excitement."

"Yeah, it's a pretty big deal around here. Locals look forward to it every year. They bring their families, shop some of the booths, and get their spot for the lighting. There's ice skating, snowball fights, hot chocolate stations. It's fun."

When we arrive at the truck, Grams and Gramps both spend a few minutes fussing over Freya. Grams makes sure to comment on how beautiful she looks tonight then shoots me a look that's full of meddling.

"Let's go before we're late." I open the door for Freya and wait until she's inside before I close it shut behind her, then open my door and slide in behind the wheel.

The drive to town is short with Grams and Gramps pointing out locations to Freya and telling her some of the town's history. I'm engrossed in the stories because even after growing up here, I'm hearing some of these things for the first time.

"Oh, Freya, look! That's where Finn broke his arm when he was seven. That darn boy. He was daring and fearless. Still is to this day, isn't that right Finn?" Grams takes my hands in hers and I feel the strings in my heart tug.

If you only knew the things that truly scared me Grams. Losing the inn, disappointing you and Gramps.

"I wouldn't say that Grams." I laugh lightly, trying to keep the subject from going somewhere darker.

"Oh, he didn't cry a tear when they had to set it and put a

cast on. His gramps bought him a BB gun after that and boy did the tears come then, because he couldn't shoot it with the dang cast!" Grams and Gramps are both laughing now, and it's infectious because Freya joins in, too.

"I told him, Finn Michael, that gun will still be there when that cast comes off. He looked at me and said, 'well Grams, it just ain't no fair!' I can still hear his little voice to this day." Her blue eyes shine with unshed tears from her laughter, or maybe at the memories that still hurt when you think of them.

Finally, the glow of downtown begins to peek through the thick of the trees and we're near town.

"Wow, everything is so beautiful. The lights, the trees, the snow," Freya says in awe. I agree.

"It really is."

Except I'm not looking at the scenery, I'm looking at her.

Tonight it's exceptionally hard to keep my eyes off of her, and harder not to take her into my arms and show her what I've been holding back for too fucking long.

When we arrive at town square, I find a vacant parking spot and pull in, parking the truck backwards so we can pull the tailgate down. Thankfully, the snow has stopped for the evening, so we can enjoy tonight without being wet and cold. I hop out and open the door for Freya, then hold out my hand so she can step down.

She eyes me warily, but still puts her hand in mine, and hops down from the truck. Her signature UGG boots cause her to slip slightly and fall right into my arms. I tighten my hold around her to prevent her from landing on the ice.

"Thanks Finn."

"No problem."

The tightness of space between the truck and the vehicle parked next to us allows for very little space between her and I, and I feel her warm breath against my lips. My hands are on the door beside her, framing her in the spot.

Neither of us say anything, but make no move to leave the confined space that has us pressed against one another. She looks up at me through dark lashes and I feel my resolve leaving by the second. I inch in closer, a mere centimeter from pressing my lips against hers and giving in to what we both so desperately want.

A throat clearing pulls us from our lust-induced trance and we both whip our heads to look at our audience. Grams stands by the tailgate, clutching her heart, smirking at the two of us.

I groan inwardly. Fuck.

Pushing off from the truck, I walk past Grams and say, "Not a word Grams."

After Gramps and I set the tailgate up with a blanket, a few pillows and some spare blankets to keep everyone warm, I help Grams up on to the tailgate and give her the thermos of hot chocolate she had me pack at the inn.

Let's be real, Grams is a complete hot chocolate snob. She says that her palate is refined, but the truth is she can't, no she *won't*, drink anyone else's hot chocolate because it doesn't come close to hers. Which is true. But, besides the point. If I'm going somewhere, I'll just drink whatever is available, but not Grams. She's got to pack her own.

"Finn, why don't you show Freya around some?"

She looks over at Gramps, who shoots her a knowing smile.

"Yeah, Finn, I'm sure Freya would love to see some of the booths and go ice skating?"

"Oooh yes! Freya you have to go skating at the rink. Heck, if these hips would cooperate, I would be out there! It's a lot of fun," Grams chimes in.

I look at Freya. With her eyes still heavily lidded with lust, she smiles up at me.

"Sure, I'd like that. If you think you can keep up Finn," she taunts.

Is she really about to challenge me in ice skating? Doesn't she realize she's the tourist here?

"Oh, is that so? You really wanna do this Princess?" I ask.

Instead of answering she takes her lip between her teeth then grins cheekily.

"Let's go."

Lately, it seems like anytime Freya and I are alone, the air gets thicker and the tension takes ahold of us both, and I'm about two seconds from taking her behind the closest building and fucking her until she can't walk. I pause a second to take a few deep breaths and try to calm the arousal that is lit like a fire inside me.

When we get to the rink, the line wraps around the side. Damn, looks like we're going to be waiting for a while. Freya's eyes light up as she sees all of the kids skating around the rink, laughing and singing along to the obnoxiously loud Christmas music.

"Is this your first time?" I ask.

"Yeah. There isn't snow in Malibu, unless it's the fake kind, and there's no way I was touching that. Plus, my dad was always too busy in the boardroom to take me anywhere that had snow. My nanny took me to do everything. I was honestly like ten before I realized that not everyone had nannies, that they weren't a part of everyone's family. Looking back now, I realize how fucked up that is."

I'm surprised that my question got this type of response from her, completely raw and unforeseen. I was expecting something short and simple to answer, but instead she revealed a part of herself that I hadn't seen yet so far. The vulnerable, real part of Freya that admits to weakness. Everything between us has been competition and a steady stream of one ups, so seeing her in an unguarded way makes her more human.

"We've all had fucked up shit in our childhood. Trust me, no family is perfect," I tell her quietly.

"Except your family, Finn. Grams and Gramps are perfect." She smiles sadly.

I'm beginning to realize that Freya's problems stem from her relationship with her father, and it makes me want to knock him the fuck out for hurting her. Sometimes I'm a gentleman, but there are times where I will fuck someone up when need be.

"Anyway, sorry to throw all of that family stuff on you. We're supposed to be having a fun night and I'm unloading all of my family drama on you, sorry." Her tone is serious, and I see the hurt behind her eyes bringing all of it up.

I reach out and place my hand on hers over the rail. "Hey, it's okay. Don't be sorry. Sometimes that heavy stuff gets too hard to hold. I understand."

She nods and gives me a fake smile, but doesn't say anything else. We wait in line silently, but her hand is still tucked beneath mine and it feels like holding her hand, as simple as that gesture is, it's how it always should be. Simple, easy. No pressure.

When we get to the front of the line, the teenager takes my money and gives us both a worn pair of skates. Mine feel like they're an entire size too big, but I don't bother asking for a new pair. My luck, he'd put us at the end of the line and Freya looks too excited.

She gets her skates laced quickly, shockingly without my help, and we make our way out to the ice. I grip her hand as she steps onto the ice, and she immediately goes down. Literally.

I can't make this shit up. The second her skate hits the ice, her feet are out in front of her and she's landing on her ass.

Hard. She lets out a half yelp, half laugh and I can't help but laugh.

And laugh.

And laugh, until it earns me a punch in the leg because she's still on the ground, struggling to get up on the slick ice.

"I'm sorry! I'm sorry. I couldn't help it." I put my fist to my mouth to hold back another laugh before she beats me up.

"You're impossible, Finn Mayberry! You don't laugh at a lady, how rude. What happened to being a gentleman, huh?"

I reach down and grab her hand, pulling her to her feet. She's clutching onto me for dear life, but instead of letting her go back on her own, I pull her closer.

"Wanna test how gentlemanly I'm feeling right now?" I whisper huskily into her ear. My breath teases the sensitive flesh, inciting a shiver from her.

She pulls back and her eyes go wide. "Finn! We're at a skating rink. With children. Behave!"

She feigns annoyance, but I can tell she's anything but. She wants this as badly as I do and it seems like all we do is dance around the truth. Except... No matter how much either of us want the other, the real truth is that she's the traitor I can never have.

I grab her arm in mine, and pull her along gently, forcing her to move from the spot she's stuck to against the wall. "C'mon, you can't stay in one spot the entire time. Just relax your body and move, you can do it."

She blows out a long, frustrated breath but glides one foot forward. A newborn baby calf has more poise than her right now and that's putting it lightly. Over the next few minutes she does get the hang of it a little better, but has fallen more times that I can count. I feel bad at this point because it's obvious that it's going to take way more than one session of ice skating for her to get the hang of it.

I grab both of her hands in mine and help her around the rink. Each time she falls, we laugh and I help her back up, over and over until I think her poor ass has had enough.

"Okay, I think that's enough ice skating for one night." I chuckle and she sighs, visibly relieved that we're getting off the ice but the competitive side of her not wanting to admit defeat.

"Sure, sounds good. I think I'm frozen all the way through."

"I think you might have a few cuts and bruises tomorrow."

She winces when I bring them up, "Yeah, I think my ass is going to be permanently black and blue with as many times as I've fallen on it. But, hey, at least I tried, right?"

Right.

Great, and now all I can think about is her ass. Perfectly round begging to be reddened by my palms.

We give our skates back to the attendant and head back, slowly for Freya, to Grams and Gramps. I check my watch and see there's only five minutes left until the tree lighting so we ended our ice skating session in perfect timing.

"I was wondering how you two fared with skating." Gramps laughs from his seat on the back of my beat up tailgate.

"Uh, I don't know if I'll be able to move tomorrow, but it was fun. Finn's a great teacher." She grins in my direction.

"Safe to say that Freya won't be leaving her career as a resort director to be a professional ice skater."

Her eyes roll, unamused. "Whatever. I didn't do that bad, you're just jealous that you don't have it the way I do."

Tease me all you want, you're still terrible at ice skating. Ha!

"Yeah yeah, funny girl. Sit, I'll get you a blanket, show's starting."

She sits down in the foldout chairs we brought from the inn and snuggles up with the blanket I give her.

Gramps is talking her head off and she's laughing animatedly at his story.

"I'm tellin' you, if it wasn't for that damn donkey we wouldn't be alive," Gramps tells her with the most serious face.

Freya throws her head back and laughs. "Is that so? Saint does seem like he is the star of every story around here."

He nods. "Never seen Finn move so fast in his life." He gives her a teasing grin.

I know exactly what story he's telling and he may be...exaggerating just a bit. But, seeing the two of them together causes an unfamiliar sensation, something deep in my stomach to hit me. Watching this beautiful woman listening intently to what my Gramps is saying, hanging onto every word like it's the most important thing in the world makes me only want her more.

She wasn't supposed to happen. *This* wasn't supposed to happen. Yet, she fits right in our world like she was almost meant to be here. Which is equal parts confusing and scary. Especially because the future of the inn rests in her hands just as much as it does mine. Every day that goes forward, I find myself veering more and more from what winning the competition would mean, and more towards what it will mean if Freya wins, and where do I fit into her perfect world.

Chapter Fifteen
Freya

Last night's tree lighting festival made my heart swell. It was magic watching the twinkling lights, and being there with Finn's family only added to that, making it a special night. All day I've been floating on a cloud of giddiness, thoughts full of Finn's charming smile. Even my sore, bruised backside from ice skating can't stop my wide grin.

The movies I love don't lie—Finn inviting me to the lighting festival was a date.

There might not have been a kiss, but he held my hand and my heartbeat fluttered with excitement whenever his gaze met mine.

Focusing on the Alpine today has been a serious challenge, one I've never faced before. My attention is divided in a way I've never allowed it to be, thoughts of Finn overtaking me when I least expect them.

By the end of the day, I'm ready to hit my favorite spot on the resort.

The night air is still and crisp as I head down the pathway leading toward the back of the resort property where the hot spring is. It's become one of my favorite spots to enjoy at night, even as Montana grows colder. I think better when I'm soaking in the natural minerals.

I'm glad the Alpine robe is plush and thick enough to keep me from freezing my butt off out here. The thought has my mind meandering, wondering if it's possible for my boobs or ass to literally freeze in this temperature.

"What are you doing out here?"

I almost jump a mile high and release an undignified shriek, whirling around to find Finn staring at me with a hint of accusation in his expression.

"Holy shit. You scared me half to death." I place my palm over my racing heartbeat. "Usually I'm the only one out here this late."

Finn has gray sweatpants on with a burgundy Mayberry Inn hoodie, and he's carrying a towel. My focus lingers on the sweatpants.

"Out here? You mean—" With furrowed brows, Finn turns, searching around until he spots the signs mounted on the natural stones lining the path proclaiming the Alpine's rules and regulations for use of the natural spring. His shoulders tense, then relax. "Oh. Right."

"Do you know about the hot spring?"

"Yeah, I..." He sighs and shakes his head, running his fingers through his hair. "When I was little, I can remember coming out here with my mom. Sorry, I didn't realize it was on your property. I'll just—"

"Wait!" I dart forward and take his hand before he leaves, lacing our fingers together. "Don't be silly. Come on, soak with me. I'm usually alone, but I'd like the company."

The uncertainty smooths from his face and he gives me a

crooked smile, back to the Finn who held my hand while teaching me to ice skate. "Yeah, okay."

The hot spring is deserted when we reach it. Steam rises above the surface and small lights hidden in the existing landscape create a dim glow. The spring has this magic quality that I love, like it's a protected secret pocket closed off from the world. Rocks surround the edge of the water and tall pine trees create a barrier around the clearing. Off to one side is a spa center that's open during the day to guests hidden amongst the nature surrounding the building.

"It's a little different than I remember," Finn says.

"We made a few changes for guest safety, like the steps and railing, but otherwise we wanted to preserve as much of the natural atmosphere as possible."

"Wet bars are natural?" His tone is teasing and he nods to the built in pool bar beneath an awning designed to look like a cave.

"If it's good enough for the lagoon in Iceland, it's good enough for us." I shoot him a sardonic look over my shoulder while I lead him to the indoor/outdoor changing area provided for guests who don't walk down ready to sink into the spring.

He snorts as we remove our shoes. "I bet."

A shiver runs down my spine as I slip the robe off and drape it over a polished cedar bench, feeling the misty heat of the spring kissing my skin.

Finn releases a soft, rumbling sound while he watches me, his gaze a sensual drag over my body, taking in my skimpy white bikini. The warmth of the spring clashes with pockets of cold from the elements, but inside I'm burning up from the desire filling his eyes. My nipples harden, but I don't know whether it's from the rush of hot and cold I get standing at the edge of the spring or from his unwavering attention.

"Your turn," I murmur, dropping my gaze to his sweatpants, where the front has tented from his hardening cock.

Damn. My teeth sink into my lower lip. *From thirsty bitches everywhere, thank god for sweatpants season.*

Finn waits until I manage to lift my eyes, holding my gaze for a beat. My breathing grows strained as he peels—*strips*—the hoodie off, revealing his bare chest with a dusting of dark hair and sculpted muscles that bunch and flex with his deliberate movement. His thumbs hook into the waistband of the sweatpants and he tosses me a glance that has my clit throbbing.

Without taking his eyes off me, he pushes down the pants. His stripping is Magic Mike level sexy, pulling a rush of heat to my cheeks as I watch the show. A breath pushes past my lips when he tosses the sweatpants onto the bench and stands before me in faded red board shorts, looking like my lumberjack Adonis, all hard muscles and broad shoulders, making my pussy clench with want.

Licking my lips, I take a step closer and peek up at him through my lashes. "Ready to get in?"

His eyes are hooded. "Yeah."

We stand there for another moment, the humid clouds of our breath mingling. The intense desire in his gaze grows stronger as we stare at each other.

"Come on, big guy." Taking his hand once more, I tug. He follows me to the edge of the spring and we slip into the welcome heat of the water. "Mm, it's nice."

Finn rumbles in satisfaction close behind me, making my stomach dip. "Yeah. Feels good."

Struck by the vibe that we're teetering on the edge of something, I move through the warm water to find the rock I like to sit on to get some much needed air. We're in the middle of the woods, but he makes me dizzy. He's not far behind me, wading up to his neck in deeper water where I can't reach the bottom of the spring. His eyes never leave me. I cast around for something to talk about to take my mind off the arousal pooling in my center.

"Riley comes out with me sometimes before she goes home for the night." Riley has become like my surrogate sister. It's nice having her here while the rest of my family is spread across the world. I play with the water, skimming my fingertips through the steam rising from the surface. It blankets us in a fog, making it seem like we're even more isolated in our own world. "It's like the shower effect. I think better out here."

Finn hums, swimming a languid lap. I watch the ripple of his shoulders as he cuts through the water. My breathing grows shallow and tingles move through my core.

"Did you come out here a lot?"

"Sometimes." The surface of the water is disturbed by his shrug, sending a small wake traveling across to reach me. "In high school mostly. With West and Riley. Haven't been out here in a couple of years, though."

"Right. If you had come out recently, you wouldn't be surprised it's part of the resort now."

His mouth curves and he flicks water my way. "Everything with you seems to be a surprise."

I retaliate with a small splash of my own, sliding off my rock seat to get him when he moves out of range. We chase each other around in circles for a few minutes, the night air dotted by our laughter echoing off the treetops. Far overhead, the dark sky is clear with twinkling stars. I can see so many more out here than I ever could at home in California.

A squealed gasp escapes me when Finn catches me, keeping my wrists trapped in his firm grip. Grinning, he releases my hands and moves down to hold me up by my waist so I don't have to tread water because it's too deep for my shorter legs to reach the bottom.

"Got you," he murmurs, eyes bright and playful in the dim lighting.

My legs slide against his beneath the water and it makes his lips twitch. The urge to wrap them around his hips is strong. I dip my mouth beneath the surface and peer up through my wet lashes. His hands fit so perfectly in the dip of my waist. I place my hands on his chest, tentatively exploring his pecs and shoulders. A rough sound catches in his throat and his fingers dig into my sides.

"I'm glad you came out here tonight," I breathe. We've drifted even closer together. Water clings to his dark lashes and droplets move in steady trails down the planes of his jaw. I want to lick them. "I like this."

His gaze is piercing. "You just like driving me crazy any chance you get. A splash war? So original, traitor."

A laugh rolls out of me. "You started that. Don't pretend you're all mature when you're only, like, a year or two older than me. I think you like anything that leads to fighting with me."

His mouth curves. "Maybe I do."

Finn's thumbs move absently, tracing circles on my skin, moving down to my hips. It feels natural to give in, winding my legs around his body. He pushes out a strained breath.

My clit throbs at the barest brush of my pussy against his abs when he grabs my ass to adjust his grip on me. I smother a faint sound in my throat and sway closer to him, feeling his breath on my lips.

We can't ignore this any longer. I don't want to pretend we're just friends or neighbors when my whole body aches to have him touch me.

I scrape my nails lightly across his shoulders, leaning closer.

"This is a terrible idea," he rasps.

His actions belie his words, hands massaging my ass and head angled to close the tiny gap left between us.

"Seems like a great idea to me," I whisper, tracing the line of his neck. "Please kiss me."

For a moment, my heart sits in my throat while my body yearns to close the small distance. I hold onto his shoulders and inch closer to him. He's already pushed me away once, and told me why he can't do distractions. It was the same argument I had against letting my attraction to him grow, but that's flown out the window.

This isn't just attraction or lust anymore. There are feelings involved now.

His attention drops to my parted lips and he squeezes my ass.

Silently I beg him not to shut me out, running my fingers up the side of his neck to touch his jaw. If I let go of him, I won't be able to touch the bottom of the spring.

"Finn, please." My voice is raw with need.

"Fuck it," he bites out before his mouth claims mine in a searing kiss.

The desperate sound I make is swallowed with the first swipe of his tongue against mine. His fingers bury in the wet strands of my hair, gripping a loose fistful to angle my head to the side. I squeeze my legs tightly around him, rolling my hips, delirious with arousal.

"*Christ*," Finn growls again against my mouth, biting the corner of it before he takes my lips in another hot kiss.

My fingers sink into his hair as we lose ourselves in kissing beneath the stars. It's perfect, even more intense than the time we made out behind Moose's.

Finn locks his arms around me and before I know it, he has me pinned against a smooth rock wall in the deeper end of the spring without breaking the kiss. He nibbles on my lower lip until it feels swollen. Liquid heat pulses in my core, my body begging for his cock.

"Please." I gasp as he grinds his hard dick right against my pussy through our bathing suits.

Finn tears his mouth from mine to nip and suck at my throat when I tip my head back. "You drive me fucking crazy," he says against my flushed skin. "Your smart mouth with those pouty lips I want wrapped around my cock all the time." He grabs my ass. "Everywhere I turn you're there tempting me. Taunting me with what I can't have. I'm wild for you."

I moan, rocking against the firm ridge of his cock, my body wracked with a shudder of pleasure.

With his other hand, he cups my jaw, thumb tracing my tender lips before pushing inside. When I automatically start to suck on it, he releases a tortured groan, gaze zeroed in on his thumb.

He takes it from me and yanks my bikini top down with a rough tug. My breasts spill free into his hands for him to tease until I'm crying out from the way he pinches my nipples.

"Fuck, fuck, I'll come if you keep doing that," I hiss, clit throbbing. "Please."

"Shit. How are you so perfect?" He stares at my tits while he rubs them, then leans in to take each one in his mouth.

My whole body trembles from pleasure. Finn leans back and I shake my head feverishly.

"No, please don't stop!"

"I have to taste you. Now," he growls, leaving open-mouthed kisses in the valley between my breasts. He rips his mouth away. "I can't wait a second longer."

With a grunt, Finn hoists me up to perch on top of a flat rock partially out of the water, my legs still mostly submerged. A chill hits my body and I shake. He smooths his hands up my thighs, spreading my legs as he hooks a finger in the panty line of my bikini bottoms. Finn glances up at me through hooded eyes, then tugs the fabric aside and drops his mouth to lick my clit.

"Ah! Shit!" I cry out, holding onto his head as he drives my pleasure higher. My eyes flutter shut. "Finn, oh my god. Please, I need to come."

His unintelligible response is rumbled against my folds. He sucks and licks, tongue flicking my clit before he pushes it into me. The scruff teases my inner thighs and folds, making my legs shake from how good it feels.

At this point, my nipples could freeze and fall off, and I would be okay with that. If I'm in danger of hypothermia from exposure, what a way to go—with a hot man eating my pussy so good I'm making noises I've never made before.

Without caring about the cold, or if I'm attracting wildlife, or if guests think someone might be dying, I moan, rocking against him for more.

"That's it. Fuck, ride my tongue," Finn commands in a deep, gravelly voice. "Don't hold back. I want to hear you screaming for me."

He stops, taking his skilled mouth away, ignoring my string of curses if he doesn't continue. In one quick move, he has my bikini bottoms peeled off and slaps the wet material down on the rock beside me. His eyes flash up at me once more and he spreads me wider, drawing one of my legs over his shoulder.

"This is nowhere near finished, little traitor. No more holding back." He watches me, tracing a finger up and down my wet folds. When I shift to get him to go further, he gives me a smirk that says he knows exactly what I'm angling for. "Let me show you just how wild you make me. I want you to come on my tongue over and over."

I give a wobbly nod, agreeable to anything if it means he'll keep making my back arch with his tongue.

With a pleased sound, he starts up again, driving me insane. He pushes a finger inside me and I bite my lip. Not long after, he slides a second in, fucking me with them while he sucks on my clit.

"God, that feels amazing," I say. "Don't stop." Finn slows down and I might kill him. Death by sexually frustrated thigh crush. "Please let me come."

"I like hearing you beg for me." He swipes his tongue over my clit and I shiver.

His gravelly chuckle vibrates against my sensitive skin, puffs of his breath coasting over me. It's almost enough to get me there from how far gone I am. He strokes my side in silent apology, giving me another languid flick with his tongue and curls his fingers inside me.

"Do you know all the ways I've been tempted to fuck you?" Finn speaks against my body, the light scrape of his facial hair and his lips making my pussy squeeze his fingers. The corner of his mouth tugs up. He likes making a mess of me.

Who knew beneath the sweet, hometown heartthrob was a sinful, dirty-minded man who takes great enjoyment in taking me apart piece by trembling piece?

"I've wanted to make you ride my cock in the truck," he says, nipping at my inner thigh. "Want your lips sucking me off anytime you shoot me those looks of defiance." He pulls his fingers free to taste me, groaning against my skin. "Fuck, baby. I want you so many different ways, all the time."

"Me too." My mind races with all the dirty images he puts there. I want it, all of it. I'm drunk on Finn Mayberry and I don't think I'll ever get my fill of him. I prop up on my elbows and leer at him, licking my lips. "What are you gonna do about it right now?"

A slow yet sultry grin stretches across his face. "*This.*"

Finn covers my pussy with his mouth, tongue lapping at my folds. He holds me by my hips and growls in pleasure as he feasts on me. I throw my head back and grip his hair as the pleasure crests.

"Oh god!" I cry out as I tip over the edge, my orgasm sending tingles rippling out from my core. "Coming, I'm coming, Finn. God, yes!"

I slump back against the chilly rocks with a whimper. Finn scoops me into his arms, drawing me back into the welcome heat of the water. He holds me in his strong embrace and kisses me hungrily. My arms go around his neck, ready to sink further into oblivion with him. I want to feel his cock inside me.

"Get warmed up. We're crazy for doing this out here," he mutters against my lips, unable to stop kissing me long enough to string full sentences together. "It's cold as shit."

"No. Can't wait," I say between the urgent, devouring kisses. "Need you inside me."

"Shit, Freya," he says reluctantly. "Are you sure?"

"Yes, I'm sure, damn it," I say in a rush. "If I wasn't, I wouldn't have said so."

He rests his forehead against mine for a beat, chuckling in exasperation. "Alright, we're doing this," he murmurs, cupping my face, brushing his thumb over my cheek. It's a sweet juxtaposition against the way he's grinding his erection against me with growing urgency. "Need to get these damn shorts off."

We both scrabble to untie the strings holding his shorts up—Jesus, the knots are tight—but a commotion on the path has both of us freezing.

Footsteps on the gravel. Laughter. Guests coming down to the spring.

"Shit," I hiss, hurrying to put my tits back in my bikini top. "Finn—"

"I've got it."

He grabs my bottoms from the rock where he ate me out, hand splashing beneath the water to hand them back to me just as the guests round the bend. A bitten off curse falls from his lips while I get my bottoms back on. He swipes a hand over his mouth and shoots me a tortured look.

I know, I mouth helplessly.

Despite the cockblock of guests arriving, his mouth curves in a wry smile while they bustle in the locker area, oblivious to what they interrupted between us.

"Come here," he murmurs, reaching for me.

Holding me close, I still feel his hard dick against my hip while he strokes my back affectionately. My palms rest on his chest. Taking my chin in his thumb and forefinger, he tips my face up to his for a soft kiss.

He touches his forehead to mine when we part. "We're not done with this."

I bite my lip and nod in agreement. Finn kisses my cheek and moves us to a shallower part of the hot spring. I watch him get out and dry off with his towel. He disappears into the locker area for a few minutes, and when he comes out he winks at me, dressed in his sweatpants and hoodie, wet towel bundled with a hint of the red shorts peeking out.

The guests clamor out from the locker room behind him, laughing and joking with each other. They're a group of guys a few years younger than Finn and I, maybe early twenties. One by one, they get into the hot spring and move to the other side, leaving me be.

"Goodnight, Freya," Finn says.

I wave, cheeks heating at the way his gaze trails over me, like he's committing me to memory.

He heads back up the path and I watch him go, wishing more than anything I could follow for more. The pull to go with him is strong. Blowing out a breath, I cup my flushed cheeks and roll my lips between my teeth.

For once, I'm looking forward to the next Jingle Wars challenge tomorrow, and it's not because of my obsession with the holiday season.

Chapter Sixteen
Finn

I woke up this morning feeling like I just won the lottery. I'm the luckiest damn man alive. Except I didn't win the lottery, and I haven't won Jingle Wars yet, but I did get to taste Freya and I would venture to say it's better than either of those. It felt so right, so damn perfect forgetting what we should be doing, and giving in to our need for each other.

It was past the point of no return, and I was absolutely gone for her.

But now I have to push my feelings for Freya aside and win this damn competition. The wind is chilling to the bone today, and the sun isn't shining, instead hiding behind the clouds making everything dark, and cold. The crowd doesn't seem to be affected by the dreary weather.

"Welcome back everyone! Day two of Jingle Wars. My, the temperature out here is below freezing but this competition is heating up! Are we excited to be here today?" Cornelius points the microphone towards the crowd to capture their cheers and applause. "Well, I for one, am glad to hear it! Today we have a very special scavenger hunt planned. A little modern day twist to our beloved Jingle Wars. Today is going to be all about social media and your way around it."

What?

My head whips to Freya who looks over at me with a guilty look on her face. Of course this would be a competition tailored to fit her. I don't even use social media aside from Facebook.

Fuck.

"Each contestant will make their way around town to various local businesses and check in, then take a picture with something they feel represents the business best for the Hollyridge Merrymaker Trail! Something that represents Hollyridge as a whole. Post in on social media and move on to the next location. There are twenty-five locations on this scavenger hunt, and you have five hours to complete your task. The person who completes all twenty-five locations and has the most creative approach will be the finalist that moves on to the next round. After this round, there will only be two remaining contestants that will move on to the final round of Jingle Wars."

This could not possibly get worse.

"Alright folks, let's get our lists handed out to our contestants." The host gestures to the stage hand to bring over a piece of paper. When the guy hands me mine, I see the first place on my list of businesses is no other than Ella's Christmas store.

And it officially just got worse.

Suddenly, winning Jingle Wars feels that much farther out of reach.

I steal a glance over at Freya who's holding her list excitedly, waiting for the host to excuse us from the stage. Unlike my sour attitude, Freya knows that she excels at all things social media. The girl was born with a phone in her hand, and a knack for marketing. Me on the other hand? I'm a simple kinda guy. I love a good cold beer, a football game, and my family. I'm good with my hands and my mind, but I don't know shit about social media or marketing.

"Contestants, you have five hours and you will meet back here with proof of postings."

The host rings the bell, signaling the beginning of the competition and the numbers begin ticking down on the clock.

This is going to be the longest five hours of my life.

I lose sight of Freya immediately as the crowd is still thick in front of the stage. Everyone's chattering excitedly, still buzzing about a new type of competition for Jingle Wars. I make my way through the crowd, stopping to shake a few hands of people I know, then make my way to Ella's store. On the way I log into the 'gram and quickly make an account, snapping a smiling selfie to use as my profile picture. The entire thing feels strange, but if I don't do it, then I won't advance to the next round. I pull my jacket tighter around me as the wind whips, and make it to Ella's store after a short walk from town square.

Through the large window out front I see there aren't many people inside, but a few tinkering with ornaments and various Christmas decor that she has displayed for sale. The bell above the door jingles as I open it. Ella immediately looks up and sees that it's me that entered.

"Look what the cat dragged in," she says with a bite.

Ah hell. I'd rather have an early prostate exam than be here right now.

"Hey there, Ella. How are you today?" I grin, trying to charm my way into her good graces even if I want to run in the opposite direction.

"Well, you haven't answered any of my calls or even called me back Finn." She pouts.

Fat chance of that ever happening.

"Yeah, sorry about I've been really busy Ella. You know, getting the inn fixed up for Grams and Gramps takes all of my attention and time."

She nods but doesn't look like she believes a word that I'm saying.

"I think we should talk about us. We're so good together, Finn. Everyone says it. Don't you think so?"

This is getting increasingly awkward and I don't want to do this, especially in the middle of her place of business with customers here.

"I think you're great, Ella, but I'm here for Jingle Wars and I don't think now is a great time to talk about this, do you?" I glance around the room at her customers, hoping she will let this go.

"Whatever, Finn. Kinda hard to talk about it when you never answer your phone, and don't bother to return my call. It's really quite rude, if you ask me. And I hear that you've been all over town with that skanky out of town girl. What's her name? Freeya or something? Honestly, Finn, she isn't even that pretty," she says, jealousy dripping from her remarks, and crosses her arms over her chest.

Now that I'm looking at Ella, I mean really looking at her, I realize she's the same "mean girl" that she was back in high school. Nothing has changed about her, and that's not some shit to be proud of.

"Ella, don't talk shit about someone you don't even know. Have you ever spoken to her? Her name is Freya and she's fucking perfect. You're the same old person that you've always been, and that's quite sad if you ask me. You'd think as you grew into an adult, you'd mature and lose that mean girl attitude, but that obviously hasn't happened. Do me a favor, don't call, don't text, stop showing up at my house, and for God's sake get it through your head that I am not into you. Sorry to be an asshole, but the second you called someone you don't even know a "skank" any of the little bit of respect I had for you has gone out the window. Have a Merry Christmas Ella."

Her mouth drops open in shock that I've just told her exactly what I think, and not even a fraction of me feels guilty for doing it. She deserved that and more. If I don't get a good score for her location, then fuck it, she wasn't going to get away with bad mouthing Freya while I sat back and did nothing in her defense.

I find a Grinch decoration on a shelf and hold it up for the shot, making sure to get Ella in the background, then post it to Instagram, tagging her store.

My caption reads: Hollyridge has no time for the #Grinch or #MeanGirls Ella Arnold with a sad face.

There. Shows her.

I don't even bother searching for Freya's name, because it'll only distract me from my task. As much as I want to see what she posts, I have to stay on track because being social media challenged is already going to slow me down in the competition. The next few hours fly by with all of my stops all over town, and I try to choose the most creative photos I can to post. Some funny, some serious, but in the end I see exactly why the committee chose this. Local business owners love interacting with everyone, and it keeps their business booming.

This would be something fun to offer every holiday season, and we could incorporate the inn in it, offer hot chocolate and some of Grams' cookies, and definitely put Saint to work with his sleigh.

Wow, now I'm thinking like Freya. Not a bad thing either.

I was quick to judge her social media marketing skills, and now I'm realizing that these skills are what helps to keep her resort relevant, and booked. Maybe it's time I change with the times.

I make it back to the stage with seconds to spare and see Freya standing there, clutching her coat, shivering. Damn, the temp really has dropped this evening. I can't believe we still have a crowd with these temperatures. A storm must be brewing. I join her on stage and stand close, hoping some of my warmth will rub off on her. If we weren't on a stage in front of hundreds of people, I'd pull her into my arms and make sure she was warm for the rest of the night.

"Welcome back!" Cornelius begins. "All of our contestants have made it back safe and sound, even if they are a little cold! I know folks, this temp sure is dropping. Our contestants have dropped off their papers to the judges with their handles and they are being reviewed. Because of the dropping temperatures, we are going to get a decision quickly so we can head home and bundle up! Everyone did an amazing job, and I can't wait to see who is going to advance to the final round."

We stand there shivering for a few more minutes before the host joins us back on the stage with his bright red envelope in hand. That envelope holds the answer to my future, and as dramatic as it sounds, it's the truth.

"What a wonderful job everyone has done! I am so here for all of these local businesses that got featured on our scavenger hunt today. Let's get down to the important stuff! The two finalists who will enter the very last competition of Jingle Wars are..." He pauses dramatically, opening the envelope. "Freya Anderson and Finn Mayberry! Congratulations to you two! We will see the both of you for the final round! Now, normally we'd let you all know what we have planned, but this time we're keeping the last challenge a secret to keep our finalists on their toes."

Wow. Part of me is actually surprised that I made the cut

with how badly I suck at anything involving hashtags. Freya on the other hand, had this from the start.

"Didn't think it would be the two of us up here on this stage, final contestants," I tell her and shoot her a grin.

"Well, that's because you underestimate me, Finn Mayberry. I told you, I let you win that tree because I didn't need it."

Sassy mouth woman.

"Oh, is that so? How about we talk about this over dinner later?" I ask. There are lots of things I want to do with Freya, and none of them involve talking. Unless you count her screaming my name while I fuck her with my tongue.

"As much as I would love to, I have to take care of some stuff. Rain check?"

"Sure. I need to get some stuff done for Gramps around the house. Good game today, but the next round is mine traitor." I tease. The back and forth between us is second nature now, and I love her playful responses. It just makes me want her that much more.

"Yeah yeah, I think you're all talk and no action. That's what I think." She huffs teasingly.

We walk side by side down from the stage towards the parking lot. I pause and quickly scan the area to see if we have any nosy onlookers, then pull her close to me, where she's pressed against my body.

"I think we both know that I proved just how much action I'm about when I had my face buried in your pussy last night in that hot spring. Need a reminder?"

Her cheeks immediately heat, the red flush spreading down to her neck. I love that my words set her body on fire. I want to play with the flames that I've created and watch as they burn.

She clears her throat and before she can object, I take her mouth in a searing kiss that leaves us both breathless.

"That's your reminder for the road. Just because I'm a gentleman, doesn't mean I can't fuck you so hard you forget your own name, Freya. Be careful getting home, the roads are slick. Stay off your phone, 'kay?" I pat her hard on the ass before hopping into my truck, leaving her with her mouth hanging open and fire in her eyes.

Chapter Seventeen
Freya

The lust-tinged daze distracts me until someone repeats my name in an exasperated tone. I give my head a little shake, swallowing at the burning heat Finn stirred, then left in his wake before he got in his truck. After what he said, I was fully prepared to tackle him in his truck. We haven't been alone since the hot spring last night, and the ache between my legs still wants him badly.

"Jesus, *Fre-ya*." Riley says my name in two drawn out syllables, waving her hand in front of my face. "Zone out queen, what's your deal?"

West is with her, hands in his pockets. They must not be pretending to hate each other today. He's standing awfully close to her for someone who's just her friend. My gaze bounces between them.

"I'm fine. Sorry." I tuck a lock of hair. God, was I really just standing around fantasizing about fucking Finn while his friends stared at me? Where anyone in the square could've seen whatever thirsty expression was on my face? *Yikes, girl.* "I was, uh, keeping my head in the game, you know?"

Riley snorts. "Sure."

"Was that Finn talking to you before we walked over?" West has a knowing smirk. "Getting to know your competition real well, I bet."

Ah, shit. He's got me there. They've already caught us passionately kissing against the wall of the bar. Finn and I can't hide what's between us from his oldest friends. Maybe it's obvious to anyone looking at us when we're together. Twitter already ships us thanks to the competition.

Riley smacks the back of her hand against his chest. "Don't be a dick, Wes."

"It was," I confirm. "We've gotten...pretty close through the competition and running into each other so often. It's good to be friendly with your neighbor."

"Friendly," Riley repeats in a sassy tone. She laughs. "Yup. Sounds about right."

Riley and West exchange a pleased look full of silent communication that comes from years of knowing someone. It's nice to watch, even if West seems like he doesn't see how Riley looks at him whenever his eyes are elsewhere.

My phone goes off in my pocket and I take it out. Once I see the alert notification on my screen, I release an excited squeak.

"What's that about?" West asks.

Bouncing on my feet, I flash my phone at him and Riley. "My luck is shining today. A new cabin listing is available! I've struck out since I moved here, but this one is mine! I can feel it in my bones."

West's head jolts with an amused snort. "You're easily excited, huh?"

"You should've seen when she spotted an elk for the first time," Riley teases. "Or the time—"

"You promised!" I hold a finger up, cutting her off.

I know she was about to tell the ski lift story again. I'll never live that moment down. Part of me is fighting back a smile anyway, even though I'm still embarrassed by it. Riley and I have grown close enough for her to rib me like we're family. I've never had that before.

My friends in California were always superficial. Riley is my first true best friend.

She holds up her hands. "I did. A deal is a deal." The corner of her mouth tugs up. "Doesn't mean I can't get you drunk and have you spill the whole story yourself."

"We should all hit Moose's tonight," West suggests. "Because this I've gotta hear."

"I can't tonight. I want to see if I can go look at this place, and Finn said he's doing stuff around the inn for Gramps."

West and Riley both lift their brows. It occurs to me after the words have left my mouth that I spoke for him, as if we're a couple. My cheeks tingle with warmth. It's not an idea I'd be opposed to. Quite the opposite.

"Soon, then," West says. "No backing out, you hear? If you're planning on staying in Hollyridge, we need to hang out more."

A laugh bubbles out of me as I dial the realtor, pressing the phone to my ear. I wave to them both as I back toward my car. "Soon sounds good. See you later!"

The call connects and my excitement rises as I hurry across the parking lot to get to my car, ready to go look at the cabin right now if I can. Everything finally feels like it's clicking into place after all my hard work.

* * *

"Come on, stupid thing," I mutter, distracted by splitting my attention between squinting through the heavy snowfall and trying to get my phone's GPS app to work. "This is ridiculous."

Once again I wish the cabin was ready for me to tour it yesterday after the Jingle Wars challenge, instead of today when the biggest storm of the season hit out of nowhere.

The realtor I spoke with to set up my viewing appointment of the cabin already called to tell me she can't stay in the storm, but that she left me the key under an antique milk jug on the porch. I'm supposed to check out the cabin on my own, then meet her at the coffee shop in the town square tomorrow to return the key. People here are so trusting. That would never fly in California. What if I was a crazy squatter?

But the chances of me making it to the cabin are dwindling as I fight with the wheel of my Mercedes against fishtailing in the snow. I am so not used to driving in winter weather yet. Despite experiencing several snow storms since moving to Hollyridge, this one is bad. Even Riley warned me to be careful before I left the Alpine to drive out here on the outskirts of the more populated residential areas toward the center of town. Those get regular plowing, but out here it seems they're waiting for the storm to finish before the roads are properly cleared.

The few glimpses I've caught of this part of Hollyridge are beautiful, the mountaintops huge and breathtaking beyond the rustic cabins and houses dotting the road I'm driving on.

Crawling along is probably more accurate.

"Just gotta get there," I coach myself, trying to remain positive.

What I don't understand is how the GPS is failing so hard. I plugged in the address the realtor told me—one for a neighboring house, because my latest unicorn cabin doesn't have a clear address.

The car fishtails again and I tense up, trying to get it under control, but it makes it worse and the car fights me.

"No!"

My heart pounds. The weird sensation of the Mercedes sliding without traction makes my heart clench in fear and the sound of snow crunching beneath the tires has me jumping. I try a little gas, hoping the jolt will get me away from the slippery patch of road, but it makes the spinning worse and with another turbulent wiggle the car finally comes to a stop with an ominous jerk. My knuckles are white on the wheel.

"Well, shit."

Praying I'm doing the right thing, I try the gas pedal again. The tires spin, but I go nowhere.

It's stuck in the snow.

"Okay." I rub my temple. "Don't panic. No reason to freak out. What was it Finn said about keeping rock salt and extra mats handy for situations like this?"

Trying to keep my thoughts from spiraling with a surge of anxiety, I think about when we helped Uncle Lyle and Jared get their tractor off the snowy embankment by putting the coarse salt down for traction.

The only problem is, I don't have any rock salt in my car. I blow out a breath, deflating my puffed cheeks. It's cool. I can totally handle this. The car has mats, doesn't it? Twisting over the center console to check the back, I nod.

Snow falls fast in thick clumps. It already partially covers my windshield, and I've only been stuck for a couple of minutes. I stall going out into the elements for a few more minutes, taking the time to gather the car mats. Since I thought it would be a quick viewing, I opted for leggings and my replacement pair of UGGs along with my pink faux fur coat instead of the wool coat. I wasn't planning on hiking through a snowstorm, dressed for fashionable comfort in an Instagram-worthy hashtag outfit of the day.

"Not worth the 'gram now," I mumble as I open the car door. A blustery wind and icy wet snowflakes assault me immediately. "Gah! Cold, cold."

My boots slip in the deep snow along the side of the road on my way to the front of the car. The wheel has jumped the build up from the last plow and is wedged in the dense snow.

"Crap."

I do my best to put the mats in front of the wheels, but I end up tripping and falling on my ass. My fingers are red when I push up, checking out the imprint of my butt. At this rate, I'll be a popsicle by the time I make it out of this situation.

Climbing back into the car, I try to drive up on the mats I laid down. The car doesn't move. With a heavy sigh, I get back out to try again. I have no idea what I'm doing, but I have to keep trying.

Despite the determination not to give up, I'm no closer to getting my car free after another slew of problem solving attempts to dig my wheels free.

With spotty cell service and no other way to call for help, I wave my arms frantically at the first vehicle coming down the road. As the truck gets closer in the near-blinding snowfall, my shoulders sag in relief. It's Finn.

He cracks the window and squints at me through the snow. "You seem to be in a predicament."

"Please help." I push my damp, half-frozen hair from my face and fight off a shiver. My boots are all soaked—another pair ruined by the Montana snow. "It's stuck and I can't get it out."

Pulling the truck off the road, he comes to my rescue with his magic jug of rock salt. He assesses how the wheels are stuck and brushes snow from the mats I tried to use.

"You did good remembering this."

His praise feels good, creating a pleasant warmth in my chest. "When I tried, the wheels wouldn't catch on them."

"Sometimes it goes like that."

I step out of the way while he works. Thick snowflakes stick to my lashes and I'm freezing. The seat of my thin leggings are causing me to shiver after the fall in the snow.

Finn gets in my car to try moving it, but the tires only spin in place, kicking up more snow.

After two more attempts, he has to change tactics, going back to his truck for his own mats. My teeth chatter and I shuffle from foot to foot trying to keep my blood pumping. The wind stings my cheeks.

Finn steps back from my car with a huff, casting a glance at the dreary darkening sky. "It's good and stuck. We should get out of this snow."

In the last few minutes of our attempts, the storm has picked up even more, the snow falling harder than it already was. At this rate it seems likely to bury my car within an hour.

"Okay." I go to head for his truck, eager to get the heat blasting, but he catches my elbow. "What? Aren't you going to give me a ride back?"

"The roads are getting worse," he explains. "They said it's bad on the radio while I was driving. Storms like this, it's better to hunker somewhere and wait until it blows over. It's too dangerous to take the mountain roads, snow tires or not."

"The cabin isn't far. I was supposed to arrive any minute before my car spun out." I point further down the road and pull up the listing on my phone to show him. "The realtor left me the key to get in."

Finn nods. "I know it, that's just up the road a bit. We'll go there, then. Hopefully it's stocked with firewood at least, so we can get warm and dry."

I grimace at the icy dampness seeping into my bones through my wet boots and socks as we trudge through the snow to reach the truck. He ducks in and hands me a Mayberry Inn hoodie from the back seat that was next to two bags of groceries.

"Come on." He sighs when he sees the state of my shoes. "Those again, huh? You don't learn. When we get there, you'll need to get out of all these wet clothes."

"Is that your way of saying you want me naked? Romantic," I tease, taking his hand to help me into the cab. Once I'm in, I peel off my faux fur coat and tug on the hoodie. It's huge on me, giving me sweater paws.

Finn shakes his head with a wry grin. "Wouldn't complain."

The heat in the car is a blessing after twenty minutes in the worst snow storm I've ever experienced. I'm eager to get in the cabin. The movies I love make the snow look peaceful and romantic, but this storm is gross to be out in.

Within minutes, we pull up to the most beautiful cabin I've ever seen. It steals my breath for a second and I lean forward to take it in. The cabin sits up on a small hill and has a wrap-around porch like Mayberry Inn's. Twin antique milk jugs sit on either side of the robin's egg blue door with a fresh holly wreath greeting us.

"It's so pretty," I murmur.

Totally the hashtag cabin goals home I've been hoping for.

Finn shoots me an affectionate sidelong glance, lingering on the hoodie I'm borrowing. "You can admire it from the inside, where it's warmer." He cuts the ignition and steps out. "There's firewood. You get the door unlocked and I'll gather wood to get a fire started."

While he heads for the wood shed around the side of the house, I pause long enough to snap a few photos with my phone. I frown at the lack of a cell signal. The mountains must mess with it.

Stepping onto the porch, I tap my boots against the step to get the clumped snow off. The key is right where the realtor said, under the left milk jug. Now I'm glad she was so trusting. Once I open the door, my eyes go wide.

The house is amazing, fully furnished and staged for showings to help potential buyers picture this place as their dream home. A stacked stone fireplace with a stained wood mantel creates the centerpiece of the living room to my right, and to the left the kitchen is cozy with a breakfast nook looking out to the mountain view behind the cabin. I imagine sitting on the bench seat with a silky smooth faux fur blanket and coffee, watching elk graze on the grass.

Finn comes in behind me, heading right for the fireplace with an armful of logs. I'm momentarily distracted by watching him work, a base part of me enjoying his competent skill. "Nice that it's furnished."

"I'll see what else it has for supplies."

"Take your shoes and socks off before you explore. Pants, too. Anything that's damp so you don't catch a cold. Leave them over here so they dry faster."

I bite my lip as a wave of hot and cold tingles travel over my body. When he gets all gruff and bossy like that it does things to me.

After toeing off my second ruined pair of UGGs, stripping off the socks, and peeling off my leggings, I walk into the kitchen. The light switch works when I flick it on and start opening cabinets.

"We have power at least," I call, poking around. "Not much else. Just some Vienna sausages. I guess those were supposed to be a snack for an open house." My nose wrinkles. "I have a bag of candy canes in my purse."

I got them branded with the resort's information to hand out.

Finn's deep laughter sounds, making me smile. His laugh sounds nice in this place, a noise that fits in my maybe-home, like we could belong together. Returning to the living room, I lean against the back of the leather couch, appreciating the view. His coat is discarded and the thick sleeves of his sweater are pushed up while he coaxes the fire to life.

"I've got some groceries in the truck. We might have to get creative though. Didn't really get much." With the fire crackling, he gets up, ruffling his tousled hair. The damp ends curl from being in the snow. He braces an arm against the window frame, watching the storm. "It's a pretty bad blizzard. We might be stuck here for a couple of days."

"Should we try telling everyone where we are?" I join him at the window and play with the cuffs of the oversized hoodie. "Riley knows I was supposed to come out here. I don't want her to worry about me."

He shrugs. "If we can get service. Mine's out."

I sigh. "Mine too. I'll keep checking."

"I'm going to get the groceries from the truck. If you do get a hold of anyone, tell them to spread the word that we're okay and we're holed up until we can dig our way out."

He steps out while I finish my exploration of the house. I like what I see of the cabin and if I can get my offer in before this one is stolen from beneath my nose, I'll finally have somewhere to put real roots down in this town. A happy glow expands my chest. I'll be able to call Hollyridge my home for real.

When I come back downstairs, I find Finn at the window again. He has stripped out of his under layers beneath the sweatshirt, leaving a flannel shirt draped over the couch. I go to his side, burrowing against him for warmth. His arm slides around my waist.

"I've never seen it snow this much here. It's already covering halfway up the fence posts! Are we really getting snowed in?"

"It's coming down hard enough. The radio said it'll be a record-breaker." He draws me over to sit down closer to the fire, putting me in his lap. "Warm up."

I lean into him and hum when his hands dip beneath the hem of the hoodie. "You gonna help?"

"I like you in my clothes." His lips find my temple and he trails kisses down my neck to my shoulder. "Like you better out of them."

"I'm on board with this plan. Is this what people do when they're snowed in?"

Finn's raspy laugh is pressed into my neck. "Mhm."

"Well, I'm liking my first time getting snowed in, then. Good choice in a hunkering partner."

More than that, he's a good choice for a partner in anything. Someone I want to have the future I've glimpsed with.

"You like it because you don't know how to light a fire."

I can hear the grin in his voice.

"I do too." I tilt my head to give him more room to kiss my neck, raking my teeth over my lip. His hands push below the hoodie, stroking my stomach. "With the help of a YouTube tutorial."

Finn's chest shakes with amusement. "Always so resourceful."

He shifts and I feel his cock when he adjusts me in his lap. He grinds against me, rumbling against my skin.

The light in the kitchen goes out, leaving us in near-darkness from how dim it's grown outside.

My lips part in surprise and I twist to meet his eyes in the orange glow of the firelight. "So much for having power. I guess we'll have to snuggle for warmth."

Finn's arms wrap around me and he tugs my back against his chest. A hint of teeth scrape the shell of my ear, eliciting a groan from me. His voice is a deep, sensual rumble. "We'll be doing plenty to stay warm."

On a scale of one to ten, getting trapped in my dream cabin with Finn during a blizzard is an eleven.

Chapter Eighteen

Finn

"Okay, I checked all of the fire extinguishers and smoke detectors. Checked the pipes, the shut off valves and the electric panel. Everything looks good. This place is a steal," I say as I walk back into the living room and find Freya gazing out of the window, watching the blizzard rage on.

After our impromptu hot and heavy makeout, I had to pull myself away even though every bone in my body said otherwise. Needless to say, my cock is not a very happy camper. But, I'm trying to be a gentleman. Even if I'm not doing the best job of keeping my hands off of her.

"I don't think this blizzard is going to be slackening up anytime soon. It's completely white out there." Freya bites her lip as she looks out the window.

Because this is her first blizzard, she has no idea what to really expect. Me? They're second nature to me. I've lived through enough of these for them to be no big deal. To her on the other hand, we're snowed in with no power so we're going to freeze to death, and if we don't then we're going to starve to death. Her assessment of the cabinets yielded nothing but Vienna sausages, which made her scrunch her nose in disgust. Thankfully on my way home from the grocery store, I spotted Freya freezing to death near her shiny black Mercedes. I'd hate to see what would have happened had the stars not aligned and fate intervened, for me to find her out here. Unfortunately, my trip to the grocery store was mostly for Grams, and I only picked up a few random things for myself for the inn. A bag of Funyuns, a six pack of Dr Pepper, and a Snickers bar. Not enough to keep us from starving, but I don't foresee us being here too long.

"You're lucky you have a strong, capable guy like me to take care of you." I give her a cheeky grin. "We have a fire, plenty of firewood, and Viennas if you get that hungry. Funyuns if you're really starving." Her distaste for Funyuns is apparently much greater than Viennas.

Her eyes roll and she laughs. "Mhm."

"Come look what I found." I call her over to the hall closet I'm standing in front of.

The power is out, but there's enough light outside and from the fire that we can see freely around the cabin, and I'm thankful as fuck that she was going to see a fully furnished cabin instead of one that wasn't. It could absolutely be worse getting stuck there during a snowstorm.

I pull down the boxes from the top of the closet and show them to her.

"Scrabble, Monopoly, and Sorry."

"You really want to play a board game right now?" she asks, eyeing me skeptically.

"Got any other ideas?"

She looks around the cabin then back at the stack of board games.

"Fine. Let's do it. Don't cry when I beat you, though. No time for tears."

I roll my eyes and scoff, "Yeah, like I'm the one with the over the top competitive nature."

"That's what all the losers say. Let's play Scrabble." She grins and sits opposite of me at the coffee table in front of the fire. With her clothes being soaking wet, she's clad in nothing but my worn Mayberry Inn hoodie and my mouth waters. The bottom of the sweatshirt grazes her thighs and leaves much to imagination.

Catching my lazy perusal of her attire she giggles. "Hey mister, eyes up here. We have a game to play."

I put my hands up in surrender. "I was just assessing my enemy, trying to see if you're hiding any game pieces in there."

She laughs and continues to take out all of the pieces from the small drawstring bag inside of the box. When she has everything arranged, we begin our game and I quickly begin making various complex words that I learned as a kid playing with Grams.

"Wow. I didn't even know you knew how to spell asphyxiation." She laughs, taunting me.

My favorite thing about her is how passionate she is. Passionate also meaning how insanely competitive she is. Except when she's bustin' my balls, that is.

"You're cheating. You have to be." She scoffs at my forty-nine point word and tosses her piece onto the board.

"Am not. And you're a sore loser. You'd never last a second with Grams in Scrabble. She's ruthless."

"Uh, pretty sure Grams doesn't cheat." She feigns annoyance, but let's be real...she's just a sore loser. Show me a time where she hasn't been even a little disappointed in losing, and I'll admit defeat, but you can't.

I didn't like admitting defeat any more than she did.

Which is why I'm winning this game of Scrabble, and her heart. I'm going to make sure of it.

"Come see, let me show you how to beat anyone in a game of Scrabble the Mayberry way." I shoot her a wide grin.

Even though she's rolling her eyes, she comes over to my side of the table, which is closest to the fireplace, and snuggles up close to me.

"Let's see it, big guy. What's the big secret?"

I'm distracted by how fucking good she smells. Cookies, vanilla and cinnamon, and her. I can't explain it but it's everything her.

"You're too distracting, I can't focus on my secret," I whisper, dropping my forehead against hers. She sucks in a sharp inhale, but leans further into me, pressing her side into mine.

"And you're dangerous, Finn Mayberry," she whispers raggedly.

Her soft, hesitant lips find mine in the dim, fire-lit living room and just like that, it feels like coming home. It's hard to explain the feelings that Freya somehow pulls from somewhere deep and hidden inside of me, but every time I'm in her presence, she does it. She makes me forget that every single time I step over the threshold of the inn there is an impossible weight on my shoulders.

When my lips capture hers, I pull her into my lap and her body is like putty in my willing hands. Lithe, and tight in all of the right places, I run my hands down her sides, until they reach her hips and she rocks against me, gasping. I can't keep my mouth or hands off of her, off her lush lips, and the sensitive skin on the top of her thighs. My mouth waters when she pulls the way too big hoodie down, revealing her tan cleavage. I press soft, sweet kisses along the swell of her breasts, sucking lightly whenever she entangles her fingers in my hair, pulling me closer to her, urging me on.

I'm so hard beneath my gray sweatpants, I feel like I'm going to fucking bust every time she rocks her warm, wet heat against me. I feel how wet she is through the sheer fabric of her lacy underwear.

She's fucking perfect beneath my touch, I want to bury myself in her heat until I forget where I end, and she begins.

Her hands snake into my shirt, up my abs and I let out a strained hiss. I'm trying to keep control but this girl, everything about her makes me feel out of control. So out of fucking control.

"Finn, I want this," she whispers, dropping her lips to mine again.

Her tongue dances with my own. I grasp the material of the Mayberry Inn hoodie in my hands and pull it over her head, tossing it to the side. I scoot us closer to the fire, so she's not cold.

The fire crackles, and sizzles as it burns, much like my desire for Freya does. Out of control and lost in the moment.

Seeing her shirtless in front of me in nothing but a lacy pink bra that pushes her tits together has me ravenous for a taste of her. I've been dying for more of her sweet pussy since the second I had it in the hot spring. I've fucking dreamed of the different ways I would take her when the moment came, and finally, god, fucking *finally* it's here.

Still perched in my lap, she reaches behind her and unclasps the bra, pulling it away from her body, leaving her completely bare from the waist up on top of me. The only way to describe her breasts is perfection. So fucking perfect that I'll spend the next fifty years worshipping them, showing her just how exquisite she is. Round and pert, sitting high with pink, dusty colored nipples that are hard and begging for me to suck them. I drop my mouth to one and suck, hard, until her back arches closer to me, and her hand fits in my hair.

"Finn, more, please," she begs, rocking against me to create friction.

"Patience, Princess. We have all the damn time in the world, and I'm not rushing this for a second." I whisper against her skin. Goosebumps break out across her arms. Whether it's the cold or her desire for me, it spurs me on.

I reach behind my head and grasp my sweatshirt by the neck, pulling it over in one motion. I need to feel her skin against mine again. I want to feel her nipples as they pebble against my chest as she writhes in pleasure beneath me.

My lips travel down her neck to her chest where I suck, leaving tiny marks that will show the world that she's mine. I give her nipples the attention they so desperately deserve, until she's a panting mess above me.

Her tiny hands travel to my sweatpants and push inside, feeling me hard and ready beneath her touch. "God, Finn, I want you. So much."

Her hand wraps around my dick and I bite back a groan. This woman. Fuck.

We're both desperate, wanton for each other. A frenzy of wet kisses, and lust. I can't get enough of her. I will never have enough of feeling her beneath me, pressed against me, moaning my name.

Here, in the middle of this cabin, on a goddamn bear skin rug in front of a fire, a cliché if there ever was one, changes everything. I can feel my heart thawing, and becoming less of my own by the second. Claimed by her every minute that ticks by.

She's spread out in just a tiny scrap of lace that leaves nothing to the imagination. God, her pussy was made for me.

Me alone. She's bare, obviously using her resort's spa services for a full wax. When I look up her body, our eyes meet and she gives me a shy grin.

"You're perfect," I whisper, dropping a tender, gentle kiss to the inside of her thigh.

She should know she's perfect, but I want to tell her everyday for the rest of fucking forever just how perfect she was crafted by the hands of all the Gods. For me.

A breathy sigh escapes her lips as I drag my teeth over her thigh, nipping lightly. My beard has marked her thighs with a delicious burn that I know she'll feel for days to come, thinking of me each time.

I pull on the lace at her hips until it snaps, and toss it to the side.

Her blue eyes hood with arousal. "That was hot. You're my very own sexy as fuck lumberjack."

I silence her giggle by placing my lips around her clit and sucking gently, causing her back to arch off the ground.

"Oh god." She moans, fisting the rug beneath her.

Taking my time, I lick her pussy, eating it like it's the last meal I'll have for days. I swipe my tongue up her pussy from her asshole to her clit and back down, pushing inside her tight hole. I want to feel her come on my face, and scream my fucking name.

I push a finger inside of her, and she's so tight it takes my breath away. God, she's impossibly fucking tight. One finger, then two, I push inside of her, hooking up, hitting her G spot over and over as I fuck her with my fingers and suck her clit into my mouth.

"I'm so close, please Finn, I need to come." She's begging for release, and I'm happy to oblige.

"Come for me, baby, now," I demand as I push another finger inside her to fuck her pussy harder, faster until she's falling apart around my fingers. Squeezing me until her creamy release coats my fingers. Nothing has ever tasted as sweet.

I languidly pump my fingers in and out of her until she's boneless, stated and happy beneath me, then I pull my fingers from her, still coated with her. As she sits up on her elbows, causing her perfect tits to sway, I suck the rest of her off of my fingers and her eyes widen with a mix of shock and desire.

It hits me as she stares up at me. More than anything, I want to sink inside of her and lose myself in the feeling only she can give me.

"I want you, Finn. I want this." Her voice comes out with conviction, and I know now that we're entering territory that we'll never come back from.

"Are you sure?" I ask, shedding my sweatpants and boxer briefs as she whispers the sweetest curse.

"Fuck. I don't have a condom. I wasn't exactly thinking I'd end up snowed in with the sexiest woman alive when I left the grocery store." I groan.

She grins in response.

"I trust you. I just visited the doctor before I left Cali and I'm clean. I have an IUD."

Bare?

Could I trust Freya to go where I've never gone before with any woman?

Do I trust Freya?

Of course I do.

"I'm clean too. I've never...been with anyone without one before. You'll be the first." I whisper as I settle between her deliciously thick thighs. My cock brushes against her center, and the wetness makes me shiver. Knowing that I was the one to give her this much pleasure brings out the caveman in me.

Her fingers run up my arms, to my shoulders and into my

hair as she pulls me down for a hot, sweltering kiss that leaves us both gasping for air. I'm consumed by her.

I line my dick up with her entrance, sliding up and down her wetness, coating myself in her slickness. The head of my cock teases her clit, and when she begins to squirm beneath me, I push inside her ever so slightly. She's so tight, it's hard to even push inside, but fuck there is honest to God no better feeling in the world than having her wrapped around me. Bare.

"Fuck Freya." I curse. My fists grab at the rug beneath her, grabbing handfuls to keep control of my movements. I want to sink inside of her balls deep but I have to be gentle with her. She said it had been a while.

I take my time as I slide inside of her wet heat, until I'm seated fully and she's adjusting to me. When her nails begin to score my back and travel down to my ass, pushing me inside of her, it's all the response I need to fuck her like I've been dying to since the second she stepped foot in Hollyridge. I put her legs onto my shoulders and pull out, then slam back inside of her with such force she cries out, begging for more.

"Please Finn, God, it's so good."

Fuck.

I get a steady rhythm in my thrusts, pounding inside of her with a force that threatens to send us both over the edge. The cabin is eerily quiet aside from the muted sounds of the fire, and the sound of our skin slapping together in perfect precision. She mewls beneath me, moaning my name, crying out whenever my cock bottoms out inside of her. I'm thankful she doesn't want to be treated fragile, and can take the heat of my desire. I am desperate for her, and she's driving me fucking wild.

I flip us over where I'm on my back and she's on top of me, riding me. My cock is buried so deep inside her, I can't possibly go any further. She places her hands on my chest and begins to bounce up and down in a steady rhythm that brings us closer to the edge.

"I'm close," she pants.

My hands are on her tits, fisting handfuls, rolling the tips of her nipples between my fingers. My thrusts meet hers until I'm driving upwards inside of her. I'm so close I can feel my ball begin to tighten and the familiar tingle at the bottom of my spine. My thumb finds her clit and I begin to rub quick circles, that I know will bring her to the brink. Seconds later, together, we fall.

"Finn, I'm coming," she screams, shaking above me with an orgasm that has taken her fully.

I push inside of her and let go. Letting my cum fill her, coat her, claim her as fucking mine.

It drips out of her and covers us both in a sticky, wet mess. It brings a sense of pride to the caveman inside of me, and I hope that she knows no matter how selfish it is, I don't want to let her go. I want her to stay here in this cabin with me, in our little slice of private heaven, and never go back to the reality of the real world.

The reality of the competition and the struggles of the inn, and the issues she has with her family.

Once we're both spent, she collapses onto me, tucking her head into the crook of my neck and snuggles close to me. I can feel the erratic beat of her heart against my own, and I want to bottle this moment up, never letting anyone inside this perfect bubble.

"This was not how I expected my night to end." She sighs sleepily.

My fingers run lazily up and down her spine, until goosebumps break out on her flesh. The languid, simple movement is just another part of this day that I never want to lose.

"Me either. But, I don't want to leave," I whisper against her hair.

I want to make sure that no matter what happens after the snow begins to melt, I've permanently etched myself inside the walls of her heart and that she never forgets Finn Mayberry.

But tomorrow, brings another day and another day brings more problems even in a perfect town like Hollyridge.

Chapter Nineteen

Freya

Being snowed in is my new favorite thing. The world is shut out and without power, the only thing we can do is get lost in each other. Zero complaints for the number of orgasms I've had in the last twenty-four hours.

After our board game and the sinfully good romp in front of the fire, we got creative for dinner with the few groceries Finn had from the store, then wound up in the upstairs bedroom for another round. Sweaty and sated, we fell asleep tangled together. It seemed like a permanent smile was stuck on my face last night, and I couldn't wipe it away as I fell asleep in his warm embrace.

The pale morning light is creeping into the room and sleep still crusts the corners of my eyes, but my body is lit up with burning flames of pleasure.

Finn has my hands pinned over my head on the mattress and my back arches.

"Mm, this is the best way to wake up," he rumbles against

my neck as his teeth tease my skin. I must be covered in his marks by now—from my thighs to my breasts to my neck, his marks undeniably claim me as his. "We should've gotten snowed in when you first got to town and fucked out our differences."

My head tips back into the pillow as a moan tears from my throat. "Less speculation, more..." I lose my train of thought when his lips close over a taut nipple. "Fuck, just more, Finn. Please."

His chuckle sends a wave of hot tingles down my spine into my core, and his grip on my trapped wrists flexes. "You need my cock again, baby?"

"Yes!"

"Hungry little thing." He leans back, a smug, sexy grin tilting his mouth. Reaching for the bedside table, he rummages in the plastic bag of Alpine branded candy canes I brought upstairs with me last night. His eyes dance with mischief as he unwraps one and pops it between his lips to suck on the end. "How bad do you want me to fuck your pussy, traitor?"

My breath punches out of me on another groan as I hook my legs around his hips, arching up to try to bring his body back down on mine. He grins around the candy cane and, fuck, that should not be as hot as it is. The sight causes throbbing heat to pool between my legs.

"Tell me, Freya," he commands in that deep voice that makes a needy ache pulse in my clit.

"Badly. So bad. Come on, Finn." A relieved gasp escapes me as he settles between my legs, shifting down so he can pull my knees over his shoulders. He takes the candy cane from his mouth and lays a kiss inches from where I'm desperate for him. "I want you again."

I fall back against the sheets, spreading my legs, only to jolt up on my elbows at an unsuspected sensation.

Finn trails the sticky candy cane over my folds and cuts his gaze up to me through hooded eyes. "You're so wet for me."

My lips part as I watch him tease me with a candy cane he was sucking on moments ago. His tongue swipes his lower lip as he rubs the hook of the treat in a torturous circle over my clit.

I drop my head back, closing my eyes. "Ah! Fuck, that feels—"

Finn's tongue follows the same path as the candy and I cry out.

"I have half a mind to fuck you with this candy cane." He shoots me another wicked look up the length of my body. "Don't think I didn't notice your resort's logo on these."

Instead of doing that, he tosses the candy aside. He lowers his head between my thighs and has me coming hard on his tongue and fingers minutes later, knowing just how to drive me wild.

"I need to touch you," I push out.

A moment later, he lets me up and we tangle together. I drag my palms over his shoulders as his hands grip my ass.

"Come here," he rumbles.

A squeal escapes me as he lifts me into his arms and carries me to the wall as if I weigh nothing. My teeth sink into my lower lip, shivering as he presses my back against the smooth, cool wood.

"You're so sexy when you go all caveman on me," I murmur.

In response, Finn smirks, then with a minor adjustment, the head of his cock nudges against my entrance and he's inching inside me. My mouth drops open on a silent cry of pleasure while he massages my ass. With the first hard thrust, my body ignites in a burst of ecstasy.

"Oh my god." His dick fills me and it feels so good.

"That what you needed, baby?"

"*Yes. Always.*"

The pace picks up until the sounds of our skin slapping together fills the room. My nails drag across his back as he pounds into me, hitting the perfect spot that makes me scream.

Finn pants and grins, muscles flexing while he fucks me against the wall. "Scream for me?"

Each word is punctuated with a sharp thrust of his cock. He presses closer, his hard chest teasing my pebbled nipples. My screams reach higher in pitch as he slams into a spot that electrifies me with pleasure. His fingers dig into my ass and he snaps his hips.

"I wanna hear you Freya," he commands.

Head thrown back, my voice cracks with my cry. "Finn!"

"That's it, baby. God, you feel amazing squeezing my cock with your tight little pussy." His lips find my neck, nibbling and sucking. He's obsessed with marking me and I love it. "Like it was made for me."

I bury my fingers in the thick hair at the nape of his neck, encouraging him to give me another hickey. "I'm—I'm close."

Finn captures my lips in a searing kiss. Everything becomes too much and I cling tightly to him as an orgasm wracks my body. He swallows my moans, slowing down his pace to keep me from tipping into oversensitivity.

"Catch your breath, beautiful," he says gently. "We're not finished yet."

While I shiver and whimper from such a mind-blowing orgasm, he holds me, kissing me for long minutes, keeping the sensations of my orgasm going with each sensual roll of his hips.

The mood shifts from something tinged in wild abandon to something more intimate as his hands drag over my flushed skin in soft caresses. His whiskey-colored eyes are filled with devotion and something else I'm afraid to put a name to, wary of chasing it away. No one has ever looked at me like that and it makes a lump form in my throat. He brushes his thumb over my cheek and draws me in for another kiss.

Finn has a way of reading my body like he's attuned to my mind, knowing how to meet my needs before I'm even aware of them. I feel safe and loved in his strong arms, worshipped like a goddess by his mouth, and my heartbeat syncs to his as he holds me close. He's reminded me how important it is to savor life and the people in it, not just barrel my way through my work. He allowed me to see what's important to him and it makes me want to do the same, to show him what I really care about.

This is the feeling my favorite movies talk about. We fit together.

I take a shaky breath.

The realization of how much he means to me makes my eyes well with emotion and I bury my face in his shoulder, trembling until he squeezes me tighter.

I think this is what I've been searching so many years for. A person who makes me laugh, who challenges me, and lets me into his world. Someone who's heart feels like a home, exuding the kind of love I've always craved.

With Finn, I no longer feel so lonely and out of place. I don't feel like I have to be as loud as possible in order to be seen or respected. In his embrace, our bodies joined and our breaths mingled between kisses, I feel loved.

"Freya," Finn murmurs, lips brushing mine.

He doesn't say anything else, but he doesn't have to.

"I know," I whisper thickly, tracing his jaw with my fingertips.

I feel it, too.

As I rock my hips and wind my arms tight around Finn's shoulders once more, he cups my ass and takes us back to bed, sitting on the edge so I'm straddling him. He controls my rhythm with his hold on my hips, guiding me to ride him. Resting my head on his shoulder, I pant into his neck.

We're no longer frantically chasing release, but savoring the feeling of our bodies connected, our warm skin sliding together. It feels like we could stay like this for eternity and it would be right.

"I want to stay here, just like this." He cradles my face when I lift my head.

Our lips meet and he falls back to the sheets, rolling us over without breaking our kiss. Hiking my leg higher on his hip, he thrusts deep, hitting the spot that is my undoing. My moans become his until I can't tell the difference. I wrap my legs around him and he drops his thumb to rub my clit.

"Finn," I murmur. "Right there."

It becomes too much once more and I utter a soft curse while pleasure ripples from my core.

With one last groan, Finn presses his forehead to mine, cock buried deep inside me. I can feel the throb deep in my body as he comes.

Neither of us say anything to break the moment. It isn't needed after our bodies did all the talking.

I push Finn's damp, curling hair back from his forehead and smile up at him. His eyes are bright with a tender happiness and he turns us on our sides so he isn't crushing me with his body. He tugs me closer, tucking me against his body, and kisses my forehead.

With my head pressed to his chest, I listen to the steady thrum of his heartbeat, knowing that even if Hollyridge isn't the place I stay, Finn Mayberry will always be the place my heart lives.

***

The snow hasn't let up yet. By the time we venture downstairs around mid-morning, the storm has transformed the landscape around us into insanely thick blankets of white snow. Winter wonderland doesn't begin to cover it.

I have the odd urge to run outside and fall back into it to make a snow angel.

"How many inches do you think has fallen so far?" I ask, tucking Finn's flannel shirt tighter around my body. The sleeves are too long, so I have to cuff them a few times, and the hem hits me above the knee. It's the only stitch of clothing I have on other than my reindeer pattern socks that dried by the fire yesterday. "This is crazy. And it's still coming down!"

"Can you see the tops of those fence posts outside the cabin?" Finn kneels by the fireplace in his hoodie and sweatpants, throwing fresh logs on the fire to warm the house.

I squint through the window. "Barely."

"Probably close to four feet, then. We haven't had a blizzard like this since I was a kid." He stands and comes to stand behind me, wrapping me in a hug. "A nearby lake froze over fast enough West and I could see the fish stuck in it." His chest vibrates against my back, shaking in amusement over the memory. "Riley cried."

It's funny to think of my tough, sarcastic friend upset over fish. I tip my head back to look up at him from upside down. "How come?"

"She thought they'd die, but they were fine when the ice thawed out. Some fish are used to being popsicles through the winter."

A light laugh bubbles out of me. "How much longer will it snow for?"

"Let's see if we can find out." He releases me to grab his phone from the coffee table. "Looks like I have service. For now, anyway. Radar is showing another day of this at least. I'm going to call Grams and Gramps to let them know we're okay. See if you have service."

While Finn strolls into the kitchen to make his call, I find a ton of missed messages on my phone. Shooting a quick text to Riley first, I skim through to find the most important ones. The phone vibrates with her response.

Riley: Glad you're okay! Alpine still has power. Roads are still pretty bad from what West said, so stay put.

"Gramps says the roads are a mess," Finn says, returning to the living room.

I hold up my phone. "That's what Riley just told me."

"Guess we're stuck here until they're cleared out."

He drops onto the couch with a content sigh. Glancing up at me, the corner of his mouth lifts and he pats his thigh. I roll my lips between my teeth, but can't hold back my smile as I set my phone aside and climb onto his lap, straddling him.

"What a shame," I drawl, bracing my hands on the back of the couch and hovering my lips over his. "However will we pass the time?"

Finn's hands find my hips, dipping beneath the material of his shirt I'm wearing and teasing my bare skin. "I'm sure we'll think of something." He gives my backside a light smack. "Like a Scrabble re-match so I can whoop your ass again."

I collapse against his shoulder, giggling at his deadpan humor. His chuckle rumbles in his chest as he palms my bare ass, absently grinding his half-hard dick against me. Sitting up once I catch my breath, I steal a quick kiss. When I break it, he cups his hand behind my neck and drags me back for another.

"You're impossible to resist," he says against my lips. "Especially when you're wearing my shirt."

"I just want to check my emails while I have service in case it goes out again," I say, escaping his hypnotic pull. "I'll be quick."

Finn drops his head to the back of the couch, mumbling a protest under his breath. Once I grab my phone, he yanks me back so I'm snuggled in his lap. It's comfortable to cuddle on the couch with him while I work, the crackling fire as background noise and his absent caresses stoking the glowing ember of happiness expanding in my chest.

"We should take a picture for Insta." I twist on his lap. "People are stuck at home and bored in a blizzard, so we'll get them thinking about how much they want to be somewhere else."

His brows pinch together. "Somewhere else?"

I nudge his sternum with my elbow. "Yes, somewhere like Mayberry Inn. Or the Alpine. It's a great marketing tactic. Let's do it."

He tips his head to the side in consideration, fingers tracing lazy circles on my skin. "Alright, fine."

My smile widens and I nuzzle close to him, holding my phone up to snap a few. The first one we look at the camera and I almost laugh at Finn's blank expression. When I turn to face him and catch his eye, still snapping selfies, warmth floods his gaze. We end up coming together in a tender kiss, his fingers grazing my jaw to tip my face up.

"There. That wasn't so bad, was it?" I tease.

"Let me see."

I show him my camera roll, swiping through photos of our kiss and the ones where we're looking at each other. The shift in his expression causes a flutter in my stomach.

"I like that one," he says when I stop on the one of us just after the kiss, our noses bumping together.

"Me too. Okay, let's post it."

I caption my picture *Being snowed in isn't so bad with this guy. We both hope we see you soon at the #mayberryinn and #thealpinehollyridge so we can show you all our beautiful town has to offer you for a magical stay this winter.*

Once I share the photos to his phone and show him how to tag me from his new account, I laugh at the flood of comments and the perplexed look on his face. Every other comment on my post is someone freaking out that we're together and comments about shipping us with the same hashtag from Twitter. Several comments ask if I'm wearing Finn's shirt.

"What the hell is that about?" Finn shows me one of the comments on his post.

"The fans of Jingle Wars. They ship us." An amused noise puffs out of me. "Guess they saw what we couldn't long before we did."

Finn shakes his head, tossing his phone to the couch. "Trust me, I saw it. I just didn't act on it." He brings his lips close to my ear. "Didn't mean I didn't want you every second I was around you." I hum as he trails a path of kisses down my neck. "Now you're all mine and I'm not letting you go anywhere."

"There's nowhere I'd rather be right now."

The truth of my statement echoes in my heart.

After a few minutes of quiet while I finish reading emails, Finn breaks the silence. "You said you were looking to buy this place?"

I cast a glance around the room and imagine how I'll decorate it with my own personal touches. It's easy to picture myself here, spending my weekends wrapped up in Finn's arms and watching my favorite holiday movies on marathon enjoying a deluxe hot cocoa with extra marshmallows spilling over the rim. In my head, he's poking fun at me for my obsession with Christmas and how I like my cocoa heavy on the marshmallow, but we're wearing matching flannel pajama pants and Santa hats.

Perfect.

"Yeah," I say softly. "I love it. And we already have memories in it."

He chuckles, tucking my hair behind my ear. "What makes you want a cabin so much? It's not what I'd picture you wanting."

I put my phone down and twist my fingers together. "It's always been what comes to my mind when I think of a cozy and comforting home. Somewhere to curl up with someone by the fireside." The memory of last night has the corners of my mouth turning up. "Something homey that feels like a hug when you come back to it."

Finn hums at my explanation, stopping my anxious hand movements when he entwines our fingers. He brings my knuckles to his mouth, brushing a kiss over them. His comfort makes me want to open up more.

"I've told you about my family a little." He nods and I take a steadying breath to clear the tightness clogging my throat. "Well, it was the worst during the holidays. I was always alone."

Finn frowns, gathering me close, stroking my hair as I talk.

"I have two brothers, you know? After my parents divorced, they moved in with my mom. She decided to live in New York, as far away from Dad as she could get. I was left behind while they went off and had their own family."

His embrace tightens around me. "Freya..."

"It's okay. Things with Dad have always been... Well, he's not the most affectionate man." I rub my face against Finn's sweater, ignoring the wetness gathering on my lashes whenever I talk about this. "Anyway, I found Christmas movies. I really fell in love with them because they helped me through some tough times."

He kisses the top of my head and the emotions bombarding me pass.

"Thanks for listening." I shift in his hold and press my lips to his neck, where he's warm and smells faintly of spice. "Ever since I got to Hollyridge, I haven't felt like that once. This town is magic. Everyone is so great."

Finn hugs me harder, plucking at my heartstrings.

"I'm glad you came here," he says.

"Even when I complain about being forced to eat Funyuns so I don't starve when we're snowed in?"

He barks out a deep laugh, shaking his head. "Especially then."

We shift on the couch to lay down, legs tangled together. The heat from the fire makes me drowsy and I rest my head on his chest.

This domestic bubble of ours is perfect. I wish we never had to leave. Forever with Finn sounds like a dream come true.

Chapter Twenty

Finn

I woke this morning to sunlight streaming into the cabin through the sheer, light curtains. The rays shine directly onto the tan, taut skin of Freya's ass. It's the first thing I've seen this morning and I wish I could wake up every morning with this view.

The fire I stoked in the bedroom fireplace has died down sometime over the night, leaving nothing but a pile of black ash and a few glowing embers. There's a chill in the cabin, but the sunlight combined with the tangle of our bodies has kept us both warm. The storm has passed and now, it's back to reality.

I pepper light kisses along Freya's, shoulder, down her back until I reach her ass, where I take a bite. She groans sleepily, stretching her arms out.

"Good morning beautiful." I whisper against her skin.

"Mmm good morning."

"As much as I hate to, I need to get out there and try and get your car unstuck. It seems like the storm has passed and some of the snow is starting to melt. Should be able to get us back on the road today."

She groans in protest. "I wish we could just stay here forever."

I grin. "Then you'd be forced to eat Viennas for the rest of your life, and I don't think you'd survive."

She looks so beautiful spread out before me, completely nude. Her body is what men like me see in their dreams. Curves and dips that beg for attention from my lips, my tongue, and my cock.

"Don't be so dramatic, I can totally survive on Vienna's and..." She trails off giggling.

"Wait, was that a dick joke, Freya Anderson?" I ask.

Her grin is wide and teasing, and fuck if I don't fall for her a little bit more. Only she would make a joke about my dick and a can of Vienna sausages.

I drop one last kiss to her shoulder, and pick up my scattered sweats, pulling them and my shirt on quickly. I need to get back to the inn and check in on everything, even if I would rather stay here for another month undisturbed. Real life doesn't stop when you need to cherish the moment, if anything those moments pass fleetingly without giving you time to stop and grab ahold of them.

"Be back in a few, going to go check on your car."

I leave her laying naked in bed and bundle up in my coat to go out into the frigid winter air. Fuck, it's cold out here. Even with the sun beaming down, it's still enough to freeze you to the bone. I walk over to my truck and see the tires aren't very deep in the snow thanks to parking under the big tree covering the driveway. Four wheel drive should be able to get me out easily to the freshly plowed road. Once inside, I turn the heat on full blast, and put it in drive, surprised when I'm able to pull out with no trouble.

Small victories.

I drive up the road where I found Freya and her Mercedes last night, and it's now covered completely in snow, but looks a lot less stuck than it did in the muddy snow yesterday. Putting my truck in park, I hope out and get to work trying to get it out of the hole she dug with her tires by constantly gassing it. That girl. She needs someone to teach her what to do when weather like this hits.

I could be the one to take care of Freya.

Less than ten minutes later, I've got her car unstuck and some of the snow shoveled away, to where she can easily get back on the road into town. When I make it back to the cabin, she's cuddled up next to the fire I started before I left, wrapped in the blanket from the bed. Much to my distaste, she's dressed, ready to head back home and a knot forms in my stomach.

I'm worried what the reality of our situation will do to what Freya and I have only just begun.

"Hey, I got your car unstuck. All ready to go." I hand over the keys before sitting down beside her.

My hands are completely numb from the cold so I rub them together and put them just in front of the fire to thaw them. Freya leans her head on my shoulder, sighing. The fire cackles in front of us, and I watch the flames as they lick and dance together.

"We gotta head back, babe," I tell her softly and I feel her nod against my arm. Standing, I help her from her spot on the floor and I put the fire out, making sure to leave everything as when we walked in the door.

"Are you going to meet with the real estate agent and sign for the cabin?" I ask her.

"I think so. It's perfect. I'm going to put an offer in."

"I like it. It fits you and it's not too far from town or me." I grin slyly.

We walk hand in hand to the truck and I open the door for her, giving her a boost up into the seat. At five foot damn nothing, she's like a tiny little pixie.

The ride back to her car is a comfortable, quiet silence. Even though there is something in the air that I can't place. I know neither of us regret what happened, we're just both determined to hold onto what it is before it's ripped away. Life has a way of doing that to you even when you see it coming.

Freya and I both have so much shit that we have to work through, it's hard to picture this working for anything other than casual, but when I look at Freya, nothing about her or the way that I feel about her is casual. Anything but. I never expected it, but damn, it's here to stay. I feel it in my bones.

Standing by her car, as it's heating up, we say goodbye begrudgingly. I place my hands on her face, framing her beauty close enough for me to kiss her chilled cheeks, her lush lips, her forehead. I take my time giving her a proper goodbye as if I don't know when the next time we'll have a moment like this.

"I'll see you later neighbor." She gives me a sultry wink, "Thank you for last night, and everything." She turns to her car, getting inside and pulling onto the road.

Just like that, she's gone.

* * *

When I finally pull back up at the inn, Gramps is in the front, shoveling snow off the walkway.

"Gramps, what are you doing?" I ask him, taking the shovel from his frigid grip. "It's freezing out here, you should be inside resting."

"Oh boy, hush, I've been doing this longer than you've been alive," he grumbles.

"Yeah, and I'm trying to keep you around for just as long, so go on, I'll get this done," I tell him as I begin to shovel the snow.

"Grams told me you were snowed in with that pretty little thing from next door." He grins. "That so?"

"Well, unless Grams is lyin', then yep, that's what happened. I was on the way home when I saw her on the side of the road up by Canyon Road, she was stuck in the snow. It was coming down so hard, I knew we better take cover before we froze to death. Good thing she was on her way to look at a cabin for sale, or we would have."

"Mhmmmmm," Gramps says, dragging out the word.

"Gramps, you got something to say?" I ask. I lean against the shovel and wait for his response, which he laughs at.

"Not saying anything, Finn, just that you been doing a lot of pushing that girl away, and now it seems like you're learning from that mistake."

I mull over what he's saying, and realize he's right.

I've spent so much time pushing Freya away, I haven't given her a chance and that isn't fair of me. I'm sure she didn't pick our Inn to try and purposefully undermine us. She's got a pure heart, and I see that now. I've seen the way that she is with Grams and Gramps both, and she'd never do anything to hurt them. I'm the fool for wasting so much time hating someone who never deserved it.

"Maybe so," I grunt, not ready to admit out loud that I was wrong.

"Love like that Finn? It only comes around once. The ones who steal your heart whenever you had it caged in so good and tight, and you never even saw it coming. Like a thief in the night," Gramps says.

"Jeez Gramps, a little premature, don't ya think?" I tell him exasperatedly.

"I know what I see boy. I'm old. I've got those eyes that see the stuff that sits beneath the surface. And it's not all about what I see, it's about what I feel."

"If you say so. I like her Gramps, but life... It's complicated and our worlds just don't fit together. We'd have to fight everyday just to be together. But, how she makes me feel is nothing like I ever saw coming," I tell him truthfully, even if it was hard to say.

"Then it's worth fighting for Finn."

Maybe he's right. Maybe my Gramps knows exactly what he's talking about when it comes to love. After all, he's got Grams.

Chapter Twenty-One

Finn

"Finn! Finn!" A far away voice jostles me from sleep, and I don't want to open my eyes and end the delicious dream I was just having.

"Wake up Finn!" Grams' voice cuts through the hazy fog of sleep and causes me to sit up abruptly in bed. It takes a few seconds for the sleep-induced fog to wear off and for me to get my bearings.

My room is dark except from the light streaming in from the hallway light, where Grams is standing over me shaking me. Her eyes are filled with tears, and she looks terrified. That wakes me up and panic sets in.

"Grams? What's going on?" I throw the covers off and swing my feet out the bed, standing in front of her.

Her bottom lip trembles when she says, "Finn, its Gramps. He collapsed when he got up to go to the bathroom..." Her voice breaks as she sobs. "The ambulance, they're here."

My heart sinks, my gut clenches, and I feel the world fall out beneath me.

I leave Grams sitting on my bed and sprint into their room where there are two EMS standing over Gramps on the stretcher, connecting wires to his chest. He looks so feeble and small right now and I've never seen him like this before. It steals the breath right out of my lungs. I'm momentarily frozen in fear, and panic seizes me inside like a vice.

"Gramps," I say to him, not even sure if he can hear me right now. But I have to say it. I have to let him know that I won't leave his side. "I'm here, everything is going to be okay. I'll be right here."

"We need to get going, one of you can ride with him to the hospital."

I nod and walk back to my room where Grams is still sitting on my bed, tears wetting her cheeks, clutching her heart.

"I...I don't know what I'll do if I lose him Finn." She sobs as I take her into my arms. Her entire body shakes with her sobs and I feel helpless, like I have so many times in the past few months. I can't fix this, even if I wanted to with all of my heart. It's up to the doctors to save Gramps.

* * *

"Mrs. Mayberry? Finn?" The gray haired doctor, Dr. Foster, walks through the waiting room doors, greeting Grams and I. He shakes my hand and touches Grams lightly on the arm.

"How is he, doc?" I ask.

"Well, son, he's not doing great. His heart is weak, and this has been a long time coming. It's why his doctor said to take it easy and not overdo it. We're still running some tests, but he has suffered a heart attack. Now, we are doing everything we can to make sure Mr. Mayberry walks out of here as healthy as he can be. With those tests, like I suspect, we will be able to determine how bad the blockage has gotten. Best case scenario, we start him on various medications, change his diet up and hopefully he'll make a full recovery. Worst case, he'll need open heart surgery."

Grams inhales sharply and begins crying into my chest as I pull her against me.

"It's okay Grams, he's going to be okay."

Dr. Foster smiles sympathetically, "He's in the best hands Mrs. Mayberry, I assure you. We will know more once the tests come back. For now, you can both sit with him, but please let him rest. He needs time to let his body heal and do what it's made to do. If you have any questions, I'll be back around in the next few hours. Try not to worry."

Right. Like that's easy to do.

"Thank you."

I extend my hand for him to shake once more and he's gone as quick as he appeared. Grams leaves me in the waiting room to go sit with Gramps. I have to call Freya and tell her what's going on. I pull my phone out of my jeans and dial her number.

A few short rings and she answers, "Hello?"

"Hey, Princess."

"You're up early. Your voice sounds funny. You okay?"

"I'm at the hospital."

"What? What happened? Is it Grams?" She asks so many questions in rapid fire, she sucks in a sharp breath of air once she's done.

"Gramps had a heart attack Freya. He's... He's not doing very good," I whisper into the phone. The hard exterior of my resolve threatens to crumble at my feet any second.

"I'm on my way. I'll be there as soon as I can," she says.

"Okay please be careful. His room number is three fifty six."

We say quick goodbyes and I walk to Gramps' room to sit with Grams until Freya arrives. There are so many emotions I feel right now but my fear of losing Gramps trumps it all. He's been the only father I've had since I was five years old.

I'm holding back tears when there's a soft knock at the door and seconds later, Freya appears. She's wearing mismatched clothes and her hair is piled on the top of her head without a lick of makeup on. She runs over to me and I catch her in the tightest hug we can manage. I need to feel her warmth, her goodness if I'm going to make it through this. Until now I never realized just how much I had grown accustomed to having Freya with me. How deep she had woven herself within my family. Woven herself into our hearts.

"Oh, Freya, thank you so much for being here for us and for Gramps." Grams pulls her into a hug. They hold each other for a few minutes before Grams pulls back and looks at her. "You are a blessing to our family, sweet girl, I hope you do know that."

Tears well in her eyes while she nods.

"There's nowhere else I'd rather be Grams."

We spend the next few minutes together in comfortable silence as the steady rhythm of the machines that are connected to Gramps surround us. He looks peaceful, and my only hope is that he feels no pain and soon he'll be awake, with us. I feel like I have so much to tell him. That I love him, and that I appreciate him. Thank him for everything he has done for me, everything that he has sacrificed. I need more time. I need my Gramps to wake up and be with us for the next twenty years, so I can cherish every single second I have with him. I'll never take time for granted again, not after this.

"Grams, I'm going to walk outside with Freya and talk for a

few minutes. Would you like me to get you a cup of coffee from the vending area?" I ask her quietly.

"That would be lovely, thank you darling boy."

We exit the room into the bright, fluorescent lit hallway. It's calm, being so early in the morning. Only a few nurses and techs in the hallway and a few patrons visiting their families. This is the ICU therefore there can only be three people inside the room at once.

"Finn... I'm so sorry. I know Gramps is going to be okay, he has to be." Her voice breaks as tears begin to fall. "I was trying to keep this inside, I didn't want to make things worse for Grams by crying, but I am just so worried about him."

I pull her into my arms and tighten them around her while she sobs quietly into my shirt. I feel my own tears well in my eyes, but I have to be strong for my girl and my Grams. I can't be the one to break down, not when they need me most.

Freya looks up at me through tear-filled eyes, sniffling, but presses her lips against mine gently.

"I'm going to go over to the inn, and make sure everything is okay there. Make sure Bell and Saint are good. Is that okay? I just don't want Grams to have to worry about anything."

This girl.

"That would be amazing. I appreciate you, babe. I don't want to leave Grams here by herself, but I have been worried that everything will go to shit if I don't check in."

"I doubt it. Everyone at the inn is great at what they do. I'll just go check in and see if anyone needs any help."

"Thank you. I don't know what I'd do without you, Princess." I give her a wry grin.

She reaches up to cup my face. "Don't worry about it."

I give her a sweet, soft kiss before she leaves me in the hallway and disappears through the double doors at the end.

The next few days will be hard. We will find out just how extensive the damage to Gramps heart is.

Grams is still sitting close to Gramps with his hand clasped tightly in hers when I walk back into his room.

"Finn, come sit with me for a minute. I have something I want to talk with you about." She pats the seat next to her on the small loveseat.

When I'm seated next to her she removes her hand from Gramps and takes my hand in her own.

"Your Gramps is really sick Finn. It feels like we just had this same conversation not too long ago. But this time, it's a lot more serious. This isn't easy for your Gramps, bless his heart. He's worked so hard for the inn to be prosperous. Given so much and sacrificed so many things for our family. It's time for Gramps and I to step down. And I mean really step down. Gramps needs to spend his time relaxing and not working, even if he'll hate to do it. I'd rather have him around than kill himself trying to do things at the inn. Finn, we want you to take over the Mayberry." She pauses, gauging my reaction.

Even though I'm surprised, part of me knew, and hoped this was coming. The inn was always meant to stay in our family. I squeeze her hand tightly in mine.

"Grams, that's... I don't even know what to say." I tell her honestly. I'm overcome by emotion.

"Say that you will Finn. It'd be the greatest honour as your grandparents to give the inn to you. I know that you'll handle it with care. Finn you are a good man. You are kind, compassionate, caring...albeit stubborn like your old Gramps." She laughs and wipes a free fallen tear from her eyes. "There is no one better than you to have the Mayberry."

I nod, my own sneaky tears falling from my eyes.

"Of course I'll do it Grams. I'd do anything for you both."

She brings her hand to my face in a soft caress. "We'll still be here of course, the inn is our home, but from here on out it's yours Finn. Let it teach you the way that it has your Gramps and I."

The Mayberry is mine. After everything, now...it's mine.
I'll make them proud.
I'll show everyone that the Mayberry is here to stay.

Chapter Twenty-Two

Freya

The thought of losing Gramps terrifies me. It sends bouts of icy dread through my veins.

But Finn needs me right now. I have to be strong.

After I left the hospital with tears leaking from my eyes, I took care of things at the inn. I know how important it is to Finn and his family, so I put my all into doing anything I can to help them. I only stopped long enough to change into simple jeans with an oversized sweater and wrangle my hair into a smoother bun than the crazed state of it when I ran out the door in a panic to get to the hospital. To get to Finn.

When I ventured out to Saint Nick's stall to feed him, I spent an extra few minutes hugging the sweet donkey, taking comfort in his soft muzzle. Those soulful eyes seemed to sense that something was wrong when it was me instead of Gramps or Finn out in the morning chill, looking past my shoulder every few minutes to search for Gramps. The sounds he made as I headed back up the path to the inn sent icy daggers into my heart as he called out.

I might not be anywhere close to Grams' cooking skills, but luckily the Mayberry Inn's cook, Bell, had it under control. The most she let me do was brew coffee, but was grateful for my company. This scare has rattled everyone who knows Gramps Mayberry. Working together—well, mostly Bell handling things, but with enough coffee brewed by me to keep us going all day—we got breakfast on the table for the few guests currently staying, then I manned the front desk with their bellhop in case there were new bookings.

Once Finn walked through the door a few hours later, my chest caved in. He looked drained with dark circles smudged beneath his eyes. We shared a sombre look and without either of us saying anything, we came together in a tight embrace to rival the way we held each other at the hospital. His shoulders shook with a slight tremor that made me squeeze him harder, trying to absorb his pain, to take it away and make it better. We worked side by side, me manning the desk and phones, and Finn going through the inn's financial reports with a bleak expression lining his face.

West and Riley show up around mid-afternoon. For a moment Finn looks surprised to see them, then the relief of having his friends here soothes away some of the rigid tension in his shoulders.

"We're here to lend a hand," Riley says, giving me a half hug. "Word's spreading around town and everyone's going to do their part for y'all while Gramps recovers."

"Come on bro, we've got this. Go rest up." West puts a supportive hand on Finn's shoulder. "We'll take over for a little while."

A lump forms in my throat. Finn has told me before how everyone in this town has each other's back. He's shown me first hand—that day I tagged along to give a hand with the favors he was returning. They all offer help and someone to lean on when things get rough.

Hollyridge is one big family.

"Thanks," Finn says hoarsely. "You're both—thank you."

I take Finn's hand, gently threading our fingers together. He casts a look at me. "Come on," I murmur. "You can't have gotten much sleep."

After scrubbing his free hand over his exhausted features, he rumbles an incoherent response and follows. At the staircase, he takes the lead, pulling me behind him.

It occurs to me as we climb the steps this is the first time I've been to Finn's bedroom. My heart gives a pang. I wish it were under better circumstances.

The room almost looks too small to fit Finn's broad-shouldered frame in it, but it's comfortable and cozy in a way I love.

Photos line one shelf along with sports trophies from little leagues and high school. One of him fishing with Gramps catches my eye. Finn is beaming while holding up his fish and Gramps looks so proud of him.

On the wood-framed bed, the covers are in disarray, like Finn got up in a hurry. My throat clogs and I rub my thumb on his hand.

Finn sinks to the bed with a heavy sigh, resting his elbows on his knees. His head hangs down. It feels natural to step into him, combing my fingers through his hair. A soft sound leaves him as I offer him this small comfort.

"I can't..." He pauses to swallow, putting his palms on either side of my thighs. It feels like I'm the only thing grounding him right now. "I can't lose him, Freya. He's more than a father to me. He's so much."

It's the first he's spoken about it since the hospital. My throat burns.

"I know. And we won't." My voice cracks and I hug his head to my stomach, willing my words to be true. "We won't. It'll be okay. *He'll* be okay. He's a strong man."

A soft, broken laugh puffs out of Finn. He nods in agreement, nuzzling into my oversized sweater. My fingers run through his thick hair.

"Yeah." Another rueful laugh leaves him. "Stubborn old man. He'll escape his health problems by sheer force of will."

Despite the rawness of Finn's tone, it's good to get him laughing. I'll do anything to shift some of the immense weight sitting on his shoulders to help him carry it.

"Let's lay down," I suggest, nudging his shoulder. "We can nap if you want, or just rest."

He puts up no resistance—a sign of just how much the last several hours have shaken him when he doesn't attempt any of our usual banter—and lays back on his bed after kicking off his boots. He tugs me down with him once I remove my own shoes. Our legs tangle together and I wind my arms around him for a fierce hug. His spicy cedar cologne engulfs me and for a beat I feel like we're in our bubble, snowed in from the world in the cabin. It makes me want to have moments like this with him forever.

I press my lips to his scruffy jaw, then settle my head on his shoulder, tucked close against his side.

"It kills me to see him in that hospital bed," he rasps after a minute, voice strained with worry. The pain and fear slices into my heart, causing an ache to radiate from my chest. "He's always been so strong—capable. When I was a kid I thought he was invincible. This year has been hell to see him struggling with managing his health. He *wants* to work. But his body isn't cooperating. It's not right to see him like that."

Finn has held it together, for me and for Grams. He's just

as strong as his grandfather. A pillar to support those around him.

"It's okay." I stroke his cheek with my thumb. "You don't have to hold anything back with me, Finn. I can be the one who holds us together for a little bit if you need me to."

He bumps his forehead against mine and exhales, more tension bleeding from his posture. "Don't know what I did to deserve you." His arms cinch tighter around me. "But you fit just right."

An affectionate smile tugs at my lips. I tilt my face up to seal my mouth over his in a sweet kiss that we sink into. His hand cups my face as his lips move against mine. With a sleepy sigh, he breaks the kiss to rest his head back on the pillow, stroking my arm.

"Are you tired?" I ask.

Finn takes a second to respond. "No. Yes."

"Well, which is it?"

A laugh reverberates in his throat. "Yes. Exhausted as shit, but I can't sleep. The doctor might call with an update on his test results."

"Tell me about him? I like hearing your stories about your family."

After taking a minute to consider where to start, Finn's body shakes with amusement. "He's always been Mr. Fix It. Anything broken? Gramps had it covered. He knows how everything works." He shakes his head, his scruff tickling my forehead. "I idolized him for it. So he's out working on the truck he used to have, changing the oil, I think."

"That's amazing he knows how to do so much."

Finn hums in agreement. As he tells the story, he relaxes some more. "So out I come—can't have been more than nine or ten—with his big toolbox I could barely lift and one of his hats sitting so low on my head I'm surprised I could see anything."

I giggle at the adorable mental image. "You wanted to be just like him. His little helper."

"Yep. So I park the toolbox next to the wheel and scramble up on it to see. And he pretended it was a bigger job than it was, guiding me through all these things we had to fix to make the engine run. He had me starting the ignition and topping off fluids—all he did was disconnect the battery. We were out there for a couple hours, until the sun was dipping behind the mountains and Grams was calling us in for dinner." I can hear the smile and fond warmth in his voice. "But he told her I was fixing the truck, so we'd be in soon."

"He sounds like an amazing father," I murmur. "You're lucky."

"Yeah," he says, angling his head to study me.

Not wanting to get swept up in the feelings of inadequacy creeping in on me when I think of my own Dad in comparison, I prop up on my elbows to kiss Finn again. He cups the back of my head, drawing me closer.

My back pocket vibrates, interrupting us.

Finn lifts his thick brows with a wry expression. "Your ass is ringing, babe."

I pull my lips to the side. "Sorry. Hold that thought."

He allows me to sit up and I pull out my phone. When I see the caller ID, I stiffen. *Dad.*

Before I answer, Finn's phone goes off. He fishes it out and chokes back a strained noise as he scoots to the edge of the bed.

"It's the hospital," he says gruffly. He answers, putting the phone to his ear. "Hello? Yes."

I hurry to press *ignore* on my phone and pull up a text message. I tell Dad that I'll call him back while listening to Finn's half of the conversation with the hospital. Dad can wait, whatever the doctors have to say is more important right now. Finn swings his gaze to me, rubbing his jaw.

"The test results are in," he whispers to me. His attention returns to the phone. "Okay. Yes." A line of worry creases his forehead. "And what does that mean for his treatment?" After another pause, he asks, "When can he come home?"

I return to the bed, sitting beside him. My fingers dig into the blankets as I wait for him to finish. Once he hangs up, his expression is grim.

"What did they say?"

Finn sighs and drags a hand through his hair. "It's not great, but not the worst case scenario they feared." He blows out a relieved sigh. "He doesn't need open heart surgery."

"Thank god," I breathe. "So he'll be okay?"

"He's not out of the woods yet, but they'll start treatment today. They couldn't give any concrete answers for when they'll discharge him, but if they see improvement he'll be able to leave the hospital."

My shoulders sag. "I'm so glad. Now that they know his condition, they'll be able to help him."

"Yeah." Finn scrubs his face and pushes out another breath.

I suspect he's holding back his emotions again. His eyes are shiny. I give him a hug that he sinks into.

On the nightstand, my phone starts making a racket again. I pull back with a frustrated breath.

"I'm sorry, I have to take this." If I don't, Dad will only be angrier I ignored him.

Finn holds up his phone. "It's okay. I'm gonna text West with the update and I should see if Grams needs anything."

Tapping my thumb on my screen, I lift the phone to my ear. "Hey, how are—?"

"Freya," Dad barks.

I don't know why I bothered with pleasantries. Silly me.

"What's up, Dad?"

Finn pauses across the room, slowly turning to watch me.

"First of all, do not ignore my calls or you'll be fired." His voice is clearer than it's been, so I guess he's feeling better. That also means he's back to being a cutthroat businessman, the king of his empire. "The investors and I will be making a trip out there. We'll arrive on the twentieth for an in-person assessment of the property."

My stomach drops. That's only a little over a week away, and the same day as the final challenge for the Jingle Wars competition.

It's such short notice, I won't have any time to put something special together to show off my hard work and present my ideas about the future of Anderson resorts. Not just my ideas, but my staff's, too.

We've grown as a team, working together to take the Alpine into a more modern approach to seamlessly blend with options like Airbnb and partner with local existing small businesses—ones like Mayberry Inn—to create a more organic and authentic local experience for vacationers. All things that could make a community thrive as one, rather than competing against one another.

A principle my father has never cared about as he crushed small businesses to build up his kingdom of luxury.

"Um, Dad, I don't think—" Blinking away the shock and ignoring the spike of anxiety, I shoot Finn a look. His expression is lined with frustration, his jaw clenched. A muscle in his cheek jumps. I return my focus to the call. "Things are sort of crazy right now. If you could push the trip back a week—"

"No. I didn't have to give you any advance notice. Be grateful for that."

With that, he hangs up. My heart races, my pulse thrumming in my neck. A different kind of dread drops like sludge in my gut. I have a bad feeling about Dad coming to Hollyridge, poisoning this picturesque town with his selfishness.

"I'm sorry," I mumble, facing Finn. More and more, talking to Dad leaves me feeling like shit. Embarrassment heats my cheeks knowing Finn could probably hear most of the call with how loud Dad talks. "He's, um…"

"What did he want?" He looks ready to punch something on my behalf.

"He's coming to Hollyridge. His team of investors want to assess the Alpine under my management."

Finn's jaw works. "When's this?"

"Next week." I close my eyes and press my fingers into the sockets to stave off a sharp twinge of pain in my head. A stress migraine is setting in quickly. "I don't know what I'll do if he doesn't like what he finds when he's here in person. He hasn't been thrilled with the weekly reports I email him."

"Fuck him," he mutters. "You shouldn't listen to him, Freya. Any man who treats his daughter the way he's treated you is worthless."

"He's not just my father, he's my boss, too. It's his company."

He makes a dismissive sound.

Worrying my lip with my teeth, I put my shoes back on and tuck my phone in my back pocket. I don't have much else to gather.

Finn grasps my arm, stopping me in my tracks. "You're just going to go? To make your dad happy? That asshole can fu—" He cuts off with a grumble. The hard lines in his face soften and he pulls me into his chest. "Don't go yet."

Leaving is the last thing I want to do. I bury my fingers in his hoodie and peer up at him pleadingly, hoping he understands why. "I have to."

His throat bobs with his swallow. He takes my chin between his thumb and finger.

When he speaks, his voice is gruff. "But I need you…"

An ache of regret pierces through me. I reach up to cup his cheek. Finn and I have come so far. Even though we haven't been together long, I can't imagine not having him in my life if this assessment doesn't go well.

"I know. I need you, too," I whisper. "I promise, I'll come back as soon as I can. I just have to do some work to prepare for Dad's arrival, then I'm all yours. Whatever you and Grams and Gramps need, I'll be here for all of you, okay?"

Another rumbling sound catches in Finn's throat as I press closer. He crushes me against him and steals my lips for a bittersweet kiss. When it ends, we remain a hair's breadth apart.

Urgent confessions clog my throat. Things I want to tell him. One important thing in particular that makes my heart thump, but I hold it back. It's not like I'll never see him again, I'm just being ridiculous and dramatic.

As I leave, I pause in the door. "If there are any more updates, let me know, okay?"

"Yeah." Finn looks like it's killing him to watch me go.

It's killing me, too.

Chapter Twenty-Three

Finn

"Finn!" Gramps calls for me from his spot in the recliner in the family room.

It's been a week since he's been home from the hospital and he has made the recliner his permanent spot. Per Grams and my orders, of course. At first, we had to threaten him with no sweets ever again if he got up out of the chair without either of us. It's too much on his heart to get up and down, and by the time he tries he's out of breath.

This morning he tried his best to get up and follow me around while I was painting baseboards, but I quickly cut that out. Grumbling and huffing, he headed back to his chair and put on Santa Clause for the rest of the morning.

Grams gave him a bell to ring when he needed us, so he wouldn't have to strain himself calling for us. We see how much good that did, because he forgets about the bell half the time and calls for us anyway.

"Gramps, ring. The. Bell. That's why we gave it to you, so you won't have to call for us." I ring the damn thing to get my point across.

He huffs. "Finn, I don't need a bell. I'm still perfectly capable of talkin' you know."

Gramps being confined to his recliner, unable to do anything makes him the equivalent of a petulant child. He's not happy, needless to say. He feels helpless and although I can't blame him for how he feels...he's got to do it. The doctor has him on a strict diet regimen to keep his heart as healthy as possible. The tests and scans revealed the extent of his blockage, and now he's on four different medications and has been told to cut back on the hot cocoa, much to his disappointment.

"You and Grams keep fussin' over me and I'm fine I tell ya." Still grumbling, he rests his head against the back of the recliner. A few minutes later he's fast asleep, snoring lightly.

"That man." Grams walks into the living room and over to Gramps, pulling the fuzzy Christmas blanket he's covered up with, up to his chest.

"Tell me about it. I'd rather him be here arguing with me at every turn than not being here, Grams."

"I know Finn, but if we don't stay on top of him he'll just end up back in that darn hospital, worse off than the last time. That's how your Gramps is. Been that way since we were kids. He puts everything before himself. The most selfless man I know, to the point where his heart is giving out and he's still worried about painting baseboards with you."

I nod. She's right, and I know that.

"Speaking of you putting in work... Are you ready for the competition?" She asks over her shoulder as we walk into the kitchen where she's baking a few pies for the homeless shelter. "It's in just a few days."

"I guess. I don't know how I'll be able to focus on anything. I'm too worried about Gramps."

Grams puts her rolling pin down on the counter and walks over to where I'm leaning against the island. Her small hands find my face and she gives me a look before speaking. "You are a good man, Finn. So much like your Gramps. He raised you that way, to be so much like him. Even though you don't see it, you are. I see it in everything that you do. He's so proud of you. What he wants more than anything is to see you be happy. You know that right?"

I nod. I do know that.

"And you know that even if you don't win this competition, he will still be as proud of you as ever and love you more than you know. Both of us will. You know money isn't everything. Family is. Love is. Because when you're six feet under, none of that money will bring you any comfort."

"I know Grams." I flash her a charming smile.

"You go to that competition and you kick some ass." My eyes widen at her cursing. "You can do it. You know... I heard from the grapevine."

Grapevine means her Pokeno group, and why she doesn't just say that I don't know, because we both know it.

"The third competition is going to be a baking competition. Gladys heard it from one of her employees who knows someone on the judging board."

Baking? Fuck.

"Grams, I haven't baked shit in my entire life. How am I going to win that competition?" I ask exasperatedly.

"Finn. Language."

"But—"

She cuts me off before I can finish my sentence. "But, nothing. We're going to spend the next day baking my secret cookies. I haven't shared this recipe with anyone, not even your daddy. Not even Gramps. But, I think this is exactly what you will need to win."

She walks over to her large cupboard where she keeps all of her recipe books and pulls out a large black book from the very back, flipping to a page in the back.

"Here it is." She points to the recipe on the paper. "This. This is what is going to win you Jingle Wars. You'll have what no one else does. A secret weapon of sorts. In the form of the most delicious cookies in all of Hollyridge. I'd bet my life on it."

Looking at it...she just might be right.

Grams' secret recipe is going to win me Jingle Wars.

* * *

The crowd today is twice what it has been for the past two competitions. Which is saying a lot, since my anxiety was proof of just how many people have been here. Being on stage is one thing, being on a stage surrounded by over five hundred people with a camera pointed in my face is an entirely different thing. Freya stands right next to me, all eyes on us because we're the final two contestants.

"Welcome back to the last day of the Jingle War competition! I don't know about you guys, but I am so very sad for it to come to an end," Cornelius says. "It has been a blast seeing all of the wonderful people of Hollyridge and everything that this jolly town has to offer. There is just one last challenge before the winner takes all. And by all, I mean one hundred thousand dollars!"

The crowd explodes in applause.

Freya is quiet next to me. Ever since I walked onto the stage this morning, she has been quiet and not herself. I can tell something's off. I want to ask her what's wrong, but with the cameras, nothing is private. We haven't had a moment alone in the last few days, with her growing too busy with preparing for her dad's arrival and me practicing Grams' recipe.

Despite my pep talk with Grams, I'm still worried about Gramps. I haven't left the house but to pick up a few groceries since he's come home from the hospital. Even then those were short trips, worried if I go too far something will happen and I won't be able to get home in time. Needless to say, this stage is still the last place that I want to be.

I steal another glance at Freya, and she's fidgeting with her nails, avoiding eye contact with anyone. Fuck, it's only been a few days but I miss her. She stopped by as often as she could once Gramps came home from the hospital, when she was able to step away from her work at the resort, checking on Gramps and stealing moments with me. I miss having her beneath me, I miss the little sounds she makes as she comes around my cock, I miss how she gets snuggly and happy once I've given her a handful of orgasms. One more reason to get this damn competition over with. I wanna get home to my girl, and my family.

"Alright folks, it's time. Let's get this competition started!" Cornelius says into his microphone. He's about as over the top as they come, decked out in a green velvet suit with a bright red bowtie to match. Last competition it was a bright red suit.

"The moment of truth," he says, followed by a drumroll from somewhere off to the side of the stage.

Its deep beat does nothing for the knot in my gut. There's only one person winning this competition, and either way the other is going to be hurt by it. It seems like there's not a real winner here no matter which way it goes. Fuck, the last thing I want to do is hurt Freya. At the same time, I need this money more than I want to admit aloud, it means everything to our family. It saves the inn.

But at what cost?

Hurting the girl I care about?

"Today's competition will be a combination of skills. Starting with knowing your way around the inside of a kitchen!" Cornelius exclaims, gesturing to behind the both of us where a deep red velvet curtain with the Jingle Wars logo is. The curtain parts, revealing two kitchen stations with various things for baking. A mixer, giant bowls, baking sheets.

Damn, Grams' intel was right. It is a cookie competition.

The knot tightens further in my stomach, knowing I may win. It's a tug of war inside of me. Happy that I have a legit chance of winning this thing, disappointed that my girl might leave here with a broken heart. Intentional or not, a broken heart is never something I wanted to give Freya.

"Your task today will involve patience, and baking skills. Are we a little worried about Finn here folks?" He laughs lightly, inciting the same reaction from the crowd. "When the timer begins, you will have two and a half hours to make the best batch of cookies that Hollyridge has ever seen. You will be judged on your final product. You have been provided everything you will need to bake the cookies, but you'll have to have your very own recipe. Manage your time well, as it's very easy to let it slip away from you. With that being said, contestants..." He gestures to the kitchen set up behind us. "Take your places." He gestures to the kitchen set up behind us.

Freya shoots me a small smile that doesn't reach her eyes. It does nothing but cause a bigger knot to form in my stomach. I'm thankful as fuck that Grams spent the last day with me in the kitchen showing me exactly what I need to do to make our secret recipe. Without her, I would have no hope for winning. None.

Up until yesterday Grams has always fed me all the treats I could possibly want, but now it's my turn to make her and my Gramps proud. Cornelius follows us over to our stations as we settle behind the counter and prepare for the timer to start. I see an apron hanging on the stand next to me, so I grab it quickly and put it on. It's a deep red with the Jingle Wars logo on front, much like the curtains that hid this entire ensemble.

If you would have asked me three months ago, did I ever see myself on a stage in the middle of town square, surrounded by hundreds of people, participating in the Jingle Wars competition...I would have told you that you were insane, that nothing would ever make me participate in that stupid competition. I would've told you that falling in love was the farthest thing from my mind. Especially with a girl fresh off the beach in California with a pair of wet, soggy UGGs and a faux fur coat. But here I am, doing things I never thought I'd do.

The truth was that somewhere along the way Freya had changed me. She brought out the man that I was always meant to be, it just took a gentle pull from the girl I'm fucking crazy over.

"Are you ready Finn? Freya?" Cornelius asks us both.

We look over at each other and I hold her steady gaze for a few beats before I nod.

"Remember, you have two and a half hours to win this competition! Best of luck to you both."

Seconds later the bell rings, and our time starts. I take a deep breath before I begin, trying to remember everything that Grams told me.

"Finn, collect everything you need before you start. Don't wait until you're mid bake. That leaves room for forgotten ingredients, error, and you'll waste time doing so."

Right.

All the ingredients first.

Not only am I doing this entire thing from fucking memory, I have to recall exactly what the measurements should be for it.

I spend the next few minutes trying not to see what Freya's

doing, but forcing myself to focus on my task instead. I gather all the ingredients one by one and arrange them in front of me in the order I'll need them. Then I spend an extra few minutes measuring each ingredient out as meticulously as possible, then place it in front of its packaging. That way, I can grab each one and have it already prepared.

Time flies by and when I glance up to check the time I'm shocked that it's already been an hour. I look over to Freya who seems to be struggling with the mixer, and I wish she would have had more time with Grams in the kitchen. I know this isn't something she's ever gotten to do, especially with her childhood.

Fuck.

She looks as beautiful as ever with flour all over her apron, in her hair—and is that a chocolate chip stuck to her cheek? Her normally put together appearance is completely disheveled, and she looks frustrated.

I pull my attention from her and try and focus on the bowl of cookie dough I've managed to put together in the mixer in front of me. I use the scooper provided and measure each cookie out individually, placing them on the baking sheet in front of me. Once finished, I put the sheet into the oven and then... I wait. I watch Freya struggle with her mess. I almost fucking just quit, and go over to help her. I can't stand to see her so down and defeated. Nothing like the woman I've come to know.

But, I don't. Because if I do, it means losing the inn. Breaking my grandparents' heart. So I stand here, and I wait for one minute before the timer dings to remove the cookies.

Grams said the secret to her recipe is not just a secret ingredient, but it's following the receipt down to a T. And I did. I followed each and every direction. Now, pulling the cookies out of the oven, I know that I nailed it. The aroma wafting from the oven is fucking delicious and I'm thankful that I get to try my hard work because damn, these smell so good.

They are perfect. A golden brown, perfectly round shaped. After giving them a few minutes to cool, I use the spatula and remove each one, placing them on the golden platter. Finally, I pick the last one up and take a giant fucking bite. I almost moan out loud because they are *that* good.

Perfect. Melt in your mouth delicious.

Not ten minutes later, the bell rings, signaling our time is up. Freya managed to finish her cookies in time, but...they don't exactly look like cookies? More like a cookie cake, all melded together in an unusual shape.

She looks like she's going to burst into tears at any minute.

Shit.

"Alright everyone, time is up, and we have two batches of what I know will be delicious cookies!" Cornelius comes over to stand between our stations, and signals us to come over together.

Freya throws her apron down on the counter, and bites her lip, holding back tears. My competitive girl.

"Let's give the judges fifteen minutes to deliberate and we'll announce our Jingle Wars winner!" He smiles for the camera, then exits the stage left. Two stage hands grab our platters of cookies and bring them to the judges table. I use the break to talk to Freya.

"Hey, what's going on?" I ask, careful not to get too close since I'm sure the camera's are still rolling. The last thing we need is more unwanted attention from the press.

"Uh...my dad. He got here early. He's here in the crowd and I'm just nervous. Overwhelmed," she says, not meeting my eyes.

Something is off, and it isn't just her dad. But, now isn't the time I guess.

"Okay, well you did great, baby, I'd eat the shit out of your cookies." I grin and a small smile tugs at the corners of her lush lips.

"I never thought I'd say this, but I'm just ready for it to be over." She sighs.

"I know, but hey, how about later we watch a Christmas movie? Snuggle up with some hot chocolate."

She nods.

"I'd like that. Thanks, Finn." She flashes me another fake smile that doesn't reach her eyes.

Cornelius joins us back on the stage with the signature red envelope and gold seal, the one that holds our fate.

I'm nervous as fuck. Worried about what's going to happen once we step foot off this stage.

"It has truly been a pleasure to come here to Hollyridge and host Jingle Wars. I am already looking forward to next year! Without further adieu, the winner of the Jingle Wars competition is..." He trails off when the drumroll begins.

I look over at Freya who's completely rigid with nerves, and I know she's feeling just what I am. Saying fuck what everyone has to think, I take her hand in mine and squeeze. I hope she can feel what I'm not able to put into words, right now.

"Hollyridge's very own, Finn Mayberry!"

The crowd goes wild, the cameras cut to me, and the only thing I can do is look at Freya. She gives me a small smile and walks off stage without a backwards glance.

Fuck, it's hard to enjoy this knowing she's hurting, whether over this or her dad.

"Finn, how do you feel right now?" Cornelius asks with the mic pointed right at my face.

"I... I'm shocked. to say the least. Appreciative. Thanks for coming out everyone." I give him a shy smile. I hate all of the attention placed on me. Always have.

I spot West in the crowd whooping and hollering and I allow myself, even just for a moment, to be happy and fucking proud of what I accomplished. I can't believe I won the damn competition. I just hope that once this is over, Freya will say yes to being mine.

Chapter Twenty-Four
Freya

I...lost.

I lost the competition.

Cornelius Frost congratulates Finn, dancing around the stage in his green velvet suit. The applause from the crowd is deafening, but the noise reaches me in that distorted, murky way like it's muffled by water. Must be the blood rushing in my ears.

Get it together, sis. Still broadcasting live on air. No crazy girl breakdowns on national television.

I take a deep breath and my racing thoughts begin to clear.

As badly as I wanted to win, I'm not as disappointed as I thought I would be.

It's right that Finn won. This challenge called for us to do something I've never had—use a favorite recipe to bake our holiday cookies. Without any family recipes of my own, the best I could do was quickly Google recipes with rave reviews at my station while trying to remember what Grams Mayberry taught me about handling cookie dough. The pressure of doing it in front of an audience, in front of *Dad*, made it hard to focus and I ended up with...

Well, at least Finn made me feel better about my kitchen disaster by assuring me he'd eat it. I want to disappear with him so we can go snuggle and drink enough hot cocoa to drown out this whole day.

But what stings is that my father's eyes are boring into me from the in person audience, his investors at his side. They weren't front and center, but I spotted them just before the challenge timer began. His cold stare rattled me more than it ever has. He got to watch every minute of my defeat. And to Dad? Losing anything means you're worthless to him.

That truth is what crushes down on me after I step off the stage with my stomach twisting in anxious knots as the broadcast ends. Finn gets pulled into hugs and back slaps as West and the residents of Hollyridge congratulate their favorite son on taking the Jingle Wars crown title.

With the money, he'll be able to do what he wanted—keep the Mayberry and make his grandparents proud.

My heart constricts with a bout of happiness for him. All I want to do is run over and dive into his arms, inhale the spice of his woodsy cologne, and celebrate with the people who have become like family to me. I want to join them, but I'm standing off to the side, an outsider once more.

"Freya." I can't stop my flinch at Dad's stony bark. It's so much worse in person than over the phone. "A word."

Reluctantly, I turn my back on Finn, West, and everyone we know celebrating his win to face my father and his flock of investors. Even the festive decorations of town square I've loved since moving here can't shield me against the way Dad's tone makes me feel like a silly little girl.

"Dad," I say lightly, pretending everything is fine.

Pretending the only reason he's here isn't because of money and business, but because he cares about me. "I hope the trip out was good. You're here a little earlier than I expected. I was going to meet you in the lobby with these great welcome drinks one of our mixologists does—a twist on hot toddies and mulled wine."

Ingram Anderson sneers at me, casting a judgmental look at the holiday cheer filling the square. "The closest airfield is almost an hour away. Ridiculous. I should never have to wait so long. My time is valuable."

I remember that from when I flew into the nearest major airport. I had to take a regional plane, then pick up my rental car and drive the rest of the way.

"It's part of Hollyridge's charm," I say, trying to smile with positivity. "We're tucked away in the mountains. It's how it's remained so quaint and untouched. People love it, they'll come from all over to visit."

"Not according to the numbers," says one of the investors flanking Dad. He has a beak-like nose that he glares down. "The Alpine is barely scraping by compared to all of the other resort properties. A severe disappointment compared to the projections before the location was opened. It's only continued to peter along in performance."

It's a jolt to hear. All they care about are the numbers, not about the guests who come to stay. They would never care about the excitement on the little boy's face who helped me show off the virtual sleigh ride, or about the couple who got engaged at the top of our ski slope last week, or the older man who proudly told me he's been coming to the Alpine in Hollyridge regularly since it opened because he loves it.

Uncomfortable with having this conversation within hearing distance of people around us who might pick up shifts at the Alpine and worry about the bleak topic, I go into people-pleaser mode. "Are you hungry? We could stop by the bakery across the street. Betsy has great coffee and killer bear claws—seriously, I'm so addicted to them. Then I can give you a full tour and present my marketing plan for the next quarter to keep us adaptive instead of reliant on holiday tourism."

"Stop wasting my time, Freya," Dad snaps. "You've always been lackadaisical in your approach. Nothing like what Anderson Resorts requires of its team members."

My words stick in my throat and I drop my hands to my side instead of gesticulating with enthusiasm.

"I already went to the property," he continues with a disgruntled frown. "Where you *should've* been. I wasn't impressed at all. And where were you? Here, doing—" He makes a jerking sweep with his arm to indicate the square. Distaste is clear on his face. "—*this*."

Maybe it's because I haven't been in the office squaring off with him and the other ruthless executives, but I'm not fast enough to defend myself. Not quick enough to make Dad listen. I've lost the edge to be ready for anything he throws at me, rusty after growing comfortable in Hollyridge, far away from him.

"You're finished at Alpine," he grits out through clenched teeth with finality. "I'll be installing someone I can trust to do things the right way."

No.

"What?" I breathe. He can't take the Alpine from me. I've worked so hard and now it's all coming crashing down around my ears. "No, Dad—listen! Just let me—"

"I'm done listening to your whims and excuses. You're not capable of running one of my resorts to the standard I expect. I should've known you were too young to give this much responsibility to."

The scathing remark blisters my ego. His standards are

impossible and too rigid. Sooner or later his company is going to come up against reality because of his refusal to change for the modern world of vacationing.

When did he stop caring about the experience his resort guests receive? Did he ever care in the first place?

Who am I kidding? Of course he didn't. It's always been about the money and renown.

"Look, Dad." I prop my hands on my hips and stare him down. "I think if you just give me one more chance to give you a tour and take you through what I have planned, you'll see my strategies are the right choice for this resort. I've spent time here getting to know the type of tourists coming through and reaching an intimate understanding of the people who live here."

From the corner of my eye, I spot Finn making his way over to me with a big charming grin. In my head, I picture what would happen if Dad wasn't reaming me out right now in front of onlookers. Finn would reach me, sweep me into his arms, and give me a kiss that leaves me dizzy.

My brain is off in la la land enjoying a victory makeout session with my sexy lumberjack while I take the brunt of Dad's callous anger. Lucky bitch.

"No," Dad says, turning away from me in dismissal. "You're done. I expect you back in the California office within two days. You'll return to your previous position. If you're not there, you're fired and cut off."

Finn freezes a few feet away at my father's clipped ultimatum. My throat feels raw.

Even with the person who makes my heart whole standing nearby, I've never felt more alone and out of place. Dad essentially said he's fine with throwing me away. His own daughter.

It's just like when I was a kid waiting and wishing for my family to be whole again.

No, this is *worse*.

At least then I had naive hope. Now I know Dad's never cared for me one second of his life. Selfish bastard.

My chest heaves with painful breaths as Dad and his entourage cross the square, scowling at the festivities and celebratory mood. He's a heartless monster, more despicable than Scrooge. Faced with the same three ghosts of Christmas Past, Christmas Present, and of Christmas Yet to Come, Dad would never learn the same lesson and change for the better the way Scrooge did.

He and his precious money deserve each other.

"Babe," Finn says as he reaches me. He's a solid wall of warmth at my side, and I'm two seconds from burrowing into his chest and never leaving. He touches my arm, casting a hard glance at my Dad's retreating back. "Are you okay?"

"Yeah." I have to nod twice before I believe it myself.

"What a fucking asshole," he mutters darkly.

I stiffen. "You overheard?"

"Hard not to when he's blustering up a damn storm like that." Finn shakes his head. Some of the brightness from winning fades from his eyes. He goes quiet. A shadow of conflicted emotions clouds his face. "So...you're leaving? Just like that?"

I open my mouth to deny it, but nothing comes out. What do I say?

Two days. I only have two days before Dad expects me back in California.

"I don't know." His eyes burn as they pierce into me. I reach for his hand. He lets me take it, but his stance is stiff. He's wary of my answer. "I don't want to."

"So don't." Finn's voice is low. "Stay."

My throat constricts. I just had the one thing I thought I wanted and worked my ass off for ripped away from me, then told if I hope to keep a job or the only blood-related family I've ever known, I need to go back to California.

"If I don't go, he said he'll cut me off," I say in a small voice.

Dad might be an egotistical, money-obsessed asshole, but...he's still the only family I know.

Finn frowns, falling back a step, dropping my hand. The look on his face cuts me deep, that hint of betrayal bleeding back into his features. I haven't seen that look in weeks.

He still thinks you're a traitor.

"You'd seriously leave because he told you to?"

"I don't know, Finn," I say in a hard voice that cracks, growing frustrated. "I—he's my father, my *boss*. He expects his orders to be followed. He expects me to go home."

The line between Finn's brows deepens as his brows draw together.

"When are you supposed to leave, then?" he mutters.

"In two days."

A muscle in Finn's jaw jumps when he clenches his teeth. "You really want to walk away from all this? Your friends here? Grams and Gramps?" He pauses, taking a step closer. His voice drops. "*Me?*"

"I—" My throat closes over.

No. No, of course I can't!

I don't really have a choice in this, even if I don't want to leave.

Dad makes demands, and I meet them.

"I have to go tell my staff I'm not their boss anymore," I say sadly.

It's not what Finn wants to hear, I can see it clearly on his face the way his handsome features close off. I hate feeling shut out and can't stand the thought of hurting or disappointing him. So much for our cocoa and movie date.

I take a step back, but he grasps my wrist to stop me. His

gaze pierces into mine. "Screw that, Freya. Screw what your dad wants. What do *you* want?"

I open my mouth, but before I can speak, we're jostled.

"Finn! We knew you could do it!"

The other townspeople still packing the square surround us, pulling Finn into their arms as they swarm him. They all want to celebrate with him, their spirits high. I shuffle back a few steps, ending up on the outskirts of the group forming around him. He looks through the crowd swallowing him to meet my gaze.

I linger for another few seconds, then leave the square to head for the Alpine without giving him a real answer.

I don't know what the answer is.

The thought of leaving Hollyridge, Montana makes my heart ache worse than it ever has, like the damn thing might fall right out of my chest any second. Can I walk away from the memories I've made here? From the people who have become my friends?

I swallow thickly.

Can I walk away from the man I think I'm in love with?

Chapter Twenty-Five
Finn

The second I pull up at home, Grams and Gramps are both on the porch waiting for me. Tears stream down her face, and for the first time since I entered the competition, I realize just how worth it that it was. Seeing tears of happiness and relief shine in my Grams' eyes makes it all fucking worth it.

"Finn! You won!" she cries, pulling me into her arms.

"I did it, Grams. I told you and Gramps that I'd make you proud." I grin, my chest puffing with pride. Gramps beckons me over to where he's sitting in the large cedar rocker.

"I'm so proud of you Finn," he says, his voice breaking.

It's rare to see my Gramps overcome with emotion, and I'd be lying if it didn't bring tears to my own eyes.

I fucking did it. I did it for them.

We're not going to lose the inn. My family's legacy is going to live on.

"I'm going to make so many celebration treats!" Grams exclaims. A laugh escapes through her sob.

"You know I'll never say no to your cooking, Grams."

"I know it darling boy. I hope you know how truly proud and thankful that your Gramps and I are for you. You didn't have to do this Finn, I know how much you hated Jingle Wars, but you put your feelings aside and selflessly did it for us." She continues to cry. "I can't thank you enough."

Fuck, I'm going to be crying like a pussy next. My grandparents are everything to me.

"It was nothing, Grams. You and Gramps...you've done everything for me. You took me in when I had no one else. I can never repay you for what you've done." My voice breaks with emotion. "I couldn't stand to think of the inn not existing anymore. I grew up here. It's my home. I'm just thankful that I somehow won."

"I never doubted you for a second Finn," Gramps says with a laugh. "Even if your Grams did."

"Oh Harold, hush. That is not true, and you know it," she chatesizes him.

"I'm just teasin'. Isn't it ironic, Finn, that you spent so much time complainin' how much you didn't like that "stupid competition", but look how much it's brought you?"

He's right.

Not only did that stupid competition save the inn and my future, it gave me Freya, and without it, I might not have ever given her the time of day. I was too blinded by my own hate to see who she really was. And now...she might be leaving Hollyridge, for good. Which is what I wanted so desperately in the beginning.

She couldn't even say what she wanted when I asked why she had to listen to her dad's demands of her. As she walked away from me in the square, all I wanted was to reach out and grab her again, hold onto her to keep her from leaving Hollyridge. From leaving me. I've already wasted so much damn time being angry and trying to hate her that now I can't stand to waste another second. Seeing the way she walked away from me in the square with her shoulders slumped in defeat was nothing I ever want to see again.

"I'm going to head in and get some supper started and put a cake in the oven. You two come in before too long. Getting colder by the second," Grams says before disappearing inside, leaving Gramps and I alone.

"I just wanted to tell you thank you, Finn. You knew how much I was worrying about the inn and stepped up, without us ever having to ask. You knew how important my pride is to me, and you never made me feel like I was failing. That's something no amount of money could ever replace Finn. Your Grams and I are so happy to have you run the inn. I couldn't imagine anyone better. Thank you." He gives me a loving look.

"I'd do it again in a heartbeat, Gramps."

"Where's Freya?" He nods toward the resort next to us.

"Her dad's here. He was in the audience when they announced I won... He said some hurtful shit to her. Made me want to lay him out right there in the middle of the crowd. He's an asshole." My fists clench at the thought.

Gramps nods.

"Now he's demanding she leave and go back to California. I don't know Gramps, I can't imagine her not being here. I hate that he's forcing her. He's taking the choice from her."

His gray brows furrow in question. "Did you tell her that?"

"I haven't told her anything. Part of me is angry that she's even considering going back, and the other part is terrified that she will."

"You'll figure it out my boy. Love's not easy. Never will be. But, it's worth it."

I nod in response and run my fingers through my hair in

unease. I need to have some time alone, straighten my head out, figure out what the fuck I'm going to do.

"Gonna head to Saint's stall and muck some, clean up a bit," I tell Gramps, rising from the rocker beside him.

"Best listener in the world, son. Been sayin' that for years." He smiles.

That damn donkey.

Daylight begins to fade from the sky and darkness takes its place while I'm still in Saint's stall, unhurriedly running the brush over his coat. I've been here thinking all evening, talking to him like he's ever going to say something back. But, the comfortable silence allows me to process everything that has happened in the past few days.

I actually *won* Jingle Wars.

As sweet as my win is, I hate that Freya is hurting and *I'm* fucking hurt that she's thinking of leaving Hollyridge.

I think back to life before Freya moved in next door. I was existing. Working, spending time with Grams and Gramps, sleeping, repeat. Nothing extraordinary.

Maybe Grams was right all along... Maybe Freya is what was missing in my life. Freya coming to Hollyridge changed something in me, and until winning this Jingle Wars and the reality that she might be leaving hit, I didn't realize how much she truly means to me.

"Saint, what do you think? You think I'm less grumpy with Freya around?"

He looks at me with his big, brown eyes and twitching ears, but damn if that stare doesn't hit me right in the heart.

"You think?"

He lets out a low "yee-haw" and bares his teeth.

"If I let her leave and never tell her how I feel, then I'll just be a fool Saint. Winning Jingle Wars was all I wanted, then somewhere along the way, she became what I wanted. I'm crazy about her."

"Heeeeee-haw."

"Saint, you're a damn genius. I'm not just winning Jingle Wars, I'm getting my girl."

Chapter Twenty-Six
Freya

Riley was sweet enough to let me pack up my entire life in the *Scandinavian Winter* room at the resort and move everything to her apartment near town square for now.

Despite having my friend's help and support, I still can't shake the strong sense I'm out of place, even in my best friend's apartment. The feeling has only intensified since I left the square earlier today. It's only the afternoon and I'm emotionally drained.

It's like I'm stuck between my two worlds—my old one in California, and my new one in Hollyridge. Right now, I'm not sure I fit in either of them, existing in this strange gray area watching from the outside. In fact, I wonder if this is how Scrooge felt looking in on the lives around him without his presence.

That look on Finn's face when I left the square earlier...it's eating at me. I didn't have an answer about whether I'm staying or not, and I still don't have one now. When I tried calling him to apologize after I left the Alpine, he never picked up.

Is he annoyed with me for not giving a clear answer? I don't want him to shut me out.

For now I push the worry down and lock it up.

"Thanks for this, dude," I tell Riley after we've brought in the last of my things. I set down a tote bag full of shoes and admire one of her pottery vases with a Hollyridge mountainscape painted on it. She's so talented. "You're a lifesaver."

My clothes are crammed into two suitcases and a duffel bag, everything a haphazard mess, stuck where it fits within Riley's space instead of the organized way I'd packed when shipping my things from California to move to Hollyridge. I've fit it where I can amongst Riley's art. Every available inch of her apartment is full of her original pieces. The first time I was here, she told me she hopes to someday show it all off in her own studio gallery.

"Of course, girl." She gives me a light, playful tap to the shoulder with her fist. "We stick together. I wouldn't leave you high and dry. Besides, you're one of us now."

A wave of love for my friend crashes into me and I wrap her in a hug. She allows me to cling to her, hugging me just as fiercely.

After Dad's ultimatum, I found out another booking was taking over my room as soon as I returned to the resort. I didn't even get the luxury of licking my wounds in the privacy of my safe space after the public reaming he gave me. Nope, one of the front desk managers let me know with a wobbly smile that I had to be out of the room in under two hours so housekeeping could prepare it for the next arrival to check in.

Riley helped me hold it together while I was essentially getting kicked out of my home here in Hollyridge.

I don't know where Dad has gone. He wasn't around when

I was announcing the news of my dismissal to the resort staff. The door to my office in the lobby was closed—something I almost never did while I was running the resort, preferring to keep an open door policy. He was probably in there undoing every unique thing about the Alpine that I put into it.

"Want some cocoa?" Riley gives me a sly wink as I take a seat on the couch. "I think I'm finally in the mood for that holiday movie marathon. One feel-good depression-buster coming right up for the mopey girl on my couch."

A short laugh huffs out of me. She remembered what always makes me feel better. "You're the world's best bestie, you know that? I'm totally getting you a mug for Christmas that declares it."

"And don't forget it," she sing-songs as she disappears into the small kitchen.

"Extra marshmallows for mine if you've got 'em!" I call.

"Obviously."

While she's in the other room, I check my messages. There's nothing from Finn. I don't know what I was hoping for. He's probably busy reveling in his win with his family.

Instead of luring myself into a montage of all our happy moments together, like a reel from my favorite Christmas movies, I open Instagram to distract myself.

Big freaking mistake.

The photo of Finn and I steals my breath.

"Damn it," I mumble.

The way he gazes at me in the photo causes my eyes to glisten. He makes me so happy, and when I'm in his strong arms, surrounded by his woodsy scent everything is perfect. I feel at home, safe, and loved.

Will I ever find that with anyone else? I doubt it. He's the first person I've ever felt like that with. The first time I've felt my heart call out to another.

Finn isn't a quick itch to scratch, he's the whole damn package. He's the guy you lock it down with and have it all—cozy little house, two point five kids, a dog. Well, in our case, a donkey named Saint Nick.

A sad chuckle leaves me.

If I walk away from Hollyridge, I could lose out on the future I want with Finn.

As I hold my phone, gazing at the picture, an idea pops into my head.

I roll my lips between my teeth, darting my gaze out the window. The late afternoon winter sun kisses the mountaintops surrounding Hollyridge.

With butterflies filling my stomach, I pull up the information for the realtor of the cabin I was planning to buy. If I put an offer in, I can stay.

It means finding a new job.

For a second, my idea stutters.

A new job.

There aren't any other hotels nearby, the only other one in town is Mayberry Inn. What else could I do?

I wonder if Hollyridge has a tourism board I could work for, or maybe Moose's has an opening. I could learn to tend bar, couldn't I? I like the thought of talking to the patrons. Connecting with guests has always been a favorite part of my work.

Before I get ahead of myself planning out my next moves, I should find a place to live. I can't couch surf at Riley's apartment forever.

Biting my lip, I dial.

"Miss Anderson," the realtor greets on the line after only two rings.

"Hi! I'm sorry it took me a bit to get back to you. There was a—" I hesitate for a second, clearing my throat. "A family emergency."

"I'm sorry to hear that," she says. "How can I help you?"

"I'd like to put an offer in on the cabin."

The realtor goes quiet for a second. "The one out on Canyon Road?"

"That's the one. It's perfect, I already can't wait to put my roots down there. I've got a whole vision board for the interior layout and—"

"Miss Anderson, I'm sorry," she interrupts softly. "I'm afraid the cabin has already sold. A newlywed couple viewed it the day after you were able to dig your car out of the snow and put an offer in immediately."

My heart sinks.

Another unicorn cabin snatched from my grasp. Not just any cabin, but my dream home where I pictured a life for Finn and I. Losing out on this one twists the knife a little deeper.

Maybe it's a sign I'm not supposed to stay here.

Defeated and worn out by this day, I curl up against the arm of Riley's couch.

Dad expects you to go. You always do what he wants in the end, my mind whispers harshly.

"I thought we were having a movie marathon?" Riley appears in the doorway with two mugs practically overflowing with marshmallows and sweet-smelling hot cocoa. My mouth waters. "Wipe that killjoy frown off your face."

Sitting up to accept the warm mug, I lift my brows. "Can't I be in my feels? I think I've earned it." I bring the mug close to my face and hum at the healing aroma of chocolate and marshmallow. "I lost Jingle Wars to my neighbor, got fired—by my dad, no less—and kicked out of the place I was living all in one day."

"Your neighbor who is definitely your boyfriend," Riley points out.

I open and close my mouth. "Well—I mean, we didn't ever officially define it. But...yeah, pretty much."

We didn't have to define it. We fell into our relationship easily once we got over ourselves. After getting snowed in, and then facing Gramps' heart attack scare together, we only grew closer, as if we'd been together for years. I can't explain it, but being around Finn now, it's like we've been together forever, even though it's only been a couple of months since we met.

As I blow on the cocoa, my brows knit together.

Is that what Finn thinks, that we're together? He has to, right? He calls me babe.

I nod to myself with conviction. Finn Mayberry is not the type to lead a girl on. I can feel it in my bones.

"Fine. I guess you deserve five minutes to be emo," Riley concedes.

"Just five? Stingy," I sass. "I thought you artsy types were all in touch with emotion to create your visions? Where's the empathy?"

Riley rolls her eyes good-naturedly and our husky laughter fills the room.

After a beat, my amusement dwindles. "I called the realtor while you were in the kitchen. That cabin I was hoping to buy sold."

Riley frowns. "Something else will come along."

I'm not so sure. If it were meant to be, I would've been able to have any of the houses I wanted. My shoulders droop with the force of my sigh.

So much for staying. Even if I found another place, I'd still need to look for something to do for a living after Dad basically disowns me like we're in Victorian England. An overwhelming sense of inadequacy engulfs me.

I close my eyes and breathe through it.

This is how I've always felt, the way Dad's influence has conditioned me over the years. I always thought I was fighting for him to hear me, to respect my input.

But in reality? He'll never respect me. He hasn't given me any of the consideration or love I deserve a day in my life. I was an asset to him. Another worker bee in the cog of his empire. All this time, I've been working my ass off to impress him, when really he's kept me under his thumb.

I thought I had earned my success, but I was wrong.

I had nothing until I came to this town.

"How long do you have until you need to make a decision?" Riley asks after a few minutes of me stewing in my thoughts.

I lick my lips. "Dad said I need to be back in two days. I'll have to book a flight, and get my rental car back." My head spins with how much I'll have to do. A weary groan leaves me. "Arrange for my stuff to be shipped back."

Riley is quiet for a moment, studying me. She's always fast to offer a sarcastic remark laced with innuendo. Seeing her so serious gets my attention.

"So you'll really go, then?" Her nail taps the handle of her mug. "You're talking like you are."

The question catches me off guard, even though it's an obvious one. It's the same thing Finn wanted to know.

"I..." My response trails off. "Do I even belong here?"

Voicing my deepest worry about whether I deserve to stay sends a tremor down my spine.

Riley scoffs, putting her mug down hard on the coffee table. "Hell yes you do. I told you, Freya, you're one of us. This is your home as much as it's mine. You don't have to grow up in Hollyridge in order to be a townie, and that's exactly what you've become." She reaches across the couch and puts her hand on my knee. "You *belong* here."

A wave of emotion crests inside me. It's exactly what I needed to hear right now to stop myself from falling into the same cycle as always when it comes to Dad's demands.

"Thank you," I whisper.

Putting my mug of cocoa down on the table, I launch myself at her, giving her a bear hug. Her laugh fills the room. It spurs me on to do what I need to. Refusing to let my fears and conditioned responses keep me down, I sit up, looking for my phone.

"So, does this mean you're staying?" Riley prompts, tilting her head with a bright glint in her pretty green eyes.

"Hell yes." I'm already dialing Dad's number. Who cares where he is, or how I'm inconveniencing him with this interruption. "Screw my dad. He doesn't get to control me like I'm his puppet."

The corner of Riley's mouth tugs up. "That's the spirit, killer. Don't let anyone be the boss of you. Only you get a say in your life."

It's more than finally making a decision one hundred percent for myself without the thought of how Dad would react. I don't only want to stay because I love Hollyridge and the people in it. I want to stay for Finn. He's the person who helped me change my perspective, who showed me the family I've always wanted is right here.

He showed me I can *choose* that family, that I don't have to suffer with the one I was dealt, who only hurt me for years.

Finn and everyone in this quaint mountain town in Montana are the family and friends I want to surround myself with.

My heart is already where my home is, and there's no way in hell I'm ever going to leave it. No way in hell I'm leaving *Finn*.

"Freya," Dad answers the call in a sharp bark. "Have you

left town yet? When you get back to the office, I expect three months back reporting on the pacific coast properties, plus—"

"I quit, Dad," I say firmly, interrupting a to-do list I'm sure is a mile long.

The line is quiet for all of three seconds.

"Yes. I fired you. You're not changing my mind. If that's what you called for, you're once against wasting my tim—"

"No, Dad. I mean I quit Anderson Resorts. I'm no longer working for you, effective immediately."

Riley gives me a wide grin while she victory dances at the other end of the couch. I leap to my feet to pace, picking up the old anxious habit in order to focus on what I need to say to Dad.

"I'm done with all of it." My pulse speeds up as I tell him off. "I'm done trying to bend over backwards thinking the next thing I do will impress you. I have good ideas, but you don't give a shit about them, or me. Otherwise you wouldn't have threatened to throw me away."

He grumbles at my accusations, not bothering to deny them. "I don't have time for this. Stop acting like a petulant child and get on the next flight out."

"No! I'm staying here. Bye, Dad. I hope the money keeps you warm at night, because you've just lost the last family member you've had. I'm walking away." With my heart thumping hard in my chest and my hands shaking from finally standing up to him, I hang up, gasping for breath.

A slow clap startles me. I whirl around and Riley is giving me a standing ovation.

"That was badass as hell." She grins widely. "How do you feel?"

"Kinda like I might pass out," I admit.

"Deep breaths, girl. That's the adrenaline rush."

She must be right because it feels like fireworks are going

off in my body and I'm still shaking, like there's an overload of energy in need of an outlet. An elated, giddy sound bursts free and I jump up and down.

"It felt so good." I can't stop beaming. "God, I feel awesome. I wish I'd done it years ago, but I kicked ass!"

"Damn right you did. Proud of you." Riley comes over and gives me a half hug. "What will you do now?"

I flash her a look full of determination as I pull away to grab my coat.

"I'll go get the man I love, that's what."

It's what I should've done as soon as the competition ended.

Not only that, I'll do this his way. I'll face him in person to tell him I want to stay in Hollyridge, that I want to stay with him.

Forever.

Chapter Twenty-Seven
Finn

Gramps once told me when love walks in, you never let it walk out. I can't remember what season of life he told me that advice in, but I know that I've never forgotten it.

Love walked in to Hollyridge and it stole my fucking breath. Took every bit of air out of my lungs, and knocked me flat on my ass.

The truth is, I'm in love with Freya Anderson. I've been in love with her since the second she linebacker tackled me in the forest. From the second she stepped into Hollyridge, she turned my world upside down. I went from hating her so fiercely, so devoutly...to hopelessly in love with her. So much that, as the man who hates being the center of attention, I'm planning to win her back in front of the entire town and I don't even fucking care.

Which leads me here.

"West, I need you, bro. How fast can you get me Riley, an extension cord, a projector, and like a fuckload of Christmas lights?" I ask, my phone glued to my ear while I brush Saint, preparing him for our journey to town.

What would a grand gesture be without her favorite reindeer-donkey?

"Umm... Wait what?" he says, confused.

During the next five minutes I fill him in on my plan and by the time I'm finished, he's on board.

"Say no more. I'll see you in an hour."

The sun is starting to disappear behind the snow-capped mountains, and it's exactly what I need for my plan to go off without a hitch.

"Thanks man. Can you let Riley know she needs to have Freya there by six thirty?"

"I got this," he says, laughing.

Fuck, I'm nervous.

"Saint, buddy, I need you to be on your best behavior tonight, okay? A lot is riding on this sleigh ride," I tell him, as I secure the Santa hat to the top of his furry head.

He gives me a dramatic "hee-haw" in response.

"Yeah, yeah. Make fun of me all you want, but I need you to help me win the girl, Saint." I grin, giving him another pet.

I check my watch and see that it's time for us to head into town, so I double check all of the supplies I've loaded in the back of the sleigh and I climb on.

I've been behind these reins many times, but this time it's different. Kismet, you could say. This time I was going to get the girl, and this donkey was going to help me win the show.

* * *

I ride into town on my donkey...ahem...reindeer-drawn sleigh, and the square is as packed as it was for Jingle Wars. The competition truly was great for the town and tourism. Patrons have traveled from all over to visit our little slice of Heaven. The television coverage changed the game. It gave our tiny town new eyes.

Town square is already decorated for the upcoming Christmas holiday and that fits perfectly with what I have planned for Freya. I see West on the other side of the square, waving me over, so I direct Saint towards him.

"Man, are you sure you wanna do this?" He laughs and holds up his armful of lights he brought with him.

I roll my eyes. "Have I ever asked you bring a bunch of fucking supplies to town square to get a girl back, West?"

"Okay, true, but I'm just sayin'."

Together, we work on stringing the hundreds of lights up around the courtyard and setting up the projector. After an hour, time gets closer and closer to when Freya is supposed to arrive and I'm proud as fuck of what we've accomplished with just the two of us. There are more lights twinkling than I've ever probably seen in one space, but I know Freya will love it. I put her favorite Christmas movie, How The Grinch Stole Christmas, on the projector...and now we wait.

Thirty minutes later, I've gathered a crowd of tourists but I wait for her in the middle of the courtyard, until I see her part the crowd in front of me with Riley trailing behind her.

"Finn?" she asks, breathless. "I've been looking all over for you, what are you doing?"

I nod at West, who cuts the street lights off and the turns the strands of Christmas lights on, illuminating the square in facets of different colors.

Freya sucks in a sharp intake of breath, and brings her hand to her mouth. Even in the dim lights, I see tears well up in her eyes.

My fucking palms are sweaty, hell I'm so nervous. But I'm ready, I'm ready to get my girl. "I know the last thing you'd expect from me is a grand gesture. I'm quiet, I'm grumpy, I'm moody. Hell, I'm the Scrooge of Christmas most days. When I first met you, I hated you, simply because of my own bitter feelings. But somewhere along the way I let you inside and you changed me Freya. You make me softer. You make me love easily."

Freya lets out a soft laugh at my admission.

I grab her hands from her face and entwine my fingers with hers. They're freezing to the touch because she's not wearing gloves, as usual.

"I almost let my own selfish pride get in the way of what we had. I'm never going to be perfect and I won't always know the right thing to say or do. But what I do know is... I love you, Freya Anderson. From the second those squishy, wet, UGGs tramped into town, you stole my heart. I never stood a chance against you."

Tears stream down her face as she cries in front of me. The balls of her cheeks are flushed with the cold, or her feelings for me. All I know is that I don't want to live another day in this damn perfect town, without my perfect girl to go with it.

"I brought you here because I wanted to show you that even though I won't always be perfect, I'll never stop trying to make you happy. The things I said I'd never do are the ones that I'll continue to do over and over if it's what puts a smile on your face." I pull her closer to me.

Everyone else around us fades away and only us two remain. The buzz of the crowd, the sound of Christmas music playing in the background, the twinkle of the light...it all fades to black. All I can see is Freya, all I hear is the sound of her soft cries as my words pierce her heart and settle somewhere deep inside.

"If you need a lifetime of grand gestures, Freya Anderson...then I'm going to be the one to give it to you. I'm asking you to choose me. Choose Hollyridge. Choose Grams and Gramps. Don't go back to California, don't leave what we have here. I love you and I want to spend the rest of my days making you happy in any way that I can." I pull her closer to me, desperate for her warmth.

She lets out a laugh that's filled with tears, but gives me a beaming smile that fucking blinds me.

"Say yes, Freya, please for the love of Saint here." I gesture to the donkey that's behind us, hee-hawing as loud as he possibly can. "Stay in Hollyridge with us. Make this your home."

I swear I stop breathing in the few seconds until Freya speaks.

"I was never leaving, Finn." She smiles.

"What?" I ask, my eyes going wide with disbelief.

Freya nods and lets out a little giggle.

"I knew after I moved my stuff out of Alpine that I couldn't leave you. I was coming for you, right after I called my dad to quit. Little did I know, you had all of this planned for me."

"So you're staying?" I ask, letting out the breath I had been holding.

"I'm staying." She throws herself at me, jumping up, wrapping her legs around my waist and her arms around my neck.

"I'm never leaving you, Finn Mayberry. You're everything I could want and more, and Hollyridge is my home," she whispers before sealing her lips over mine.

The crowd erupts around us, bringing us back to reality. I forgot that we were even in the middle of town square.

She laughs, bumping her nose against mine. "You know they'll never let you live this down right?"

"I know it, baby, but guess what? I don't fucking care, because it made you happy, and that's all that matters."

* * *

Hours later, I'm wrapped up with Freya in bed while she runs her fingers lazily down my stomach, teasing the line of hair that leads downwards. Each slide of her fingertips causes my dick to rise back to life.

"Everything feels so easy with you, Finn," she whispers hotly against my skin before she throws her leg over my waist and straddles me. So fucking perfect. Completely comfortable with herself and her body, she doesn't shy away from my eyes when I drink in her curves.

"That's what happens when you find the love of your life ya know," I say, mimicking Gramps.

"Why does that sound like something Gramps would say?" she asks and lets out a squeaky laugh when I surge my hips up against her wet heat.

I groan. "Let's not talk about Gramps while you're sitting naked on top of me please."

Jesus H.

"I'd much rather focus on you," she whispers with a husky edge to her voice that I've come to love more than I can fucking say.

"You sure you can handle another round, Princess?" I tease.

That's what makes us, us. Our competitive edge. Our constant drive to one up the other, and test each other's limits.

"Oh? Are you sure you're up to it, big guy?"

She shifts around, then her tiny hands find my cock beneath the thin sheet and she pumps me, once, twice, three times until my hips piston off the bed.

"Mmm. Who can get the other to the finish line first?" Freya whispers challengingly.

Is my girl taking this to the next level? Who can come first?

"I'll always win this, baby. Your body was made for me. I can play in the dark with my eyes closed."

She sighs happily, and bends down, licking a path down the column of my throat, then flashes me a cheeky, smug grin.

"Well you know what they say... All is fair in love and Jingle Wars."

Chapter Twenty-Eight

Freya

"Okay, okay." My breaths come in gasps as I collapse next to Finn in bed. Maybe more like face plant. "You win."

"What was that?" His tone is full of satisfaction. "I couldn't hear you, Princess."

With what little energy I have left, I blindly aim a weak punch. The soft *oof* that gusts out of him makes me think I caught him in the side. Strong arms come around me and once he has me resting half on top of him again, he strokes my back.

"So you concede defeat at last?"

I make an approximation of a response. It's mostly a groan. Finn chuckles. He has zapped all of my energy.

"Fiend," I mumble into his shoulder.

"That's right, baby." He reaches down to smack my ass lightly.

Little does he know, I'll challenge him to a rematch because I love competing with him.

As soon as I come down from the insane orgasm he gave

me. And maybe recall how to string full coherent sentences together.

Finn traces my spine and a content sigh escapes him. "So, since you're staying in town, will you put an offer in on the place we got snowed in at? I liked the porch on it." He hums with mischief. "Liked the bedroom, too. And that wall I fucked you against."

Laughter catches in my throat. "Definitely a highlight." Sighing, I shake my head. "I actually called the realtor earlier to make an offer, but she told me it sold. Some couple stole it right from under my nose."

He makes a sympathetic sound and kisses the top of my head. "Well, that makes my next question easy, then."

I lean up so I can meet his eyes. "And what's that?"

"Where are you planning to stay until you find a place?" There's a glint in his eye.

"Well, my stuff is at Riley's for now. She offered to let me couch surf." I pull a face, scrunching my nose. "I'll have to up my real estate game. Make sure my thumbs are lightning-quick so I can achieve hashtag cabin goals."

Finn snorts. "Did you just use hashtag in a real sentence? Out loud and shit?"

My mouth pops open in mock-offense. "Don't knock my goals."

He grins, affecting a more southern drawl to his Montana accent. "Darlin', I would never."

I dissolve into giggles when he tugs me down for a kiss.

"Now," Finn says after he's kissed me soundly. "My question."

"And what would that be?"

"Will you stay here?"

For a man who stepped out of his comfort zone to give me

an amazing grand gesture earlier tonight, I'm struck by the emotion flickering in his eyes.

I blink, then a bright smile stretches. "Yeah?"

He blows out a breath. "Yeah." His palm smooths up my side. "Stay here at the inn with me instead of Riley's couch."

"I'd love that."

Finn gives me that charming smile that I love and with the kiss I give him, we get started on round—who knows. I've lost count. All I know is when I'm with him, my heart soars.

* * *

A few days later, the distant sound of Christmas music and the delicious scrape of Finn's open-mouthed kisses on my neck draws me out of a dream that left a smile on my face. His bed is a cocoon of warmth. I hum, stretching so my body arches against the smooth planes of his naked chest.

"Hi," I murmur sleepily.

He leans back from teasing my neck and smiles at me. "Merry Christmas, beautiful."

The deep rumble of his voice sends a throb of heat between my legs. I slide them together, the material of his flannel— which I've officially stolen as my favorite sleep shirt—skims my bare thighs and ass. It's the only thing I have on.

"I love waking up with you in my bed," Finn says, lowering his head to resume his slow, seductive torture.

I sink my teeth into my lip. "I do, too. Especially when you —*ah*—do that."

His gravelly chuckle vibrates against the column of my throat. I swallow back a moan, not wanting to broadcast to the entirety of Mayberry Inn what's going on behind Finn's door. He tugs me closer, pulling my leg around his hip to position himself between my legs. My breath hitches at the hard ridge of him exactly where I need him, only separated by his red plaid sleep pants. He buries his face against my neck and shoulder as our hips rock slowly.

"Finn," I plead with a breathy sigh.

"What do you need?" He nibbles a patch of skin beneath my jaw.

"I want to kiss you, caveman," I sass.

"Is that right?" His fingertips skim my cheek as he angles my face toward him.

My arms lock around his neck and I pull him down. He makes a pleased sound and kisses me languidly, both of us smiling into it.

"I see Santa decided I was a good girl this year," I say between kisses. "He brought me this sexy as hell lumberjack with a kind heart. Best Christmas present ever. I'll have to send a fruit basket to the North Pole as thanks. Do you think Edible Arrangements can do snowflake shapes?"

Finn chuckles, sliding a palm down my body to massage my ass while he slowly grinds his erection against me in lazy rolls of his hips.

"Can you not talk about other men while I'm doing *this* to my girl?" He makes my breath catch with the movement of his hips. After another kiss, he pulls back to gaze at me. "Maybe it's the other way around and I wished for you."

My smile stretches and a warm glow of joy blooms in my chest. He makes me so happy. "Love you, you big softie."

Finn huffs out a laugh and kisses my cheek. "Love you, too, beautiful."

We settle back into snuggling, in no hurry this morning. We have all the time in the world.

"What does your family do for Christmas morning?" I ask.

"When I was a kid, I used to try to be the first to wake up. Grams always beats me, she's attuned to Christmas morning.

She looks forward to it all year." A sad look twists his handsome features for a moment. "They've always made it special. Holidays make me miss my parents more, but it's also a reminder to be thankful we have each other."

I tighten my arms around his neck in support. He rubs his hand up and down my back. We hold each other and remain quiet to honor the memory of his parents.

Once the moment of grief passes, he continues. "As I've gotten older we have coffee together before we exchange presents. You can hear from the music, they like to start early."

My mouth curves and I snuggle closer. "I love it."

Waking up to holiday music is perfect. The fresh scent of something baking also wafts upstairs. It feels so much different than the holidays I've grown up with. The love filling the house is palpable. No one could feel lonely or unwanted here.

"Should probably get up soon," Finn murmurs, skimming his fingertips beneath the flannel shirt to caress my skin. "Grams is probably dialed up to eleven already."

A soft giggle shakes my shoulders. "I thought I loved Christmas."

"No one loves Christmas more than Grams Mayberry. No. One." Finn levels a serious look at me, but he can only hold it for a second before his eyes crinkle in amusement.

My heart thumps and I cup his face, pulling him back in for another kiss.

A knock comes at the door.

"Are you two up yet?" It's Grams. "You can make moon eyes at each other downstairs, where there's coffee and fresh cinnamon rolls. Get your behinds in gear, it's Christmas!"

Finn drops his head to the crook of my neck. I can't hold in my tiny sound of delight. He shushes me, pinching my side, which only makes me squirm with more giggles.

"Hurry along now! Don't make me come in there and drag you both downstairs."

A stricken look crosses his face as he props up on his elbows. The expression makes me smother a snort.

"Let's get up," I murmur, poking him in the chest so he releases his strong hold on me.

"We'll be there, Grams," Finn calls.

"You better be, Finn Michael Mayberry."

I waggle my eyebrows at him. "*Ooh*, full-named, huh?"

Smirking at my sass, Finn kisses me, swallowing my giggles until I'm clutching his shoulders and breathless.

"That's what I thought," he says as he draws back, leaving me in a daze. With a smug tilt to his mouth, he pats my ass. "Consider that a promise for later."

"Can't wait," I breathe.

We climb out of bed and steal more intimate touches as we dress.

Downstairs in the family room off the kitchen, Grams wraps me in a hug, then Finn. Gramps is all grins, doing much better since his heart attack. A huge spread of cinnamon rolls and fresh coffee is ready, and the music sets the mood in the background, filling the whole inn with the festive spirit of the holiday.

"Merry Christmas," Finn says to each of them.

His affectionate smile fills my heart.

"Coffee, Freya?" Grams offers. She's glowing with love for her family on her favorite holiday. "Try the rolls, too. My secret is I put a bit of orange zest in them. Perfect for the winter season."

"Sounds amazing," I say.

"Good enough to eat your weight in the little buggers," Gramps says with a hungry gleam in his eyes.

"You can only have one," Grams scolds, stealing the second

cinnamon roll Gramps was putting on his plate. "That was the deal. No sneaking more."

"But I want the sweets," Gramps grumbles. "You know these are my favorite thing you make, love."

"Doctor's orders, Harold Mayberry." After a beat, Grams smiles and leans in to kiss Gramps on the cheek. "There, that's the sugar you can have."

I bite down on a grin while Gramps makes a happy noise and pulls Grams in for another sweet kiss. They're adorable.

The rustic room is decked out in fresh pine garlands wrapped in tinsel and the biggest Christmas tree I've ever seen stands in the corner. I haven't had the chance to admire the decorations since coming to stay at the inn, so with coffee and a tasty cinnamon bun in hand, I give the Mayberrys a few minutes to themselves while I take in the tree.

It's beautiful with an assortment of ornaments from vintage to local treasures. Some are handmade and a delighted sound escapes me as I lean closer to one of Finn's creations. It's a red-nosed reindeer made from popsicle sticks and a red pom pom with a picture of him as an adorable little boy, his tousled brown hair unruly and curling over his forehead.

"I love this," I say over my shoulder. "Finn, you were such a cute kid."

He stops talking to Gramps and turns toward the tree. "Grams, please tell me you didn't put the embarrassing school ornaments on the tree this year?"

"Don't be silly," she says. "Of course I did. Those are my favorites in our collection."

Finn comes up next to me and groans under his breath. He puts an arm around my waist and tosses me a wry look. "How can I bribe you to forget you saw that?"

I pretend to think it over. Leaning closer, I drop my voice to a sly murmur, "It'll cost you." I allow a short pause, then add in a husky tone, "But you'll definitely enjoy doing it."

I finish off the last bite of my cinnamon roll and lick the sticky icing from my fingers so only he can see.

Heat flares in his whiskey-colored eyes and his hand flexes on my hip. "You'll be the death of me."

Laughing softly, I take his hand and take a seat on the leather couch. Finn's arm drapes across the back, playing with the loose strands of my hair. Grams and Gramps join us, each settling in the arm chair and recliner.

"We can do presents after another cup of coffee," Grams suggests. "What does your family like to do on Christmas, Freya?"

A pang hits me in the chest, but Finn squeezes my shoulder, tucking me closer against his side. I shoot him a grateful look.

"They were never as big on the holidays as me. Christmas is my favorite, though." I share a look with Grams that chases away the brief shadow. "I'm happy just to have the gift of spending time with you all."

Grams makes a touched noise. "We're glad to have you here, too." Her gaze shifts to Finn. "You make our boy happy."

I swallow back a wave of emotion and put my head on Finn's shoulder. He rubs my arm and drops a kiss on my head.

"Freya loves holiday movies. Why don't we put one on after presents?" Finn suggests.

"I'd love that," I say.

"Let's do gifts, then." Grams gets up to freshen our cups of coffee. "Finn, you start."

Finn rummages in his pocket and pulls me off the couch. When we're by the tree, he smiles at me.

"Got something special for you." He tucks my hair behind my ear. "It was short notice, but I think you'll like it."

A rush of surprise makes my stomach swoop. "You didn't have to get me anything."

Taking my hand, Finn puts something small and warm in my palm. When I unfurl my fingers, I suck in a breath. It's a key.

"I know you couldn't get your cabin," he rumbles, tipping my chin up. "But I want you here with me. It's a key to the inn. You can keep staying for as long as you want, or if you buy a house in town, you can come and go. You're my girl, Freya, and you're right where you belong."

"Finn," I whisper. A beaming smile overtakes my face and I stand on my tiptoes to hug him. "You're so—I love it. Thank you."

He hums and holds me close. Grams and Gramps offer us warm smiles as we take a seat on the couch again. Presents are exchanged, along with laughter. When we're full on Grams' delicious cinnamon rolls, Finn puts on a movie and we wrap up in blankets. Gramps falls asleep and Finn distracts me with kisses, but it's the most memorable Christmas ever.

I don't need to wish for my life to be as perfect as a Christmas movie anymore. I have it now. This year I finally get to have the holiday moments I've always longed for, making memories with Finn and his grandparents that have welcomed me into their arms as one of their own. Every day new memories fill my heart up.

Finn Mayberry and his family chose me as much as I have chosen them.

Like so many holiday songs go, this is all I could ever want for Christmas.

Epilogue
Finn

Six Months Later

"Freya! Do you know where the Christmas lights are? I would've swore that I put them up here. Right next to the damn donkey blow up," I call from the attic.

My beautiful girlfriend waits by the ladder below.

"Back left corner, in the box labeled 'lights', Finn Mayberry," she says exasperatedly.

"He does this every year, I swear." I hear Grams whisper to Freya.

"You know that I can hear you, right?" I grumble.

"Yep." Grams and Freya share a laugh.

The two of them together is more than I can handle sometimes, but then that's where Gramps comes in.

"Oh, both of you leave that poor man alone," Gramps scolds them both.

"Gramps, I literally color coded and labeled everything in that attic not even four months ago."

That she did. She got tired of going up to the attic and not being able to see squat or find anything we needed, so she made it her own personal project to label and color code everything in the attic. Which I must say is quite helpful, but still doesn't solve my issue that the string of lights she's looking for is nowhere to be found. Or so she thinks...

I climb back down the rickety ladder, and fold it back up, the door closing with a final thud.

"Sorry, babe, not sure where they are," I tell her and it earns me a stink eye.

"Finn..." she warns.

"What? I looked everywhere. No lights."

Grams rolls her eyes next to Freya, then pulls Gramps back into the kitchen, leaving us alone.

I tug on Freya's hand and bring her upstairs with me, to our room in the inn, where we've been staying for the past six months.

Yep. Freya officially moved into the Mayberry with me right after I gave her a key on Christmas morning. I didn't want to be apart from her any longer than necessary, so buying or renting another place in Hollyridge was useless. After our big scene in town square, she spent more nights in my bed than on Riley's couch, and Christmas sealed the deal.

The past six months have been pure bliss and I mean that in the most manly way possible. Having Freya here with me, Grams, and Gramps has been everything. She fits in our family like she's always belonged.

"Finn, why are you dragging me upstairs? I have so much work to do!" She huffs.

She's been planning a Christmas in July event for the Mayberry all month, and all of her hard work is finally paying off. We are fully booked with no vacancies. The inn is thriving better than it has been in years and Freya gets most of the credit for that. She has used social media to turn the inn around. While I stay as far away from it as I can, except for the occasional selfie that she asks for, she's the star of the show. Well, her and Saint. She loves him despite the smell.

"Shh. I have a surprise, close your eyes," I whisper into her ear as I guide her down the hallway.

I open our door and cover her eyes with my hands, because she might peek and I wouldn't put it past her.

"Finn, what in the world!" she exclaims.

"Can you promise not to look if I take my hands off?"

She huffs. "Fine."

Grinning, I remove my hands from her eyes, walk over to my spot, and drop down in front of her. I pull out the box that holds our future inside. An engagement ring that's every bit worthy of the love of my life. Gramps and I spent an entire day trip to Great Falls to pick it out and when I saw it, I instantly knew it was hers.

"Freya," I whisper.

She creaks her eyes open one at a time and finds me on one knee in front of her, surrounded by the very Christmas lights she spent the past hour grumbling about. The entire room is lit by strings of lights, and there are rose petals on the bed. Her eyes light up when she takes in the room around her.

Her body goes completely still and she takes in a sharp breath. My girl is surprised just as I had planned.

"Freya Anderson, my little traitor girl, the only person I'm ever going to call Princess. I'm the hollow bones of a man without you in my life. You're everything to me. I love you more than I can ever explain and I promise to love you forever. To be the best husband I can be to you and hopefully our children. To love you free, and love you wild. To help you reach your dreams, to bring you face to face with the fears that stand in your way. Will you marry me? Will you be my wife?"

Freya releases a watery breath and fresh tears spill from her shining eyes. She nods over and over before sinking to her knees with me.

"Of course I'll marry you, Finn Mayberry!" she cries, holding out her trembling left hand so I can slide the ring on her finger.

I pull it out, then set the box down on the ground next to me. She makes another soft, happy sound when I slide the rose gold, two carat solitaire onto her finger.

"I love you so much." She throws her arms around my neck and kisses me with so much love, I feel the breath leave my lungs.

She came into my life as a traitor, out to steal everything from me... But in the end, she gave me more than I could have ever wished for.

Epilogue
Freya

Three Months Later

"Oh, and Evie Lark, let's add her to the list," Grams suggests. "She was Finn's elementary teacher."

Grinning, I add the name to the guest list. A couple of magazines are on the coffee table, along with my iPad with a Pinterest vision board. Our wedding is shaping up to be the biggest in Hollyridge's recent history. I have no complaints about that. I'm looking forward to setting a big cozy vibe for the day Finn and I tie the knot.

No matter what, I'm excited to promise Finn my forever.

Grams and I are seated in the family room with cups of tea while Finn is out back with Gramps down at Saint's stall. I bet anything he's sneaking the donkey a Jolly Rancher. Finn can't say no to that droopy face with those soulful eyes.

My life is like a dream now. I've found the family I've

always longed for, and a man who makes me feel like every day is Christmas. I still love my holiday movies, but now I get to enjoy them in his arms with our matching mugs of hot chocolate.

The back door to the mud room opens and both Grams and I look up as Riley comes in.

"Hey, Riles." I wave my best friend over. "Come make sure I have the address for your parents right."

"Hey." She glances around like she's searching to see if the coast is clear, then joins us in the family room. "Maid of honor, reporting for duty."

I chuckle, bumping my shoulder against hers when she takes a seat on the other side of me.

"Coffee?" Grams offers.

"No thanks, Grams." Riley takes in the array on the coffee table. "So what'd I miss?"

"We're working on the guest list again," Grams says.

"Should I still leave your plus one blank for now?" I ask. "I know you said you didn't want one, but you can bring another friend, or—"

"Uh, actually." Riley coughs, shifting her gaze to the side. Color floods her cheeks. It's rare to see her confidence and sarcasm tempered by shyness. "I sort of...*maybefoundadate.*"

Grams and I exchange a look, brows lifting.

"Oh?" Grams has that matchmaker tone she gets after time spent with her Pokeno group. A gleam brightens in her eyes. "It's nice to see you opening yourself up, dear."

"So tell us more about this date." I prop my elbow on my knee and rest my chin in my hand. "Give us the goss, dude. Who is it? Do we know him?"

Hollyridge is only so big and the tourist season is only just starting. She'd have to be going with someone we all know.

"You do," Riley hedges. "It's, um. It's West."

Silence falls over the room for all of three seconds before I release a high-pitched squeal of excitement and Grams nods knowingly. Riley turns a deeper shade of red.

"Well, it's about dang time," Grams mutters under her breath, tilting her face up like she's thanking a deity.

I give Riley a half hug. "Finally bagged your crush, huh?"

"Yup." Her tone is strained.

"I'm going to make us a snack." Grams gets to her feet. "You dears want anything?"

"No, thank you," Riley mumbles.

Once Grams is out of earshot, I lean closer. "What's the deal, shouldn't you be more excited and like *yay*? I see the way you look at him."

I'm sure the whole town knows how Riley feels about West. Their history goes all the way back to when they were kids. The only one who can't see her pining for him is West himself. I want to just grab his shoulders and shake him so he'll understand, but Finn tells me we need to let them work it out for themselves.

"I—he..." Riley pushes out a breath. Her shifty gaze travels the room once more, even though we're the only two in here now. Most of the inn's guests have ventured out to enjoy the town. "I'll tell you later, okay? I'm gonna need a whole ass bottle of tequila to get through this explanation."

My brows jump up. It's that serious? "Okay, dude. Whatever you need. You know I'm here for you."

"Thanks girl." Riley groans and slumps against my side. I stroke her hair comfortingly. Under her breath, she mumbles, "Can't believe I got myself into this mess."

"Do we need a night at Moose's so you can dance all your feels out?"

"Yes," she mutters in a mock-petulant tone.

"You've got it, girl. This Friday, you and me. No boys allowed."

Her laugh is muffled. "Will Finn be able to keep away if he knows you're going off to Moose's for a girls night? He always gets all growly and possessive over you when the other townies leer."

"They can check my ass out all they want, it's got a big stamp on it that says *belongs forever and always to Finn Michael Mayberry*," I sass. "He knows my heart only beats for him."

The mud room door opens again and I recognize Finn by the heavy footfalls of his boots. I can hear him stop in the kitchen to talk to Grams, his deep voice drifting through the door. A smile spreads across my face as he pops his head in. When his eyes land on me, the corners of his mouth lift.

"Hey, handsome," I greet.

Finn saunters over, drawn by an invisible magnetic pull whenever we've been apart for more than a few hours, and bends to drop a kiss on my head from behind the back of the couch.

I tip my head back. "Did you grab a picture for the daily Saint Snap on our Insta?"

"Yeah, here. You know he loves it when it's time for his spotlight. Now that he gets it year-round instead of just at the holidays as our local reindeer, he's turning into a little diva."

Riley snorts. "Is that why you decided Saint is your flower donkey for your wedding?"

"Exactly." I look up at my fiancé with fondness. "Plus, it's right to have him there. He's family."

Finn hands me his phone and I coo at how cute Saint Nick looks with his tongue poking out to take the carrot from Gramps.

"This is perfect, babe."

Using his phone, I log into Mayberry Inn's Instagram account and post with our hashtag for Hollyridge's favorite donkey. Messages and comments pour in, many excited for their upcoming bookings. These days the inn is booked solid for months in advance throughout the year, tourist season or not.

It's funny to think Finn used to be against my methods, but now we share our ideas. The inn is doing fantastic with both of us at the helm. We've even been doing well enough to expand our property line, purchasing the hot spring we both love so much and some of the land the Alpine occupied when it was suffering through the off-season during the summer. Dad's resort is still next door, but it's half the size it used to be because his stubborn methods don't work for the kind of vacation people visiting Hollyridge want.

I've tried to email him with a few marketing plans I've put together with first-hand knowledge of what tourists and locals in Hollyridge respond well to, but they go unanswered. We haven't spoken often since I quit, but that's fine with me. Finn and everyone in my life now are the family I choose.

My younger brothers have even reached out. They happened to catch a Facebook Live event Finn and I put on for the Christmas in July party with Saint Nick's annual transformation into Hollyridge's only reindeer-donkey.

Social media is a funny thing, connecting and reconnecting people all over the world. Maybe that's why I've always loved it so much.

"Can I steal you away from wedding planning for a minute?" Finn asks.

"Of course." I take his hand as he comes around the couch to pull me up. "Be right back, Riles."

"If you makeout for longer than ten minutes, I make no promises that I can stop Grams from hunting you down." Riley holds up her hands.

Huffing with laughter, Finn shakes his head and leads me onto the porch. Even though we're at the tail end of fall, it feels like it might snow.

Lacing his fingers with mine, Finn tugs me close for a kiss, cupping my face with his free hand. I hum into it, absorbing his body warmth from the early winter chill creeping into the Montana air.

"What was that for?" My eyes are still closed and I can't contain my smile.

Finn's thumb caresses my cheek. "Just because. Missed my girl."

"Missed me? You see me all day," I tease. "You barely let me leave our bed this morning."

"Never can get enough of you, beautiful," he murmurs. "I can't wait to marry you."

"Me either."

I press on tiptoe to steal another kiss. His arms wrap around my waist, keeping me toasty as a cool breeze moves through the front lawn of Mayberry Inn. As the kiss ends, we both look out at the beautiful view of the mountains surrounding Hollyridge.

The feeling I get looking at this view still takes my breath away. Between the mountains and the hints of Finn's cedar and spice scent tickling my nose, I know I'm where my heart is happiest.

Home.

* * *

Thank you so much for reading JINGLE WARS! We sincerely appreciate your support. **Please leave your review on:**

Amazon | GoodReads | BookBub

Or any of your favorite book communities, like **Instagram** and **Facebook**!

Curious about how that wedding date will go down between West and Riley? Return to Hollyridge for their story. Sign up for R. Holmes' and Veronica Eden's newsletters for more Hollyridge news.

ACKNOWLEDGMENTS

Readers, we're endlessly grateful for you! Thanks for reading this book. It means the world to us that you picked up this book. We hope you enjoyed your read!

***

From R. Holmes—

There are so many people to thank when it comes to this book, but first and foremost I want to thank V for being the best writing partner, like ever. She made this process SO much fun and so easy. I can't wait for our NEXT.

Next, I want to thank Katie Friend who I literally had the idea to write this book for! She has more Christmas spirit than any person I've ever met. Her spirit is infectious and I am so thankful for her. This book would not be what it is without her. Truly. Much love babe!

I want to thank my entire team for always taking my words and making them something great. Without you, I would just have words on a piece of paper. I can't thank you enough for everything that you do! To my AMAZING assistant Amber who I love so so much. You are a Godsend. Seriously an Angel. Without you I would be a mess. I am so thankful for your organization and ability to run my life from like over two thousand miles away. I. LOVE. YOU.

To my betas Ofa, Sabrina, Jan and Brittany. You get to see things when they're still ugly and help me make it something beautiful. To Pang and Jan both for always making me the most beautiful graphics EVER. You girls spoil me, and I am forever grateful for you both. To Clarissa for being the ultimate hype girl and always being my sounding board. To my Dirty Girls street team for always sharing and getting the word out. I love you guys! To all of the bloggers/bookstagrammers who have read, reviewed and shared our book baby. To my best friends for putting up with my shit every day (insert halo here).

Last but not least, to my family, especially my husband for allowing me the time to write this. You all sacrifice so much to make my dreams come true and I'll never be able to repay you. I hope that one day I can make yours come true.

***

From Veronica Eden—

With every book, it always seems to take a bigger village and I am thankful that my support circle grows with each release. First, to Ramz, girl I am *so* glad we did this. I'm so thankful to have you as a friend and I love working with you as a writing partner! From start to finish, working on this with you has been a blast!

Thank you to Najla Qambar for taking our vision and creating the PERFECT illustrated cover! Your work is incredible, and we appreciate you so much for working with us on this.

To our alpha/beta team, thank you so much for taking our raw words and helping us polish this into a beautiful and touching story with your thoughtful considerations of the characters. Thank you to Rachel and Bre for always being with me and for never blinking whenever I roll into your DMs like *surprise* this is what I've got for you haha!

To my street team and reader group, y'all are the best babes around! To see you guys get as excited as I do seriously makes my day. Thank you for your help in sharing my books and for your support of my work!

To the bloggers and bookstagrammers, thank you for always being the most wonderful and welcoming community! Your creativity, excitement, and beautiful edits are something I come back to visit again and again to brighten my day. To the new bloggers I've met while working on this book, I'm so thankful to get to know you! You are all incredible and blow me away with your passion for romance! Thank you so much from the bottom of my heart for sharing, reviewing, and reading this book!

Thanks to my husband for being you! He doesn't read these, but he's my biggest supporter. He keeps me fed and watered while I'm in the writer cave, and doesn't complain when I fling myself out of bed at odd hours with an idea to frantically scribble down.

ABOUT R. HOLMES
VILLAINS THAT WRECK YOU

R. Holmes is from a small town in southern Louisiana where she lives on a farm, with her husband and two little boys. Whenever she's not chasing around the goats and her boys on the farm, she spends her time watching ridiculous amounts of Netflix and is almost always stuck with her nose in a book. She thrives on horror films, sarcasm, and reruns of Harry Potter. A perpetual night owl, you'll find her in her office locked away until the wee hours of the morning. She loves to meet her readers and discuss her latest favorite books and her upcoming projects!

* * *

CONTACT + FOLLOW
Email: rholmesauthor@gmail.com
Website: rholmesauthor.com
FB Reader Group: R. Holmes' Babes

facebook.com/rholmesromance
instagram.com/rholmesauthor
bookbub.com/authors/r-holmes

ALSO BY R. HOLMES

Sign up for the mailing list to get exclusive news! **Follow R. Holmes on BookBub** for new release alerts!

MC Series

Sins of my Father (COMING SOON)

Standalone

Misfit

The Beginning of the End

Hate to Want You

ABOUT VERONICA EDEN
ROMANCE WITH DARING EDGE

Veronica Eden is an international bestselling author of new adult romances romances with spitfire heroines and irresistible heroes.

Typically her playground is more on the dark side, but she loves a feel-good read. She loves exploring deep (sometimes complicated) feelings, magical worlds, epic adventures, and the bond of characters that embrace *us against the world*. She has always been drawn to gruff bad boys, clever villains, and the twisty-turns of morally gray decisions. If they're moody, broody, and broken—she's here for it. Veronica Eden also writes romance as Mara Townsend. When not writing, she can be found soaking up sunshine at the beach, snuggling in a pile with her untamed pack of animals (her husband, dog, and cats), and surrounding herself with as many plants as she can get her hands on.

* * *

CONTACT + FOLLOW
Email: veronicaedenauthor@gmail.com
Website: http://veronicaedenauthor.com
FB Reader Group: bit.ly/veronicafbgroup

- facebook.com/veronicaedenauthor
- instagram.com/veronicaedenauthor
- bookbub.com/authors/veronica-eden
- goodreads.com/veronicaedenauthor
- amazon.com/author/veronicaeden

ALSO BY VERONICA EDEN

Sign up for the mailing list to get first access and ARC opportunities! **Follow Veronica on BookBub** for new release alerts!

Sinners and Saints Series

Wicked Saint

Tempting Devil

Ruthless Bishop

Savage Wilder (COMING SOON)

Crowned Crows Series

CCOTP (COMING SOON)

Standalone

Unmasked Heart

Hate to Want You

Printed in Great Britain
by Amazon